"WHO ARE YOU?

A woman's voice was on the other end of the line, strained and wary.

"Raul Sá." He pulled the phone away from his ear to glance at the screen. No traceable caller ID.

"I was calling the Search and Protect Organization." The woman hesitated. "I'm looking for Arin Siri."

"She's working right now. Must've forwarded her calls to my line."

There was a long pause. "This is Mali, Arin's sister. Please help me."

PRAISE FOR PIPER J. DRAKE

TOTAL BRAVERY

ALSO BY PIPER J. DRAKE

Extreme Honor
Ultimate Courage
Absolute Trust

TOTAL
BRAVERY

PIPER J. DRAKE

FOREVER

NEW YORK BOSTON

Copyright © 2018 by Piper J. Drake
Excerpt from *Absolute Trust* © 2016 by Piper J. Drake
Cover design by Elizabeth Turner Stokes
Cover illustration by Michael Heath
Cover copyright © 2018 by Hachette Book Group, Inc.

Forever
Hachette Book Group
1290 Avenue of the Americas
New York, NY 10104
forever-romance.com
twitter.com/foreverromance

First Edition: April 2018

Forever is an imprint of Grand Central Publishing.
The Forever name and logo are trademarks of Hachette Book Group, Inc.

The Hachette Speakers Bureau provides a wide range of authors for speaking events. To find out more, go to www.hachettespeakersbureau.com or call (866) 376-6591.

The publisher is not responsible for websites (or their content) that are not owned by the publisher.

ISBN 978-1-5387-5953-0 (mass market)
ISBN 978-1-5387-5954-7 (ebook)

Printed in the United States of America

10 9 8 7 6 5 4 3 2 1

OPM

Dedicated to my coworkers and colleagues, in both my careers. Because team means everything.

TOTAL BRAVERY

CHAPTER ONE

Tomorrow, I get coffee first." Raul Sá fumbled with the keys he'd been given to the team house. "Some of us need caffeine to face the morning, even in paradise."

Taz, Raul's new canine partner, dropped his jaw and let his tongue loll out in a doggie grin.

"Yeah, I figured I wasn't going to get much sympathy from you."

First day reporting in to the new Search and Protect Corporation and he'd taken Taz out for a run immediately, before the tropical morning got too hot for the German Shepherd Dog, or GSD for short. Back and ready to get to the more onerous duties, he stared at the duty board on the wall. He was on kennel duty. All week. Great.

Well, he and Taz were the newest additions. He'd spent some time on the East Coast, training with Taz prior to finalizing the acquisition of the highly trained canine. And damn, the men at Hope's Crossing Kennels trained some fine dogs. Now they'd both arrived ready to get to know their new team.

This time, he was going to build the most positive impression possible. This time, he wanted to be part of the team and not just a temporary extension of it.

"We'll both get to know the dogs first," Raul murmured to Taz. "Then we'll do our best with the humans."

Taz tilted his head up to regard Raul with a calm, dark-eyed gaze. After a moment, Taz uttered a quiet woof.

"Yeah, I like dogs better, too." Raul headed for the stairs. Before he reached them, the smartphone he'd been issued sounded an incoming call alert. He pulled it out of his back pocket and swiped the screen with his thumb to answer. "Sá."

"Who are you?" A woman's voice was on the other end of the line, strained and wary.

"Raul Sá." He pulled the phone away from his ear to glance at the screen. No traceable caller ID.

"I was calling the Search and Protect Organization." The woman hesitated. "I'm looking for Arin Siri."

She spoke his teammate's name with the proper pronun-ciation, even getting the soft *r* that sounded more like an *r* and an *l* than the rolling *r* some Spanish or Latino speakers fell into. She'd added a lilting, tonal quality to Arin's name, too—something Raul had learned to hear but had never man-aged to pronounce even after years of practice, even though he considered Arin his best friend and had put a lot of effort into getting her name right. So this person had been speak-ing Arin's name a long time. "She's working right now. Must've forwarded her calls to my line."

Arin had known he'd arrived late last night.

"You're a...coworker?" There was hope in that voice, but still a thread of fear.

"Yeah." Raul considered for a minute. "And a friend. I wouldn't be here if it weren't for her."

"A friend?" Suspicion remained.

He was losing patience. Honestly, he had work to do, and no matter how menial it was, it was the next step in making a good impression. But something about the strain in the voice on the line made him offer one more reassurance. "The kind of friend who knows the origin of Arin's last name, her full last name."

Arin Siri was first-generation American, like him. His family had come from Portugal. Her parents had come from Thailand. Thai names weren't often so short and easy to pronounce, especially not the surnames. Upon coming to the United States, Arin's parents had made the choice to shorten their surname to something more easily accepted by English speakers. Still, many cultures placed deep meaning in names. Arin's was derived from an older dialect and carried meaning that continued to have value to her, so she had always held her full surname close. It wasn't something she shared with any but very close, trusted friends.

He was one. The person on the other end of the connection might be, too.

There was a long pause. "This is Mali, Arin's sister. Please help me."

CHAPTER TWO

How can I help you?" The man on the other end of the call didn't laugh or crack a joke in response to Mali's request for help. Honestly, it'd come out as a plea, and she'd been half expecting him to dismiss it. He didn't ridicule her or tell her he'd get her sister to call her back when she returned.

He was paying attention, and he was absolutely serious.

She swallowed against a fear-parched throat, relief and hope trickling in past the constriction in her chest. "There's someone—several people—chasing me. I think I lost them in the crowds at the big shopping center."

"Are you safe where you are?" His tone was calm but managed to convey urgency, too, and it helped her focus.

She glanced around her. "Maybe? Probably not. I walked fast, but I walked, didn't run. So they might not have seen me leave the mall area. I tried to blend in with the tourists."

The moment she'd seen her pursuers, a childhood memory of her sister's voice played through her head, telling her to never run from immortals—or predators in the real world—because running attracted their attention. So she hadn't. Random, maybe, but here she was with a chance to evade some very scary people. She'd take advice in whatever form it came.

"Can you get to the Search and Protect office building?"

She laughed, the sound harsh to her own hearing. "That's why I was near the Ala Moana Shopping Center. I was trying to get there."

God, had she even said the name of the place right? She was so not a local. This guy didn't sound like one either. Would he even know how to find her?

Taking a deep breath, she fought for calm. "I took a taxi there first, trying to get close to the office building. But then I spotted the people chasing me waiting nearby and left."

They hadn't been standing right out in the open, but they'd been dressed in suits. In the heat of the day, not even the office workers actually wore full suits as far as she knew. Not on Oahu or any of the other Hawaiian islands. It'd set off alarms in her head, and she'd veered off, falling into step with tourists headed from the mall to the other shopping areas.

"Okay." His calm acceptance helped her settle. "If you walked away from the mall and stayed with the crowds, are you near the beaches now?"

"Yes." *Hurry*. They both needed to communicate faster. "Around the big hotels. I figured there'd be more security near them."

"It's mid-morning, still cool out. Good time for shopping until people get hungry and start looking for places to eat lunch." His words were coming quicker, too. "There's always catamarans over there, launching from the beach for a sail out to deeper water. Vendors sell tickets to tourists all up and down the streets. They go out for an hour, maybe two.

Do you see any signs for those? You can buy tickets right on the beach."

"Yes." Once he'd told her to look, she spotted one or two right away. "There's one right between two of the big hotels with boardwalks."

"Good. I know where that is." His tone took on a crisp quality, full of confidence. "Get on one of the catamarans. Don't drink much but do what you need to, to not stand out. That'll take you out of reach until I can get to you. I'm headed there now. When you get off the cruise, I'll be at the ticket booth waiting for you."

"How will I know it's you?" She'd never seen any of her sister's friends, not from the military or whatever Arin did now.

"Look for the guy with the service dog. I've got a GSD."

"A what?" Even as she asked, she hurried toward the ticket booth and fumbled for her tiny change purse where she kept her cash, one credit card, and ID. She struggled to juggle it and her phone while she tried to keep aware of her surroundings. The thing was cute but it was a pain in the ass to get what she needed out of and back into it.

There was a sigh on the other end. "German Shepherd Dog. He's big, black and tan, a lot like Arin's partner. We probably won't blend in with the crowd."

That was okay though, right? Once he came to get her, she'd be safe. No one was going to just grab her with some badass mercenary.

"It'll be okay. Get on the catamaran." His voice was soothing and sounded so good. She wanted to know what his lips looked like shaping those words.

"I'll get a ticket." And maybe she could take the time on the waves to reassemble her scattered mind.

"Go ahead, Mali. I'll be there as fast as I can." He ended the call.

She tucked the phone into the back pocket of her shorts. When she reached the small booth, her heart plummeted. The catamarans went out at the top of the hour. She had at least a forty-minute wait. Buying a ticket and a floppy hat to protect her dark hair from the sun's heat, she tucked the ticket into her change purse and tried to maintain a casual attitude as she scanned the area around her.

Suddenly, being between the big hotels didn't seem like such a good idea. The streets between them were more like alleyways, shadowed by palm trees, with lots of random doors and archways to get pulled into. There was nowhere to run on the narrow boardwalks, and it wouldn't be easy to jump over the waist-high walls into the private pool areas. Maybe a hot action movie star could vault those retainer walls and sprint across the hotel grounds to lose his pursuers, but she was a skinny postdoc who could at best be described as vertically challenged.

She'd left the sidewalks along the street thinking it'd be harder to grab her and stuff her into a car, but was the beachfront area so close to the hotels much better?

Every man walking past her seemed to be staring at her through his sunglasses. Every woman seemed to be looking the other way. The women who did look in her direction could've just as easily been after her, too.

She rubbed her palms together. It was the beach, though. She'd spot suits a mile...

Cold fear washed through her, and her stomach twisted hard as the distinctive black fabric of men wearing ridiculously hot suits appeared at the far end of the boardwalk. They were so far away that they were barely more than dots but they stood out in stark contrast to the sane people wearing light colors and airy warm weather wear.

They were still trying to find her. They had to be. They couldn't know exactly where she was because they'd have made more of an effort to sneak up on her. Wouldn't they? If she could see them coming so easily, she still had a chance to fade away before they spotted her.

Time to walk in the opposite direction. Removing her light-colored hat so it wouldn't catch the eye as she moved, she held it close at her side. She forced herself to move at the pace of the people in front of her, only passing tourists on the narrow boardwalk when others were. There were the occasional picture takers halting to capture a memory here and there. She slipped around them and counted each as one more obstacle between her pursuers and her.

Her heart raced as she tried to catch sight of the people behind her in any reflective surface. Suddenly, every person wearing sunglasses was a rearview mirror. She didn't dare bring attention to herself by looking over her shoulder.

Her memory of her big sister's advice came back to her again, echoing in her ears over the harsh sound of her own breathing. She even remembered the childhood movie that'd inspired her sister. The lesson had been simple. There'd been two things to remember. Don't run. Don't look back. These weren't immortals and she wasn't a unicorn, but they were definitely predators, and she didn't want to attract their attention if they hadn't spotted her yet.

The boardwalk ended, and the beach spread out in front of her. Too many people stood idle on the path ahead. Her thoughts crystallized almost painfully as it occurred to her that the men behind her could be dressed so conspicuously to drive her into an ambush ahead of her. It'd been a miracle no one had grabbed her yet.

She couldn't keep walking. They might have others ready to meet her where the path led back to the street. Getting shoved into a car would end her chances of being rescued by Raul Sá and his GS— whatever.

He'd told her to do what was needed to keep from standing out.

Her gaze passed over the beach dotted in sunbathers. The awesome thing about Waikiki was the way some people came prepared with towels and beach bags, but others just showed up on a whim and laid out on the sand using nothing but their shirts.

She began unbuttoning hers.

In moments, she'd slipped up close to a scattered collection of local girls, all laying out. Some had shirts, some didn't. They were all gorgeous. The best Mali could do was be thankful she'd always tanned easily and had been on the island long enough to develop summer color. Her Southeast Asian heritage gave her dark brown skin with golden undertones, not quite the same but similar to the local islanders. She wouldn't stand out as tourist-pale among them.

Wearing a bikini under her clothes had been a regular thing for the last several days as she and her fellow postdocs took advantage of the locale to enjoy the beaches every bit as much as their research. She was leveraging the habit to hide in plain sight.

Dropping her shorts, she laid them out and spread her shirt over the sand. She stretched out on her belly quickly, hiding her dark hair under the floppy hat, and watched the feet of passersby. Hopefully, people couldn't see her trembling.

*   *   *

"Damn." Raul fumed at the delay as he and Taz threaded their way through the crowds on the sidewalks. Even in late morning, traffic headed into the Waikiki area—or "town," as locals called it—was insanely slow. On the island of Oahu, it seemed like it was tourist season year round, and Waikiki was overrun by them.

He headed down the side street he thought would bring him out at the beach closest to his destination. It was a risk because he was going by memory from a vacation years ago. He hadn't had time since he'd arrived to refresh his knowledge of the area.

Hopefully, Arin's little sister was going to see him coming and give him a sign or he was going to be screwed trying to spot her right away. Hawaii, especially Oahu, had a huge number of Asian visitors and locals with some Asian ancestry, so it wasn't as if the woman was going to stand out in the crowd just based on physical features. He could spot Arin in a heartbeat, even in a crowd, but Arin had told him that she and her sister didn't share a strong physical resemblance. It was a family joke. Beyond that, Arin didn't talk much about her family besides how incredibly smart her sister was. Intelligence didn't help when Raul was trying to recognize her on sight. And considering the places he and Arin had served in, neither of them had carried pictures of family or those close to them.

His best chance had been looking in the hallway closet. He'd traded instant messages with Arin the night before, the way they did a couple nights a week. Arin had told him how she'd met with her sister for dinner. How it was funny her sister was on the island for some sort of research thing and Arin hadn't known ahead of time. Mali had simply texted her out of the blue. Mali had forgotten her jacket at dinner, and Arin was holding onto it, expecting to meet with her again.

There'd been one jacket in the closet that looked like it belonged to a young woman. It was more of a light-weight hoodie in teal. Arin rarely wore anything outside of a monochromatic black and white color scheme so Raul had grabbed it, guessing it belonged to her sister. The rest of the core members of their team were male, and Miller's wife was of a completely different build. No way did the hoodie belong to her.

As he and Taz came out on the beach, Raul headed straight for the catamaran booth where tickets were sold. The catamarans came back up on the beach in right about the same place. To his left and right, big chain hotels rose up and towered over the beach.

No one else was waiting around the booth. The next sail wouldn't go out until just before sunset. A quick scan up and down the boardwalks extending in either direction revealed no suspicious characters. Of the people out and about, he and Taz were actually the most conspicuous. Then again, there weren't a lot of big dogs on the island, and Taz was wearing a service dog harness.

Stealth wasn't one of his objectives today. In fact, if his presence scared off whoever was after Mali, all the better.

There were a bunch of women wandering past. Several of them glanced at him with interest, but there was no flash of recognition. None of them approached him. Just about every female in the area was with a partner, friend, or group of friends. No lone woman anywhere, much less one looking nervous or waiting for someone.

"Taz."

His partner looked up at him immediately, ears forward

and ready to work. If they'd been working alone, he wouldn't even need to use the dog's name. But here, in a crowded place, it was best to make it clear he was addressing Taz.

Raul retrieved the baggie containing her hoodie from the small backpack he'd slung over his shoulder. He held the plastic bag open for Taz, showing him the scent article inside and allowing his partner to sniff it liberally. "*Zoek.*"

Track. Taz was trained to respond to Dutch commands, one of the standard languages used to train working dogs, and this was his primary skill set: finding people.

His partner went to work. The big dog ranged back and forth in front of Raul, sniffing first the ground and then lifting his nose to catch additional airborne scents on the breeze. Taz proceeded forward once he'd systematically checked everything within the current grid, from the sand to the side of the booth to a nearby retention wall. In a few minutes, Taz froze, his stillness deliberate.

He'd found a trail.

"*Braaf.*" Even as he praised the dog, Raul's heart pounded. Just because Taz had hit on the trail didn't mean Mali was safe. It just gave them something to follow to her, so long as the trail remained clear and wasn't disrupted farther ahead. Raul also didn't know if Mali had left the area of her own free will. If she'd been taken or if she'd had to run, there was no way to tell from the ground around the booth. The loose sand and the passersby left no hints. All he knew was that the woman he'd come to help wasn't where she was supposed to be, and his partner had a trail that might be hers. He needed to assume the worst and hurry as best he could. "*Zoek.*"

Excited by the trail, Taz surged forward to the full length

of the six-foot lead. If this had been a sanctioned search and rescue in coordination with local law enforcement, Raul would've let Taz off leash. In this case, he kept the GSD tethered. If they were stopped by police or other security, he wanted to be with the dog when they approached so he wasn't mistaken as lost or without a handler. But considering the urgency, Raul let Taz set the pace.

They moved at a fast walk. Taz followed the trail along the narrow boardwalk past the huge hotel. Despite the heavy foot traffic, the big dog proceeded with confidence. He was locked into working mode and wasn't allowing anything else to distract him. They paused once or twice as Taz sniffed the ground and the railing before continuing.

She must've paused in each of those places.

A few minutes later, they were moving out onto the broad expanse of Waikiki beach. It was getting to the hottest part of the day, and Taz was panting now between sniffing the air to catch scents. Heat rose up off the hot sand.

Raul called Taz to a halt and gave the big dog a quick drink, making sure his nose got good and wet. The water served two purposes. Taz's well-being was paramount. A handler always thought of his dog before anything else. The second reason was the impact of the harsh sun on the bare sand of the beach. As the area dried out from the morning, scent particles would be harder to catch unless the dog was well-hydrated. Taz's panting, the increased saliva, and a wet nose maximized Taz's ability to keep and follow the trail.

It took only moments and Taz was back on the trail. The dog veered away from the path. Mali must've decided not to go back toward the street. It was a smart choice, but where had she gone? Raul saw nothing but sunbathers and tourists lounging out on the beach.

His partner wasn't relying on sight, though. Taz weaved his way through tourists and locals.

"Don't touch the dog, please." Raul smiled to diffuse the disappointment as people sat up or leaned toward Taz. "He's working."

Even with a service harness on, there were a lot of people who tried to pet a working dog. Though a decent number of people scooted away when they caught sight of Taz, too. At around eighty-five pounds of muscle, he was a good-size canine. His mostly black face, with only hints of tan, was intimidating.

Despite the reaching hands, Taz remained focused on his task, nose to the ground here and lifted to the air there. It was Raul's job as his handler to run interference so Taz could do his job.

They had a lady in distress to find.

In moments, Taz approached a group of girls. Raul hesitated, keeping his eyes on his dog, but Taz was all about the trail. The big dog sniffed right up to a petite sunbather with an amazingly shapely, tight behind and poked his nose right into her golden bronze hip, then sat, looking back at Raul expectantly.

"Taz." Raul was scandalized. Jesus, the hoodie must not have been Mali's. Instead, they'd ended up molesting some random girl…

The bikini-clad, dainty woman stirred and peered up at them from under a bright white, floppy hat. The face…

…was a ghost of Arin's, about five years younger, with a more delicate jaw and rounder cheeks. The biggest difference was in the eyes; the skin folds of the upper eyelids covering the inner angle of the eyes.

Maybe most other people didn't see the resemblance, but he did.

Taz leaned toward the woman's face, sniffing, and then gave a soft bark.

No doubt about it, Taz had found his target. Raul pulled a well-chewed tennis ball from his pocket and tossed it to Taz as his reward, then turned his full attention to the woman. "Mali Siri?"

"My full last name." Her voice was hoarse. "You said you knew it."

Fair. Even if Taz was proof that Raul was the person she'd spoken to on the phone, she was smart to get confirmation that he knew her older sister as well as he'd claimed.

"Srisawasdi." He fumbled over the pronunciation a little. The *r*, the last *s*, and the *i* were almost silent but he tended to miss the correct intonation. Intonation mattered in the Thai language, he'd learned, and could completely change the meaning of the word. So he spelled it out for her, too. "It was strongly implied that it would be better for your parents to shorten their surname to something easier to pronounce when they immigrated to the United States, so it was shortened. But Arin never forgot the full name and the meaning behind it."

Mali closed her eyes then opened them slowly, her expression weary. "Neither did I, but she's always been angrier about it. It's a long story. I'm just...tired."

Raul looked sharply at her face. Her lips were cracked, they were so dry. "How long have you been laying here?"

He kneeled immediately and handed over a spare water bottle. Now that he wasn't embarrassed out of his mind about his dog poking a strange girl's butt with a cold nose, he took a more serious look at Mali Siri. Her golden bronze skin had a red undertone to it. She'd been in the sun long enough to burn. "Sip that slow."

She did as he advised, her movement sluggish and her hands trembling. She spilled some water down her chin as she sipped.

Muttering a curse under his breath, he scanned the area to confirm no potential threats were nearby and then he draped her hoodie around her shoulders. "Take your time. You're safe now."

CHAPTER THREE

We'll take you up to the main house once we've got you cooled down," Raul called into the bathroom.

Good. Mali hadn't wanted Arin to see her with salt and sand in her hair, ready to pass out from overexposure and about to have a heat stroke. She'd asked for the chance to put herself back together. Raul Sá had hesitated but offered the use of his hotel room.

Her sister's friend was cute. Under different circumstances, she'd have taken his offer as an invitation. But at the moment, her nerves were a mess. She'd spent long minutes expecting people to find her, yank her off the sand, and make her disappear like the others.

Somehow, she'd gone past terrified into a semi-conscious state out there, hiding and waiting. Never had she realized how hard it was to be still when all she wanted to do was break cover and run. Only there'd been no cover. She'd been exposed with no alternative but to hope they didn't notice her. It'd taken about an hour, her heart pounding in her ears and the sun burning down on her back, before his dog had found her.

Turning on the shower, Mali set the heat to a gently tepid temperature. It'd help cool her down, and she could use the hotel lotion to treat her skin. There was no getting away from the sunburn, but she could do her best to minimize the damage.

If she wasn't well, her older sister wouldn't listen to a word Mali said until Arin was satisfied Mali was taken care of. It was a quirky silver lining that Raul had answered when she'd called her sister's line.

There was a precise knock at the bathroom door. "I had room service bring up water with cucumber slices and a plate of fresh fruit. If you can sip and eat, it'd be good for you to rehydrate. It'll be right here in the room after you come out of the shower."

Mali stepped toward the door. "Okay."

There was a pause then. "I'll leave Taz in the room. Leave the bathroom door unlocked. If you feel faint or something, just call. He'll let me know to come help you. Otherwise, I'll be out in the living area so you can have your privacy."

"Thank you." She didn't have the energy to say more as she stepped under the cooling trickle of water. Never had she been so thankful for the gentle fall of a rainfall showerhead.

He was kind. A lot of men in her life were sincere enough in that they consciously made an effort to be nice. As men of academia, they were intelligent and sophisticated, schooled to a higher level of thinking and applied theory. But many of them lacked a gut understanding of why they did what they did. They required explanation and logic, a concise hypothesis and sufficient supporting evidence to take action. They'd have tried to calm her down earlier today until she'd simply disappeared.

But Raul had acted. And now, he was taking action again. His kindness, his consideration, was intuitive and came from a desire to help a friend's sister or a damsel in distress. He probably wasn't thinking too hard about it. He was just doing the right thing. And for that, she was grateful.

It wasn't until she tasted salt on her lips that she realized she was crying. Ducking her head under the water, she let the shower clean away the fear of the day. She breathed in the steam and detected the faint scent of eucalyptus. She tried to order her thoughts, organize them so she could take the next steps.

"Field research involves risks." She was muttering, but the words were for her anyway, not for anyone else. Hearing the sound of her own voice helped her find her own center.

Her colleagues, her friends, needed her, and she needed to pull herself together. They'd all been downtown conducting interviews to gather data earlier this morning when her principal investigator had blown his alert whistle in a shrill warning. It'd scattered her routine and sent her through the streets, looking for safety. She was a professional researcher and had acted in accordance with her training and established procedure. The time for fear was past, and she should consider what came next. But she wasn't over it.

A funny noise echoed in the shower, the sound of her teeth chattering. She wrapped her arms around herself and leaned against the tiles. Damn, damn, damn. As much as she wanted to pull herself together, she was shaking herself apart just like she used to as a child.

Arin wouldn't be like this. Her older sister would've done everything differently, would turn everything around.

Maybe, if it'd been Arin with them in Chinatown, they would all be safe and simply continuing on with their research. Maybe...

Something cooler than the shower water touched her hip. Instinctively, she shrank away and pressed herself harder against the tiles. "What?"

Mali blinked water from her eyes and looked down into dark brown eyes. Taz looked up at her, one paw in the shower with her, and whined. She didn't know dogs the way Arin did—and maybe it was her imagination—but this dog looked concerned.

She swallowed. "Shh. Don't bring him yet. Look, I'm getting out of the shower now."

Having a large canine practically in the shower with her was new. It was weird enough to shake her out of her mental spiral, and for that, she was grateful to the big dog. Gingerly, she turned off the water and reached for the towel.

The big dog gave her space but remained within arm's reach as she wrapped the towel around herself without bothering to dry off and made her way unsteadily out of the bathroom and into the bedroom. As she slid onto the bed, she reached for the cool glass of water to sip.

Only then did Taz relax and sit back on his haunches, still watching her intently.

"Thanks." She studied him. "Did you turn the doorknob? Seriously?"

She could've believed it if the door had a handle like some of the more ornate décor one might find in nice hotels. But the door to the bathroom had a round doorknob. That was a lot harder to turn when one didn't have thumbs. Hell, she had trouble turning a doorknob when she put too much lotion on her hands.

The dog only opened his mouth and panted, his ears up as he watched her.

Her stomach was roiling with nerves but she took a piece of pineapple and nibbled at it. What she really wanted was a musubi or onigiri. There was nothing like a good rice ball to settle her stomach and she'd been spoiled the last few days with the availability of good ones here on the island. Back in Boston, she had to go to restaurants specializing in Japanese cuisine, and even those might not have her favorite snacks in favor of Americanized sushi.

Actually, she couldn't remember seeing Spam anywhere. Musubi were a new passion.

Taz placed a paw the size of her fist on the edge of the bed. Once he seemed sure he had her attention, he withdrew his paw.

"Are you allowed to eat pineapple?" He was looking at her face and not the pineapple in her hand, and she didn't think well-trained dogs were allowed to beg. The plate of fruit on the nightstand was well within his reach, and he wasn't paying any attention to it either. "I don't speak dog."

She had a PhD in Human Rights and Transnational Studies and was struggling with communications issues across species. The situation was heading into the surreal.

Someone knocked at the bedroom door and she jumped, dropping her piece of pineapple. Taz discretely picked up the fallen piece of fruit between his teeth and placed it on the edge of the plate.

* * *

Raul made sure to give it a solid three count from when he heard Mali give permission to enter and when he opened the door. He didn't want any chance of misunderstanding and catching her by surprise. When he saw the looks of guilt on both Taz's and her face, he wondered if he should just turn on his heel and head back out.

"I didn't feed him." Mali's immediate reassurance had Raul looking at Taz.

Taz had his ears back a touch and his head angled as if leaning away or exposing his neck. There was dog denial in every line of his posture.

Some might believe animals incapable of the kind of reasoning and nuanced decision making generally attributed to human consideration. But Taz was incredibly well trained and also possessed a strong predisposition toward caretaking. Whatever food might be in a person's hand, Taz would never take. Nor would the big dog ever beg for a handout from a weakened individual, which Mali was at the moment.

Raul tried hard to remember she was unwell, but damn. She was sitting on the bed wrapped in nothing but a towel. Her hair was still wet, only serving to accentuate the sweet shape of her face and to make her eyes look larger. Her knees were bent, probably to keep the sunburned backs of her legs away from the fabric of the bed covers. Even air contact was likely to be hurting her right now. The effect, though, was incredibly distracting because she was gorgeous in so many ways.

"I was just trying to figure out if he's allowed to eat pineapple." Mali pressed her lips together, looking more uncomfortable than could be blamed on her sunburn.

Taz just kept looking at him. It wasn't like the dog could speak in his own defense.

"To be fair, he didn't seem to want it," Mali added in a rush. "And I just dropped a piece by accident, and he didn't eat it. Actually, he cleaned up. Put it back on the plate."

Ah, well that would explain Taz's guilt then. Generally, the dog had been carefully trained not to take food from anyone. But he'd touched it, which was an undefined area of action, and Taz probably wasn't sure how Raul would react. Not that Raul had ever seen Taz put something back on a plate ever.

He cleared his throat. "Concierge sent up some aloe. I thought it'd help make you more comfortable before we head up to the main house."

Yup. Mind on the mission. He'd rescued the damsel, and now he needed to get her back to her family. Because her sister was absolutely capable of erasing him from existence if he entertained any of the distracting fantasies forming with every minute he spent in this room. Arin Siri might be primarily a search-and-rescue handler in the present, but she'd been a sniper in the past and had her share of hand-to-hand combat experience, too.

"Ah. Thank you." Mali's lips twisted in a very cute grimace. Then she managed to tuck her legs under her so she could rise up on her knees to reach for the bottle of aloe lotion.

He took a step forward, figuring she looked unsteady. She shouldn't be leaning to get something when he was perfectly capable of bringing it to her. He'd managed to take a couple of steps, then Taz was standing, too.

When eighty-five pounds of dog is suddenly in your way, you either stop or trip over him. Momentum played a part in Raul's decision. He fell forward and spread his arms wide to catch himself on the bed rather than accidentally catch a handful of Mali's towel.

He caught a face full of her towel-covered cleavage instead.

Mali squeaked.

Raul rolled to the side.

Taz barked.

"Sorry." *Jeezus*. He tried to get out his apology, his eyes clamped shut. He was not going to remember how good she smelled, a mixture of honey and sea salt and the indefinable, delicate scent of woman. Nope. He wasn't. Nor was he going to ever think about how nice her cleavage had been. Just enough to bury his face and let him nuzzle without being so full he'd suffocate. The palms of his hands burned with an insane desire to feel her soft skin cupped in his grip.

Mali backed away and then hissed in pain.

His head cleared, and he opened his eyes to see nothing but ceiling. "Did I hurt you? Do you need help?"

She leaned forward into his range of view, one hand clutching the front of her towel over her breasts. That was a really hot image, too. "No. I just sat back too fast and put weight on my sunburn."

"Oh." He had no idea what to do. He couldn't sit up while she was leaning over him and rolling to the side seemed awkward as hell. Of course, so did lying flat on his back in front of a woman in nothing but a towel. "Is there something I can do to get out of this situation without Arin wanting to kill me?"

Mali's eyes widened, and she froze for a moment, her lips forming a seriously naughty-looking O. Then she blinked and laughed. "No. Probably not."

It was either laugh with her or pull her down for a kiss. "I'm doomed. Dead." He paused. "Once I get you safely to Arin, that is. No worries. We'll get you to her before I report myself for molesting her little sister."

Her laughter faded, and her dark brown eyes sparkled with mischief. "Well, if you're going to get in trouble anyway..."

She bent then, leaning a hand on his chest, and pressed her lips to his.

CHAPTER FOUR

Mali's lips burned against his as she pressed against him. Her sunburn might explain the temperature but it had nothing to do with the way heat scorched through his entire body as she pulled back just enough to lick his lower lip and then settled her mouth over his for a deeper kiss. He opened for her, letting loose a low groan as her tongue explored and teased.

Apparently that worked for her, because she answered with a pleased sound of her own and tilted her head for a better fit.

Flat on his back and at her mercy, he balled up the bed covering in his fists to resist the urge to run his hands over her. Not that he didn't want to. Damn, but it was taking everything he had not to wrap her in his arms and tumble her right out of her towel.

"So good," he muttered the words against her lips.

"Mmm." She'd settled on top of him, her hands flat on his chest.

A nervous whine broke through his awareness, and suddenly her weight was gone. Raul opened his eyes to see her sitting beside him looking toward the side of the bed.

Taz sat there with ears canted slightly back and a glazed expression in his eyes. The dog had an amazing sense of smell, and right now, he was probably drunk on all the pheromones. Raul sat up and shook his head. He was pretty overwhelmed, too. Obviously.

"We need to get you back to your sister, and I have kennel duties to finish." Shit. He hadn't even started. Leaving the way he had without a word to anyone, he was sure he'd left behind a crap impression. This had obviously been more important.

Mali was biting her lip, one hand clenching the towel over her chest. She nodded. "Yes. I don't know why I… We really need to get to my sister and your team. I need help."

She had started to tremble, and her jaw was clenched hard enough to make the muscles stand out.

"Hey." He tried for a soothing tone but he wasn't good at comfort. He started to lift his hand, remembered the state of her skin, and let his hand drop. A person needed calm to project it, his mother used to say, and Raul hadn't been the type to keep calm inside him. He'd been the kind to fake it. "It's okay. People have all kinds of reactions after they've been in danger. You can take your time to tell us what happened. You're safe now."

She laughed, the sound strained by her chattering teeth. "I am. My PI and the rest of my research team are out there, though. I'm hoping they're safe like me. But I need to find out for sure."

PI. Private investigator? No. Raul wracked his brain for what he knew about her. "You're here conducting some kind of research."

She nodded. "The main research is my principal investigator's but my secondary research was under his supervision. There's another postdoc on the team and we've been here on the island gathering testimonials. We're close to the same age, obviously not law enforcement, so the individuals we're trying to interview are more willing to talk to us than the older researchers."

Raul nodded. The details weren't completely fitting together right now but he was taking mental notes and would see if he could make sense of them later. He wanted to encourage her to keep talking but he didn't want to drain her either. This needed to happen at her pace.

It must've been the right thing for him to do because her shaking eased. She reached out carefully for the water glass and took a sip. When she spoke again, she was somewhat more settled. "The police are limited help with the research. Hawaiian laws are still evolving to protect the right people so most of the victims we want to interview aren't willing to talk to us for fear of being arrested, but we'd started making progress with local contacts. Even if we weren't looking to buy what they were selling, they were willing to chat if we made it worth their time and didn't get in the way of potential...clients."

Raul tried hard not to let his eyebrows rise up into his hairline. If this was going where he thought it was going, he was very sure Mali had gotten tangled up in some bad news. "I'm guessing you weren't trying to interview street vendors selling knock-offs or produce."

Her gaze met his and there was a fierce spark in her dark brown eyes. "No. Human trafficking is a serious problem around the world. Places like Waikiki and Honolulu are key hot spots because of the sheer waves of tourists coming and going year round."

Considering the mention of clients, it was unlikely that the people Mali and her postdoc friend had been trying to interview were manual laborers. More likely, Arin's little sister had been approaching prostitutes to interview them for her research. Prostitutes could be dangerous, yes, but worse were their pimps. Arin was going to have a stroke. Raul rubbed his forehead. He wasn't maintaining his calm thinking about this either.

"You said men in suits took your friends this morning." He tried to focus on the details that didn't fit. Tried to get her talking again so she could release her pent-up tension, ease the shaking more.

Mali blinked several times but she maintained eye contact. "They weren't standard pimps, obviously. I don't know who these new men were. We were doing early morning interviews because work is slow for the ladies then and the pimps sleep in late. These men pulled up, and we thought they might be government officials checking up on our research until they started talking to my PI. I was farther away, down the street but still able to see everyone. We always kept in sight of each other. But then they made a grab for my PI, and he blew his safety whistle in the pattern for us to scatter. We all bolted in different directions."

Relief flashed through him, and then he paused. "Usually safety whistles are to call for help. I'm glad you all split up to get out of there; don't get me wrong. It's just unusual."

She lifted her chin. Her back straightened, and she was proud sitting there in nothing but a towel. Proud and confident and gorgeous in that moment. "Our studies on human rights take us to a lot of places. Not all of them are safe. Sometimes it's smarter to call for help to come to you, and sometimes everyone should split up and regroup. We have whistle patterns for either scenario."

The moment passed, though, and she sank onto her heels a fraction.

He didn't want to take away from her confidence, the strength she had despite her fear and exhaustion. Despite sunstroke, she was holding up amazingly well. "Let's get you to your sister and our team. Then we'll regroup with your PI and research colleagues. Okay? One step at a time."

Her gaze rose to meet his. He wondered at the mahogany red hue of her brown eyes. Amazing.

Then tears welled up, and she blinked them back, but a few spilled over. "I don't know if they're safe. I haven't got a call yet, and when we scatter we're supposed to meet up the next morning at the hotel. It'll be a whole afternoon and night before it's time to meet." Her shaking increased, and her hands tightened into fists at the top and bottom of the towel, holding it and herself together.

Raul got off the bed. He searched his closet for something loose and light for her to wear. Her burned skin wouldn't do well in her smaller, closer-fitting clothing. "Then we have time to take care of your health and talk to the team. What you saw wasn't just a thug issue. And if they came after you, we should be prepared to handle them before the situation escalates."

Truth was, she would need to tell the team all of this again and then probably the police. It wasn't a good sign when men stood out the way Mali had described and didn't care that they did. If they'd followed her all the way from downtown to the mall area and even farther to the hotel beach area, they had a good idea of what she looked like. They were going to come after her and her colleagues again.

He didn't know the island law enforcement yet but maybe one of his new teammates did. Raul had left a message on Arin's voice mail, but she wasn't likely to answer a call until she'd completed her current mission and was on the return trip. Raul wasn't sure when that would be, but Arin would go to the team house first to check in. Raul could call the police here to the hotel, but it might be better for them to come to Mali at the team house or even in town at the corporate office. Miller would know better but Raul definitely didn't think it was in Mali's best interest to take her down to the closest police station. She needed Arin.

And he planned to be right there with Mali, too.

* * *

Raul opened the front door to the house and gestured for Mali to go ahead. She smiled as Taz also waited for her. The two of them were a contrast to what she thought she'd encounter when she met her sister's coworkers.

Growing up, she'd viewed with trepidation the way her older sister went out into the world. Arin was straightforward, living out loud with no time for subtlety. Her sister preferred confronting people to get to the crux of any given situation. Mali hadn't appreciated it in their younger years. It meant fighting and raised voices. It meant discord and people disgruntled at her because her sister made them uncomfortable. She'd always imagined the people Arin would work with would be coarse, impatient, and intimidating.

Instead, Arin's best friend had dropped everything, at a single phone call, for Arin's little sister. And she hadn't been completely forthcoming with her sister the last time she'd been here.

Guilt tightened her chest as she stepped past Raul and Taz through the small foyer area into the comfortable living room. She'd had a lot of misconceptions previously and she was about to prevail upon them for even more help when she hadn't previously appreciated how important their work could be. Needing to ask for help was uncomfortable on a lot of levels.

Nails clicked on the cool stone tiles covering the floor as one of the big red hounds ambled into the room from down the hallway. The dog regarded her as it panted for a moment and then sat.

She'd met him when she'd come for dinner with her sister. At least she thought it was the male. There were two, and she'd mostly seen them together. They belonged to Todd Miller, the kennel master. He and his wife lived here at the team house, so Mali had met them when she'd visited previously.

Mali let the cool seep into the soles of her feet, too keyed up to sit on one of the couches nearby. She'd thought it an odd choice to have stone tile floors instead of some kind of wood flooring but Arin had explained to her how the stone tiles helped wear down the dogs' claws in a small way. Plus no wood floor would survive so many dogs coming and going at all times of day. The people in this house were practical.

Before their recent dinner, Mali and Arin hadn't spoken beyond the occasional brief text or email for years. Arin had always been away overseas and working. Mali had been buried in her undergraduate, then advanced, studies. They'd become only familial acquaintances, and Mali had no insight into what Arin did aside from doing dangerous work for the highest bidder. Arin never talked about it, and Mali decided she didn't care to know.

It'd been easier, more comfortable, to simply exchange pleasantries through those brief messages than to check in and really get into what was going on in their separate lives. This entire reunion with her older sister after years of adulthood had been a reset in the way Mali viewed what their relationship could be. Needing to call for help didn't reduce her unease at all, obviously.

"This is unexpected." Todd stood in the hallway, his other hound at his side. The silver-haired man smiled at her. "Welcome back. Arin hadn't mentioned you'd be visiting again."

The bigger hound—Dan, she remembered belatedly—moved to sit on Todd's other side. The female's name was Ann. Arin had explained to her that they were Redbone Coonhounds. Mali wouldn't have remembered at all if it hadn't been for the subsequent discussion on dog breeds they'd had and the kinds of traits a team like theirs looked for in their canine partners. It'd been surprisingly interesting, and more startling, talking about dogs had made her sister smile. Mali had few memories of Arin smiling. So here she was, looking at Dan and Ann, two aging Redbone Coonhounds flanking their master. Maybe it'd been a few seconds, or several minutes, because Mali wasn't sure how long she'd been lost in pondering them.

She lifted her gaze, belatedly hoping Todd didn't think she'd been staring at his legs. The man stood with his weight evenly balanced between his good leg and a high-end fitness prosthetic. If he thought her rude, it didn't show in his expression either. He was simply waiting.

"Abrupt change of plans." Mali gave him her best smile despite her struggle to think through swirling emotions. "I called Arin but Raul answered the phone. I asked him to pick me up."

"That so?" Todd's gaze lingered on Raul where the other man stood in the doorway. "Was wondering what would induce you to abandon your post."

Mali scowled. She didn't want Raul to get into trouble. The team hadn't seemed so formal when she'd visited Arin for dinner. Todd's words were cool, and his phrasing sounded distinctly severe to her.

"I made a decision." Raul's tone was respectful but his words were concise, not conversational. "It was urgent."

Todd considered Raul for another long moment before looking at Mali again, and his smile returned. "I'm guessing this'll be a good story then. Kalea happens to be in the kitchen right now. Raul can get back to what he was doing this morning, and why don't you and I head into the kitchen to see what Kalea might be cooking for lunch? Arin and Zu won't return from their mission until tomorrow but they should be calling in soon and we can get a more exact ETA."

Mali tensed. Arin wasn't just away for the morning. Asking for the team to help until her sister returned was too much of an imposition. But where else would she go and what should she be doing while she waited?

Raul stepped up behind her then and gave her a light nudge with a hand at the small of her back. "Sounds like a good plan. I'll be nearby if you need anything."

There were undercurrents, but Mali was too sun-tired to really understand what was going on. The idea of Raul and Taz walking away caused a sharp hitch in her breath, and her vision darkened. "No. Don't go. Don't leave me."

The room contracted and tilted sideways in her field of view. Her chest constricted.

A cold nose touched her thigh, and Taz slipped his head under her hand. The big dog pressed against her leg. Raul murmured gently, "We won't leave you."

Mali swallowed hard. She wasn't prone to panic attacks in recent years but she'd had them enough as a kid to recognize what was happening. She opened her eyes wide and looked around the room, filling her vision with the homey items in the simply decorated place. This was a place to rest.

No black suits. No guns. The sounds were of dogs panting and someone cooking in the kitchen. There were no safety whistles firing off a shrill warning pattern for her to run.

"I guess it might be better for all of us to go see what's for dinner." Todd's words were low as blood rushed through her ears at a dull roar. He gestured for them to head toward the kitchen.

Mali jerked her chin up and down in an affirmative, but her feet remained frozen in place until Raul stepped to her side and offered her his arm with a rakish grin. The ridiculousness of his expression startled a smile out of her. Her jangling nerves settled and gave her a chance to suck in some air. She slipped her hand into the crook of his elbow and let him lead her to the kitchen. There was the large table off to one side, big enough to seat six or even eight people if they got friendly and still be out of the way of anyone cooking. There was a lot of counter space, too, and a big range top over a full-size oven.

Kalea glanced up as they entered, her dark eyes landing on Todd first. She gifted her husband with a warm smile before focusing on Mali. Mali tightened her grip on Raul's arm. It wasn't that she was afraid of Kalea or anything. More the opposite. She was sunburned and off balance. Years of traditional Thai upbringing welled up with expectations of being a good, proper, polite guest. Mali wanted to try; but at the same time, tears of exhaustion welled up in her eyes.

She was a mess.

Kalea murmured something lyrical and gentle. "Aloha. Welcome back. I've some nice iced tea and fresh cut pineapple to cool you down. Why don't you sit?"

Mali wavered. "Fruit sounds very nice. Thank you. Um, mahalo."

Kalea came to her and folded her into a huge, gentle embrace. "No worries here. You've had a hard day. Anyone can see that. You just be you. We'll get a little bit of food into you and then a nice nap, yeah? Your sister will be back tomorrow, and that will be soon enough. Raul can tell my Todd what is needed now."

There was more, though. Mali wasn't sure how much she should tell all of them but they didn't know everything yet. A part of her dreaded voicing the rest out loud because she couldn't think straight, couldn't explain why she'd made the decisions she'd made.

And she was horribly afraid her choices might have caused all this.

But it was the last fear that forced words to tumble from her mouth. "We need to call the police. They need to look for my colleagues, my friends. I need to tell them what I saw and remember every detail. I had my rest. I can't wait any longer."

Todd stepped forward. "Sit first. Breathe."

She was sobbing. She didn't know when she'd started, but here she was. As a chair was pulled up for her, she sat and gritted her teeth. Damn it. She didn't want to be crying. She wanted to be collected and able to express herself clearly. She wanted to get back the logical part of her brain. Only it was burned away from overexposure to sun and fear. It hadn't been this bad at all when she'd been cooling down at Raul's hotel room. But during the car ride over here, she'd been thinking over and over about what she needed to tell her sister and what she needed to remember for the police. She figured they'd have questions, and she was trying to recall the university training for these situations when researchers went abroad. But then she wasn't abroad. She was still in the United States. Yet looking at the inside of the kitchen and the plate of assorted fresh cut fruit Kalea placed in front of her, this felt more like her childhood visits to Thailand.

Her thoughts were disjointed and tumbled together. She wasn't making any sense.

"It's okay." Raul was kneeling next to her. "We're listening to it all and I know enough to connect the pieces we need to figure out what to do next. It's okay."

She'd been talking the entire time, she realized. Her fingers closed convulsively over Raul's. He'd been holding her hand. "There's no reason to be this hysterical."

"Ah." Kalea made a comforting noise. "You've been in the sun too long. No one thinks straight after that much exposure. Let the boys do what they do with the information we already have. You rest."

Todd nodded. He was sitting at the table now and pushed a tall glass of tea in her direction. "Sip slow. Take your time. Kalea's ginger peach tea will settle your stomach while you rehydrate."

Mali clutched the cool glass. Her mother used to make her ginger tea to soothe her sore throat and settle her stomach. Better than water, her sister used to say, because drinking too much water when you were overheated could upset a person's stomach more.

There were so many childhood memories rushing up to crowd her thoughts today. Too many.

"I've got a friend at the local police department," Todd was continuing. His mention of police added a new drop of reality to the ripple effect going on inside her. "Instead of taking you down there, why don't I invite him here for dinner so we can keep this an informal chat? It'll be easier on you than formal questioning down at the station."

Mali sipped. "Is that allowed?"

Todd nodded kindly. "If it'll help you feel more comfort-

able and communicate easier, then definitely. What's important is that you give us as much information as possible. We
can go with what works. Far as Raul tells me, your teammates could also be making their way back to the hotel
overnight. They might be fine. You weren't directly as-
saulted. Your team might not have been, either, if they all
managed to stay out of harm's way as well as you did. So to
be honest, there's technically no incident to report. We'll just
make sure he has a heads-up in case things did go south."

True. She could be making a big deal out of nothing.
Scattering the way they did was intended to have this exact
outcome. It was a way to avoid harm and also ensure they
were free to carry on with their research without any fuss
from local law enforcement.

She laughed unsteadily and took a sip of the tea. It was
cool with a light flavor, the peach and ginger balanced but
not too sweet. Her stomach warmed a bit as the ginger hit.
There was obviously real ginger in there, not just a hint for
flavor. "I'm sorry to be so upset over nothing."

"Hey." Raul waited until she met his gaze. There was his
kindness again, patience. He'd let her go at her own pace
all day today, and she appreciated it. "This isn't nothing,
and there isn't anything wrong with your sense of urgency.
Better to know what we can do now than to wait without
worrying. If the need arises, we'll be ready to react because
you prepared us. Being upset, being afraid is absolutely real.
Bottling it up will only hurt you."

She didn't know what to say. She was frustrated with
herself but instead of trying to talk more, she sipped the
tea. Maybe having her big sister nearby, calling Arin for
help, had been a knee-jerk reaction. In Mali's confused state,
she was floundering and reverting back to the days when
she'd relied on her big sister to make things right. She didn't

like admitting that she was second-guessing herself despite Raul's reassurance, but it was exactly what she was doing.

The exercise of logically working through her emotional state helped settle her and made it easier for her to decide on what she could do for now. "Let's talk to your police friend, please. Then we'll see if my colleagues are back safe tomorrow."

Raul sat back on his heels and smiled. "Sounds like a plan."

CHAPTER FIVE

Raul climbed up the stairs from the basement level, tired and maybe a little punchy. He had one nagging concern eating away at him. There were any number of things he could be doing next, but Mali's situation kept occupying the forefront of his mind.

Miller was still in the kitchen, his chair pushed back so he was easily visible as Raul hit the landing. Dan and Ann lay on the kitchen floor by his feet. Like their master, they were showing their age but the two Redbone Coonhounds were still lean and muscular. Raul hadn't expected the breed, even if he recognized them, but then again, this private outfit was unique and their primary object was search. Hounds were excellent scent dogs.

The older man lifted his chin as their gazes met. "You made good time cleaning out those kennels."

It was no surprise the kennel master had waited up to ensure the job was done. The care and well-being of the dogs was Miller's utmost priority, and in a military environment he would outrank all of the handlers but Zu. Raul figured Miller would be going down to check on the quality of the work, too. Raul was new, and any good kennel master would see to it that the dogs received the best care possible. Most likely, the man would provide a few notes but Raul had been thorough. There shouldn't be any complaints.

The kitchen light was the only one on, but it was more than enough to see by so Raul headed into the kitchen with Taz at his side. "Nice setup you have down there. I like the direct access to the yard out back. Appreciate the big sink to wash up, too."

Miller extended his prosthetic under the table, using it to push out a chair at the kitchen table, an invitation to sit. "This morning was all hustle, getting Zu and Arin out to provide supplementary search support to the police on one of the other islands. Otherwise, I'd have been around to brief you on our general hours of operation and give you more of a tour around the house."

Miller pronounced both names with the ease of frequent use. Zu was uttered as "zoo" and Arin was pronounced "ah-rin" with a softer *ah* and *r* sound rather than the way most U.S. personnel tended to try to turn the name into "Erin."

It was a sign the team had gotten the chance to get to know each other in the few weeks before Raul had managed to join them. Arin, he'd known from prior service. And hell, she was probably his best friend in the English-speaking world. But he wanted to be sure he got along with the rest of their team, too. A soldier's existence could be uncomfortable at best or far worse than miserable when he didn't fit in with his team. His previous time on active duty had been closer to the latter than the former. Here, with this team, he'd wanted to start off on a positive note and he'd failed, for a good reason but that might not matter.

"There's been a lot going on today." Raul took a seat, giving himself a mental shake.

Dinner seemed like a long time ago. Miller's police friend, Officer Kokua, had joined them and Mali had told her story. She'd been calmer with a solid dinner in her, but reliving it had obviously taken her to the end of her energy reserve. When Kalea had suggested she rest the night in Arin's bed, Mali had immediately agreed. He'd gone down to kennel duty and even making good time, it'd been a couple of hours.

"Could say that." Miller paused, then grunted. "My wife, Kalea, left you some musubi in case you needed a late-night snack." He tilted his head forward to indicate a plate in the middle of the table.

"Appreciated." Raul awkwardly thought about how to bring up his concern about Mali while he had Miller here. As he considered ways to broach the topic, he lifted a snack sealed in plastic wrap from the plate. Miller did the same and unwrapped his without hesitation.

It looked to be a block of tender rice topped with a portion of omelet and a slice of . . . Spam, all wrapped together with a thin band of seaweed.

"Can't remember the last time I had Spam," Raul commented, then took a bite. Flavor burst across his tongue in a savory combination of salty and the barest hint of sweet. The rice was soft with every grain still holding its own shape. It was so much better than the mushy, overcooked stuff he'd had out of his eight-dollar rice cooker back on the mainland. "S'good."

A grin spread across Miller's face as he tossed the other half of his into his mouth. "You can find these in any convenience store on the island. Some are just the Spam and the rice. Others are made with different kinds of soy marinade."

"Betting the convenience store musubi aren't as good as homemade." Raul tripped over the unfamiliar name of the snack but he figured he'd get used to it quick.

"You think?" Miller raised an eyebrow.

Raul shrugged. "Nothing store bought ever is. These are real good. Please pass on my thanks."

Yeah, complimenting a cook's food was brownnosing some, but he was sincere. He bit in a second time and savored the flavors. Taking more time to taste, he thought he got a hint of sesame oil on the Spam along with the stronger presence of soy sauce. Sugar must've been added to make the flavors pop. The omelet was fluffy and a contrast from the rice and the firmer Spam.

Miller reached for another. "Well, you're welcome to these any time they're here. If my wife says she'll feed you, you are welcome in this house."

A simple concept, being welcome. One Raul had never realized was so very important until he hadn't been in the past. He was hungry for it here. To have it offered even after today's SNAFU had him swallowing past a hard lump in his throat. He covered the awkward moment by taking another bite and chewing carefully.

"Thanks." Raul studiously avoided glancing over at Taz. His partner and the coonhounds were all lying on the cool kitchen floor watching them eat but Raul didn't feed his partners at the table. Besides, marinated Spam would probably give Taz all sorts of gastrointestinal issues later. Raul preferred to maintain as healthy a diet as possible for a canine under his care.

That line of thought reminded him of the pineapple earlier in the day, and Mali.

"Sir—"

"Miller or Todd will do." Miller waved his hand. "We're

not as formal in this team. Zu is the founder and our lead. If he needs formality, it's usually in front of clients. When we're working among ourselves, we can keep it familiar."

Raul nodded. "The situation with Mali seems handled for the time being, but the more I consider what happened, the more concerned I am about what comes next."

Miller grunted. "You mean if her colleagues don't show up at their designated meeting place in the morning?"

Raul shook his head. "Even if they do, whoever made them scatter is still out there. I've only met Mali Siri today, but she doesn't come across to me as someone who walked all that way from downtown to the Waikiki beach area because she imagined men in suits were following her."

"The suits are weird," Miller agreed. "It's not local behavior, not even among the more affluent criminal elements here on the island. It's either incredibly stupid or making a statement to send your men out dressed like that in the middle of the day."

"If it's the latter, they're not going to be satisfied with scattering a few scientists." Raul wished it would've been enough. He didn't think Mali had thought beyond the need to know her colleagues were safe. "Your police friend is going to do some preliminary investigation, but is there any additional intel we can gather?"

Miller's bushy eyebrows came together as he considered and then nodded. "Might not turn up any hits before dawn, but we can get together the descriptions and send them on to a contact here on the island, a sort of intelligence specialist."

Even if it meant a sleepless night, Raul would give up the rest to ensure the fear in Mali's eyes could fade away. "Anything we can get on these men would be good. Once we locate Mali's colleagues, even if they're fine, they won't be able to continue their research."

If they tried, whoever had sent those men in the first place would be forced to escalate. The next time, someone could be hurt or worse.

"Best case, the scientists are going to have to leave off their current research." Raul kept his voice low, in case Mali was a light sleeper. He had no idea how thin the walls were. "Worst case, they're all going to need security detail until they can leave the island and go back to the mainland."

That was the worry eating away at Raul. If Mali's pursuers were still looking for her, she was in danger.

CHAPTER SIX

Mali lay staring at the ceiling in her sister's room, torn between wanting to sleep more and being driven to find out if the rest of her research team was okay.

Guilt immediately crashed over her again, and she sat up. Of course, she should be headed back to the hotel to meet up with everyone else. Hopefully they were all safe, and they'd be worried about her if she didn't check in soon. They had to be there, all of them.

She rubbed the heels of her palms over her eyes, still blurry with fatigue. Her limbs were all heavy and sore. Yesterday had been a marathon of adrenaline spikes and tension. After the evening spent speaking to Todd's police friend, she'd been worn out. Talking through the events of the day had wrung out the last bit of energy she had.

Going through it all again had calmed her, though. She'd been borrowing guilt, worrying about her line of research and related activities. Those were things that could wait, though. They hadn't caused yesterday, and she needed to check in with her PI before getting back to her research.

She picked up her phone from the bedside table and swiped sideways to unlock the security screen. There were no notification, no text messages, no messages on the app they tended to use for instant messaging. Nothing.

"Don't panic." She whispered the words to the room. It was still very early. The team members could still be making their way to the hotel from wherever they'd found to stay overnight.

She began to leave a message in the app and then hesitated. Their procedure was to hold on all messaging until they'd met. As much as she wanted the reassurance, she wouldn't see messages until people had gathered face to face. No one else had broken their procedure so she shouldn't either.

Mali grimaced as the skin across her face itched with dryness. As much advantage as she had with her complexion, her skin was tight from yesterday's sunburn. She probably looked hilarious too because she'd spent the entire time waiting for Raul on her belly with her face hidden. So her shoulders, back, and legs had taken the most exposure.

Where had everyone gone? They'd probably stayed in town. It would've been easy to blend in with tourists like she had and gotten a room at a different hotel.

If the men who'd chased her had also been as persistent with her colleagues, staying in town might not have been enough. Her worry spiked as she explored the myriad of possible outcomes. There had been one vehicle and a handful of those shady suits. She hadn't seen more. If she'd been the only one they'd come after, why her?

She swallowed against a dry throat. The water bottle on the bedside table was mostly full and had a slice of lemon in it. She reached for it and sipped slowly. It wasn't refrigerator cold anymore but it was still soothing.

Sitting here alone was not a good idea. She'd only work herself into a spiral of panic, asking questions to which there were no clear answers. She needed to get moving.

Mornings sucked at the best of times. She'd never been able to wake up at dawn the way Arin could. When Mali did wake up early, it took forever for her rambling thoughts to focus enough to push her body into moving. Or if she did get moving, her brain hadn't had the chance to wake up yet, and she might as well be sleepwalking for all the recollection she had of what she'd done before she'd had a good cup of coffee.

Coffee. Caffeine would be good. Kalea had said there'd be coffee this morning, and the woman had mentioned she'd make breakfast. Mali wasn't sure she was ready to eat breakfast yet but coffee would kick her thoughts into a higher gear. Right now, she was close to useless.

It took some effort to swing her feet over the side of the bed. Another long minute passed before she put her feet on the hardwood floor and stood. Her thoughts scampered around in her head, randomly. Sense and nonsense. She shivered as the cooler air of the room whispered across her exposed legs.

She'd slept in the shirt Raul had given her back at the hotel to wear here to the team house. It was a nice white linen shirt, light and broken in from enough wearings to be soft. It smelled of detergent, fabric softener, and faintly of him. She'd tried to sleep in the nightgown Kalea had loaned her, but the garment's lace edging had rubbed against Mali's sensitive skin. Arin didn't have any actual sleepwear—she tended to sleep in old tees and shorts. So Mali had switched back to Raul's shirt.

His scent and the memory of his lips had warmed her and distracted her enough from yesterday's fears to lure her to sleep. And her dreams had been very naughty.

This time, the heat in her cheeks wasn't from sun exposure. Raul was a very good kisser and in her dreams, she had imagined him to be equally good in other intimate things. Maybe better.

But about that coffee...

She found a pair of soft knit shorts in Arin's drawers. Her older sister was a couple sizes larger but the shorts had a drawstring. There was also a stretchy camisole Mali managed to slide on over her tender skin. Arin had luscious taste in fabrics even if all her clothes were in a monochrome range of black, white, and gray, with maybe a splash of navy blue for adventure. Every piece of clothing was good quality and of super soft, light fabric.

Dressed, Mali paused and reached for Raul's shirt. She didn't need it. She could probably plunder her sister's entire wardrobe. But having it in hand calmed her nerves so she put it on again over the camisole and shorts. It was oversize and comforting.

Random clattering and the sizzle of something savory became apparent as she opened the door to her sister's room. The hallway was empty but obviously someone was cooking in the kitchen. Mali padded down the hallway, her bare feet safer on the cool polished wood than socks would've been.

Kalea was at the stove, hovering over not one or two, but three pans. Mali had grown up thinking her older sister Arin was big, but Kalea had broader shoulders even than Arin, with amazing curves and a solid presence to fill out her frame. Kalea filled a room with herself, her delicious food, and a sense of welcome. She smelled of coconut and butter. She made this place a home, and it wasn't until Mali had come to visit Arin here that Mali had believed Arin had really found a family away from home.

The sight of Kalea chased away the lingering anxiety twisting in Mali's chest. It'd been the right decision to leave the solitude of the room and come out to the kitchen.

Kalea turned from the stove and halted when she caught sight of Mali. "There you are. The boys ate up all the breakfast so I made a fresh batch and was going to come wake you. Come. Sit."

Mali smiled and slid into the indicated seat at the kitchen table. "Is there coffee?"

Kalea grunted. "Coffee. You all look for coffee first thing. How can anyone think without a good breakfast in their bellies?"

Despite her words, Kalea snagged a pot from the coffeemaker. She set a mug down in front of Mali.

Mali breathed in the rich scent of strong coffee. She might wake up just from huffing it. "Thank you."

"Cream is in the fridge. Sugar is on the table. You sit and drink your brew." Under the brusque tone was a soft warmth. Kalea was a nurturing soul. "I'll have a plate for you in a second."

A far as Mali was concerned, good coffee needed neither cream nor sugar. She took an experimental sip first to find out if she'd need to add anything. A combination of bitter with a hint of sweet and almost chocolatey richness filled her mouth, and she almost groaned with the pleasure of it. "Oh, this is good." She should've known it would be, based on the rest of Kalea's cooking.

Kalea chuckled, bustling at the stove. "Apparently."

Coffee was a wonderful thing. Mali sat with her hands wrapped around the mug, sipping and enjoying. In moments, Kalea set a plate in front of her. "If you're still hungry, there's plenty more. Don't hold back. You had a rough day yesterday and you need the fuel to recover, find your balance again."

"Mahalo." Mali gave Kalea her first genuine smile of the day. Setting aside her mug, she lifted a fork and started in on the plate full of food. The warm interaction had encouraged her appetite as much as the fortifying dose of coffee.

There were scrambled eggs, soft and fluffy and rich with just the right amount of milk and cooked with butter. You'd think scrambled eggs were just scrambled eggs, but Mali had learned there could be sad things done to eggs which even scrambling couldn't save. Served alongside the generous helping of eggs were browned slices of Spam and Portuguese sausage. These were flavorful, and Mali figured she needed the salt content to continue rehydrating after her day in the sun yesterday.

The island of Oahu was hot and humid, though the breezes helped ease the heat most of the time. A person could sweat a lot without realizing how much moisture they were losing. It was easy to become dehydrated, and Mali had learned in the first few days of the research project to drink water every chance she got and enjoy a few salty treats to help her retain fluids.

Kalea remained in the kitchen, unsubtly hovering. The woman's hands flew from the stove to the countertop where she had a huge Japanese-style electric rice cooker. At the counter, she was making musubi.

Mali made sure to eat at least a third of her food before asking a question, otherwise she bet Kalea would refuse to answer until she ate more. "Is anyone around this morning?"

Kalea didn't look up from her task. "Mmm. Zu and Arin aren't back yet, but we expected them back late tonight. Todd—all the boys and Arin call him by our last name,

Miller—he's out back working with one of the dogs. Your Raul is downstairs on kennel cleanup."

He wasn't her Raul but Mali had a mouthful and didn't want to spit scrambled eggs making the correction. Besides, Kalea might be fishing. Instead, Mali speared a piece of Spam and kept her mouth full as she tried to get her brain thinking pertinent thoughts.

"Heard my name as I was coming up the stairs. What did you need?" Raul walked into the kitchen with uncanny timing. He was dressed in plain work pants and an old button-up shirt with the sleeves rolled up. Inside, his dark hair appeared black. It was a striking contrast with the bland tan of his clothing and his incredible green eyes.

Mali choked on her piece of Spam and reached for her coffee mug. She downed it in one gulp.

Kalea waved a spatula at him. "Not one step farther into my kitchen until you've showered and changed."

He'd been on kennel cleanup duty, Mali remembered. No one should be allowed to make work clothes and kennel cleanup smoking hot. No one.

Suddenly, she was grateful for Kalea's menacing spatula. Then Mali hoped Kalea had several backup spatulas to continue cooking in case Kalea actually whacked somebody with one.

Raul held up his hands. "Freshly washed up to the elbows and I left my boots downstairs. I promise I won't come one step closer."

Kalea grunted. "Mali was asking who was here."

"Ah." Raul paused. "Taz is with me. Ann and Dan are napping downstairs. There's one unpartnered Belgian Malinois in his kennel, and the other one is out back with your husband."

"Of course you'd know where all the dogs are. Todd will

like you." Kalea didn't turn to Raul, but she did reach back to offer a freshly made musubi.

Raul took it. "Thanks."

"It seems like you've only recently joined." Maybe it was morning grogginess or a need for more coffee, but Mali wasn't clear on a few things. "What's your role on the team? Will you be working closely with my sister?"

"Yesterday was my first day." Raul chuckled. "Taz and I can work on our own, or we can be part of a joint search and extract operation with the other handlers and their canine partners. It'll depend on the contract and what's needed. Zu wanted to keep us as adaptable as possible."

Kalea grunted again but didn't enlighten them with any further commentary.

"I thought you knew my sister really well. If not here, how have you worked with her in the past?" Mali drew her brows together. Maybe she did need a second cup of coffee.

Raul bit into his rice ball and chewed for a second. "We were assigned to the same unit when we were on active duty. After we both got out, she joined this team first, then recommended me. We've been friends a long time."

The kitchen fell silent except for the sizzling of Spam and eggs. Kalea continued to make a small mountain of musubi, wrapped in clear plastic wrap.

Mali pushed the last of her scrambled eggs around the plate. "Arin didn't talk much about the people she worked with in the military."

Actually, Arin hadn't told her or their parents much at all about her time in the military. She'd gone; she'd come back alive and whole. Arin hadn't ever gone into details about who she worked with or where she'd been.

"Not surprising." Raul finished his musubi. "There's not a lot family would be interested in knowing. A lot of stuff we can't talk about even if it would make for good dinner conversation."

"I want to know." Mali snapped her mouth shut. Old frustration bubbled close to the surface. It wasn't going to help at the moment, though, and this was more for Arin than him. "Of course family would want to know things."

"No." Raul's gaze caught and held hers. "There's no going back once you do. Trust me. It's better to love her the way you do right now and let her tell you things when she can."

Mali shifted in her chair, suddenly uncomfortable. This was the first time she'd broached this topic with one of Arin's friends or coworkers. Usually this was a family discussion. Raul's was a different perspective and having him push back on her comment was unexpected.

"I was hoping to go back to my hotel right now to see if the rest of my research team checked in yet." A change of topic seemed prudent. It was also chipping away at her calm, and her gut was starting to compact the delicious food she'd eaten into a heavy ball in her belly. "According to our procedure, we were supposed to meet back up in the morning. It's morning." Yes, she was stating the obvious, but it bore repeating to back up her request.

Raul was silent a minute longer. He leaned against the doorjamb. "No one is answering their personal phones?"

"We're not supposed to call or text until we meet up face to face." She chewed at her lip. "People's phone batteries could've died by now." Maybe "die" was the wrong term to use at the moment. It had an ominous feel, and she didn't want to worry even more than she already was.

"You could call their hotel rooms and leave a message if they don't answer right away." His logic was solid, his tone lifting at the end of his suggestion in a positive way.

Mali shook her head. "I hate to be an imposition, but after what happened yesterday, I think it'd be good to stay here for at least another night until I can talk with Arin about what I'm going to do next. Arin might want me to stay here for a few days, or I might book a different hotel. Either way I need to pick up my clothes and toiletries. Going right there and checking in person would kill two birds with one stone."

The line of Raul's jaw was angled and strong, small muscles jumping as he chewed on her request. "Arin's not back yet. You shouldn't go until she's here and can go with you."

"That could mean waiting all day. We were supposed to meet in the morning. Please." She made the entreaty quietly. "I need to go do something. This is constructive."

"You shouldn't go alone, and your sister would be a better option than me, mostly because she'd tear into both of us for going without her." Raul made the statement flat. He studied her, though.

She stared right back at him, sitting up straight and letting him know he wasn't going to make her back down from her intent. It'd be smarter to have help from somebody here, but she would do it on her own if she had to.

Raul sighed. "I've finished kennel duty for the morning. Let me shower and I'll take you. I'll clear it with Miller."

Kalea huffed and turned away from the counter, setting a small plastic bag on the table by Mali. "Here. I packed you a few musubi to take along."

* * *

The research team's hotel was a low- to mid-range establishment belonging to a common U.S. chain. The lobby was spacious, with doors open at front and back to allow a natural breeze. It was a few blocks from the higher-end shopping and hotels along the beaches. Raul studied the staff standing casually behind the front desk and the older lady in the lobby waiting with a couple of toddlers while her companion had gone out to the parking lot to pull up their rental car. All this he knew because the lobby was so quiet every conversation carried.

It wasn't a bad sort of quiet. With the doors open, the hustle and bustle of the street floated in with the breeze. It was just peaceful, laid back, sleepy. It was a good hotel for a relaxing vacation. The only spikes in noise were the exclamations from the toddlers when they caught sight of Taz.

The older woman with them hushed them, not allowing them to bother the nice working doggie. "See he's working? Look at the harness."

Raul was glad he wouldn't need to deal with the additional attention drawn if he'd have to take the time to keep kids from petting Taz. He'd thought about leaving Taz back at the house or in the car, but Taz was his partner and it was easier to watch out for Mali with two of them.

"Okay, let's head out the back."

Mali blinked up at him in surprise. "What?"

She had asked her question quietly, matching the ambience of the lobby.

He gave her a quick grin and jerked his chin toward the back entrance. There was an outer stairwell visible from where they stood. "Let's take the stairs."

Mali took his proffered hand, falling into step beside him. To anyone else, they might be dating. He led her out the back and over to the stairwell, Taz keeping pace alongside them. The area appeared clear both at street level and on the balconies facing the hotel, at least for the moment. The stairs were enclosed but the lower entrance was an open arch with no door. He glanced up the stairwell, getting as much of a visual as possible.

Stairs sucked, but elevators were even worse kill boxes. Given the choice, he opted for the route less likely to be watched with the most room for him to maneuver. The men who'd approached Mali's research team hadn't made any effort to hide themselves, and they'd probably known they were approaching a group of academics. It was likely they'd be watching the lobby and the elevator if they had figured out where the group had been staying.

"Fourth floor." Mali's tone had a hint of a grumpy rumble to it, but she began the climb readily enough. Taz ranged out ahead of her by a step or two, taking point automatically.

"Let's take our time." Raul didn't want to frighten her. Caution was the primary goal at the moment. He'd be better able to spot a potential problem if they weren't rushing up there.

She was in good shape, heading up at a steady pace. Her fingertips coasted over the railing, ready to grab hold if she stumbled or lost her balance but she didn't use it to pull herself up the stairs the way some people did. Her breathing came easy. She had decent cardio. Four flights tended to leave the average person at least a little out of breath.

When they hit the landing of the fourth floor, he lightly wrapped his left arm around her shoulders. They crossed the open breezeway from the stairwell into the hotel hallway with her tucked against his side, sheltered from the casual glance of people on the street. They were just a couple, heading to their room. Nothing unusual to see.

"Your room on this side?" he asked.

She nodded, the motion only minimally jerky. "Yes. It's a few doors up on the left here. It overlooks the back driveway and koi pond."

The hallway was empty and straight, stretching way to the other end of the hotel. He could make out the arch of the elevator doors about two thirds of the way down the hallway. All clear.

"When we get to your door, I want you to stand against the wall on the other side of it and use your key to unlock it." He kept his voice to a low murmur, for her ears only. "Let me go in first, then come right in behind me. Stick to my back like glue."

He needed to clear the room but he was not leaving her out and exposed in the hallway while he did it. Sure, it might be overkill. But caution now was better than regret later.

Mali only nodded, her lips pressed into a line. He was scaring her. He'd apologize to her for it later.

They reached her hotel room. She did a great job of following his instructions exactly. Raul watched Taz carefully, but the big dog gave no signals of detecting anyone or anything alarming. They entered with no trouble, and once they were inside, he let the door close behind them and pressed her slight frame into the corner of the small entry area. Leaving her there, he methodically cleared the small hotel room and bathroom. It didn't take much. The entire room was visible from the doorway. Taz explored the nooks and crannies, sniffing the floor and wall.

The two full-size beds were set on frames just inches from the ground. There was no place for a child, much less an adult, to hide. Bathroom and closet doors had been left open so he had a clear line of sight into those as well. One bedside lamp had been left on, and the curtains were wide open.

Certain the room was empty, he strode to the curtains and twitched them closed. After all, someone might be keeping watch on her room from afar. Maybe. It didn't hurt to be paranoid.

"Does anything look like it's been moved?"

Mali shook her head. "Everything is pretty much where we left it. I share this room with the other postdoc, Terri."

The two of them weren't exactly neat and tidy. Bras hung on the backs of the chairs at the small table in the corner of the room. Shorts and T-shirts lay strewn across the floor like fallen butterflies. The ladies enjoyed bright colors. As Taz made his way around the room, the big dog placed his paws carefully, choosing not to step on any article of clothing.

"Been here a while?" He tried not to guess which bras and panties belonged to Mali. He could guess, though. There was a distinct, if not significant, size difference in the unmentionables. He was a boob guy and pretty good at guessing size.

Mali liked lace.

So did he.

She brushed past him and pulled a tote bag almost as big as her out of the closet. Setting it on the nearest bed, she unzipped the bottom compartment and tossed in a pair of sandals she'd scooped up from the carpet. "A few weeks. This is my side of the room. Don't make any assumptions, though. It looks like this as soon as I check in to a new hotel room. I like to explode my stuff and spread out."

He decided it'd be wisest to stay where he was while she collected toiletries from the bathroom to dump into the bottom of her bag. "Makes sense to make a room yours if you're going to be here a while."

Taz sat in the middle of the room where he could watch both Mali and Raul.

"Something like that," Mali grumbled. "There's just a lot to see and do, interviews to conduct and data to work through when we get back to the room."

Her packing style was easygoing, too. She tended to roll

her shirts into tight cylinders before stuffing them into the
top of her tote. In a few minutes, she had several choices of
clothing and a sweatshirt packed. She'd also slid a compact
laptop into the side.

"Ready? What room would be the meeting place for your
colleagues?"

She stood in front of him, her brows drawn together with
worry. "I'm good to go. Terri hasn't been back to the room,
though. I was hoping she'd be here. We only ever talked
about meeting back at the hotel. No room was specified."

He figured her roommate hadn't been back since she'd
said things were where they'd left them. "Could be in someone else's room if she was spooked. You were unsettled last
night after your experience."

"We're all here on the same floor." Mali flicked a hand to
indicate the hallway beyond the hotel room.

He turned and opened the door, taking the time to check
the hallway again. Taz waited at his side until he murmured
a quiet command. The big dog proceeded into the hallway
and then paused and turned back to look expectantly at Raul.
Still clear. "Let's go down and knock then."

They did, and he was happy to observe Mali following
the instructions he'd given her for approaching her own
room. She stood to the side at each of three other doors and
knocked. He stood where someone could see him through
the peephole in each door, close enough to hear if a body
brushed against the door to look through. Nothing. Every
one of the rooms sounded empty. Taz didn't sit to indicate
he detected anyone.

"Let's go down to the front desk." Raul figured there might
be a message there. It was less likely that anyone would con-
front Mali in such a public space so it'd be safe enough.

He accompanied her back down the stairs and through the

front doors to the hotel lobby this time. Mali stepped right up to the front desk with a sweet smile. The old man behind the counter returned hers with a smile of his own. "Miss Siri. How are you today?"

"Fine. I was out late and wondered if any of my companions left a note for me here?" She delivered her inquiry in a quiet tone, not loud enough to carry too far but not conspicuously hushed either.

Sensible.

The old man frowned. "There's two messages here for you. I took the first over the phone for you. The second was left here. It must have been delivered while I was on my morning break."

Mali held out her hand. "Hopefully they aren't waiting too long for me. Mahalo."

"Of course." He handed her the folded notes with a deferential nod. "Have a good day."

She turned away, moving to the side by a step or two in case someone else approached the front desk. Her expression was decidedly pleasant as she read the first. "My PI says they checked in for me early this morning, and I wasn't here. They'll be looking to meet up with me later today."

She opened the other note. Her hands trembled slightly. After a moment, she knelt to ruffle Taz's ears, and then she looked up at Raul. "One of my friends is inviting us out sightseeing."

He raised his eyebrows. "Yeah? Sounds good."

She rose, handing him both notes and threading her arm with his as they walked out of the hotel and back toward where they'd left the car.

Raul was a patient man. He kept his attention on the area around them and on his partner as they walked down the street. The rental car was waiting just as they'd left it, and he saw Mali comfortably seated in the passenger side. Taz hopped into the backseat and settled down with little fuss. It wasn't until he'd driven them away from the area and gone several blocks that he pulled over and took a good look at the second note.

"Who is this?"

Mali had been patient, too. She'd drawn her knees up to her chest, sitting curled up in the passenger seat, waiting as they'd been driving. "One of my contacts. I didn't see her yesterday, but she wants to meet us at the plantation after lunchtime. Maybe she knows where the rest of the research team is waiting."

"I thought you said—"

Mali shook her head. "Maybe my PI called the front desk. Maybe they already checked for me, and I wasn't at the hotel. It's part of our procedure. But if they didn't find me, why didn't they wait at the hotel for me? Why didn't Terri go back to our room? It feels wrong."

Her instincts were good. She was taking an analytical approach, and she had sensible questions. He was inclined to agree with her.

"I don't like it." Raul scowled. "I should take you back to the house."

"I don't have a contact number for her." Mali didn't raise her voice as she reached over to tap the second note. She didn't cajole or get sharp with him. Instead, her tone remained completely reasonable, logical. "This woman could be there waiting to give me a real message, and then my team will think I'm in trouble if I don't show up. This is the quickest way to find out if we're all freaked out for no reason or if there really is a need to take action."

Raul tapped the steering wheel as he thought it through. "Seems too complicated."

But then her research team were academics. They had established a fairly complex set of actions to take in the case of various circumstances. They weren't military or law enforcement. Maybe this was just the way these people thought.

"I need to know." Mali's voice cracked a little as she spoke. "Is it that much more dangerous than coming out to my hotel in the first place? It's a totally public place. You and Taz will be with me. It makes sense to find out as much about what's going on as possible."

Maybe. "This goes against my better judgment."

"But you are not my keeper." Again, she didn't push with her tone. She simply stated fact. "I appreciate your help so far. I am really glad you're here with me. But you're not my bodyguard, and I'm not under any kind of protective custody. We're not even sure if there is a situation to speak of, really. Whatever it was yesterday could have blown over by now. We need to know more."

"You saw men in suits yesterday." He understood the desire to downplay events, doubt what she'd seen. She might be second-guessing herself at this stage. After all, she was calmer today and probably more inclined to rationalize what she'd experienced. "You feel like something is off about the message from your PI. That's your gut instinct talking, your intuition. Have faith in it."

Mali was silent for a moment. She released her knees from her chest and stretched her legs, extending them and giving him a good view of her toned thighs. "I feel like waiting is the wrong thing to do. We need to get more information. Please. You're with me. Take me to find out what my contact has to say. If we get there and you see any sign that there's something wrong, we'll leave. Right away. I'll follow every instruction you give me."

Raul growled. If she'd cried or yelled at him, argued in any kind of strident tone, he'd have overruled her and taken her back to the house. But she was chipping away at him with her reasoning. She'd demonstrated both yesterday and today how good she was at thinking on her feet. And she was right about needing more information. He couldn't go get it for her. The contact wouldn't speak to him, even if he did figure out who the heck it was. Mali needed to be there.

"Fine. Let's go find out what's going on."

CHAPTER SEVEN

I t's drives like this one that really make me realize this is an island." Mali stared at the front entrance of the visitor center at the pineapple plantation as Raul pulled around the parking lot and chose a spot. "North Shore is only another ten or twenty minutes away. We crossed the whole island in a couple of hours."

"It's a weekday. There's only light traffic, but I'm guessing it wouldn't take that much longer even on a weekend." He opened his side of the car door and got out. "Let me come around and open the door for you."

A flush of pleasure spread through her core at the gesture. She watched him through the windows as he came around the car. He wasn't looking back in at her, though. His gaze swept across the parking lot and the surrounding area, scanning for things she hadn't even thought to look for. The butterflies in her middle dropped, dead weight in the pit of her stomach. He even let Taz out of the back seat first.

She'd asked him to bring her out here, and he was watching over her, ensuring her safety. He protected people. It was his job. And he was doing this because she was his best friend's little sister.

When he opened the car door she started to get out on her own, but was brought up short when he extended a hand to help her.

Damn it. She blushed as she placed her hand in his. "Thank you."

"No problem." His tone was warm, even if his gaze wasn't on her.

They started walking toward the main building, and he let her get a half step ahead of him before placing a hand at her lower back. His touch sent shivers up her spine and down her tailbone as they continued forward. She bit her lower lip, willing her body to leave her alone.

"To your point, the island isn't big." He raised an eyebrow when she glanced up at him. There was a Big Island, and he might have been making an oblique pun but she wasn't sure. If he had, he wasn't giving her more of a hint than the incredibly sexy ghost of a smile playing on his lips. "When you can drive shore to shore in a couple of hours, where we're used to taking double the time to drive across some states, it does make you realize what it means to be on an island."

"Yeah." She smiled, surprised he'd come back to her talking point. Conversation with him came naturally, and he had an easygoing way about him. Things weren't working out the way they were supposed to, but having Raul and Taz with her made her confident she could find out what had happened.

"Our research has been in town so we haven't come out here yet." She veered to the right and paused on a porch overlooking ticket booths. People were promoting a few of the activities on the plantation. "This is basically a tourist attraction."

"Not a bad place to meet." He shrugged. He'd brought them to a stop with their backs to a wall between windows rather than standing with their backs to the clear panes. Taz sat at Raul's left side.

"Public place." She tried to follow his example and study the area. Everyone around them looked like them, tourists. There were a lot of parents with kids. If she thought about it, there weren't many couples or single adults. "We're supposed to go into the maze. It's perfect for a meeting."

He snorted. "What makes you think that?"

The ticket booth for the maze was directly across from them. She stared at the hedges and the sign advertising the attraction.

"Well, no one is going to see us wandering around in there. We could go in, and my contact could be in there, too, maybe talk to us through the hedges." As she spoke, she got more confident about her rationale. This was definitely what her contact had in mind. She was sure of it. "She could give us any information she has, and no one would know we spoke directly."

Silence. When she glanced back at Raul, he was struggling with a huge grin and not trying hard enough to hide it.

She frowned. "What?"

"I'm guessing you like to watch a lot of movies, maybe some police procedurals?" He wasn't laughing at her outright but there was obvious amusement in his voice. "I'm betting you definitely like action movies featuring hit men and spies."

"So?" She kept her tone neutral.

She didn't think he was patronizing her. There was no smirk or lean in to pat her on the shoulder or back, yet. From experience, she'd made it a practice to never let it show even when she was feeling defensive. It only encouraged know-it-alls to wax eloquently on their comprehensive knowledge of life, the universe, and anything worth knowing.

Raul's grin faded, and his expression became serious. "It's important for you to learn places like the maze aren't a good idea. As easy as it is for you to wander around in there, it's a great place to sneak up on you. Too many ambushes could be lurking around the corners. Anyone could be listening from behind another hedge. Your line of sight is completely limited in there. There's no way to know what could be coming at you from any direction and too many places to hide a surveillance device or worse."

Images of hands reaching out to grab her popped unsummoned into her mind. Despite the heat of the day, a cold shiver raised goose bumps over her upper arms. Over the last few years, she'd started to think of herself as fairly aware of her surroundings, street smart. The perspective Raul was offering was a completely different level of observation. Maybe he was doing it to freak her out and maybe he wasn't. She didn't know him well enough yet but she didn't think he was the type to scare anyone unnecessarily.

His lips were pressed in a grim line as he lifted his chin toward the far end of the maze. "This maze is directly adjacent to the parking area. You could be snatched and dragged right through the hedge to the parking lot where a vehicle would be waiting to take you out of reach before you can call for help. We're not going in there."

Who was he to tell her what she wasn't going to do?

She bit back the angry retort and considered his comments. They made sense despite his joking about movies and television shows. Her knee-jerk reaction had been to prove to him he couldn't tell her what to do, but it'd be spiting herself for sheer pride. He was the reason she was here at all, safe and in a position to look for her PI and research group. This was his area of expertise—and her sister's—so at least she could give his perspective equal consideration.

She took another look at the tall hedges of the maze. Her imagination may have led her to the unwise assumption of a maze being a good idea but the same creativity let her envision what he was suggesting, too. He had a strong point, and it was a lot scarier.

"Okay," she agreed, and if her voice was a little high pitched, hey, she was capable of vivid visualization. "Next steps then?"

"Your contact knows what you look like, right?" He was still waiting, watching, taking in everything around them. He wasn't gloating about having won his point.

As nervous as she was now with his warnings in mind, she found his proximity very reassuring.

"Yes. I haven't seen her yet, but she always tended to see me first in town." Mali tried to picture the woman's face. "She'd walk into my path and tell me to follow her to wherever she felt comfortable talking for a few minutes. It was never longer."

"Fine. She's here then, and she's spotted you, most likely." Raul slipped his hand behind her back and began to guide her inside the building. "Let's get some of the soft serve and find a nice, open place to sit."

"Seriously?" Mali paused for a moment, but his hand at her back urged her forward.

"As a heart attack." He opened the door and accompanied her into the cold rush of air-conditioning, Taz close at their heels. "When you're going to meet your contacts in the future, consider controlling the meeting. You've been researching and trying to encourage these women to come to you, so you've been letting them choose the time and place of their approach. The situation has changed. Now we pick our position."

He followed words with actions, taking them through the massive gift store. In fact, he really did buy her a cone of pineapple soft serve. Then he led her out the back doors to a wide-open seating area and picked a table in the center of the space. Taz settled on the ground under the table, taking advantage of the shade with a grunt.

Mali sat in the chair he pulled out for her and licked the cool, tart, frozen treat, bemused. "If you'd asked me to guess where you would sit, this would've been the last place I'd choose."

Raul huffed out a laugh. "Situational variability."

"Please don't tell me that's a real phrase." She scowled at him. He had to be joking with her.

He shrugged, enigmatic. "This spot gives me a clear line of sight in all directions. No one is going to sneak up on us. There's also no way your contact can miss seeing you and she has got to be panicking since we walked inside the build-ing. If this is a trap, I'll see it coming and have a chance to get you out of harm's way. If she really cares about you and your research team, she'll pull her courage together and walk over to us. Either way, I figure you have time to enjoy your cone."

Mali licked her soft serve and considered his words. He made a lot of sense again. She wasn't sure if she believed everything he had to say, but at least when it came to their safety, she was going to put her faith in him.

"This is delicious, by the way." She had to hurry to lick around the base of the cone before the frozen pineapple melted in the heat of the outdoors. "You should try some."

"Hmm." His response was noncommittal.

She leaned forward so he wouldn't have to stop keeping watch. "Here."

His gaze flicked to the cone, then her chest beyond the cone, and then rose immediately to lock on her eyes. "You are tempting me way too much."

If he'd been teasing, she would've laughed it off. Instead, his gaze had burned into her. And his voice—wow, his voice—had taken on a rough warning tone. She froze in her pose, forward and holding out the cone, very aware her nipples were tightening in response. His voice unraveled her in the best way.

He stared at her for another heartbeat— or forever—and then looked away and around her. "You finish your cone. It's good to see you enjoy it."

She swallowed and sat back in her chair. He hadn't missed her reaction, couldn't have. Maybe she would've been embarrassed but she was too focused on him. Suddenly, he was more than safe and comforting. He was magnetic and mutually attracted to her.

This was getting complicated.

* * *

No. Nope. Not a good idea. Raul mentally threw his attention back into the tasks of scanning the area around them and keeping watch for this alleged contact. He couldn't put one hundred percent of his focus into those things, though, because a part of being good at what he did was always being aware of his charge as well. To be honest, there was no way he could ignore her.

Everything about Mali Siri drew him to her. From her deep brown eyes and sweet, kissable mouth to her sharp intelligence and sparks of energy even when she should be exhausted. She didn't need to drop twenty-dollar words in every other sentence to prove how smart she was, either. It was in the way she heard and absorbed everything said to her, remembered details, and processed the information she'd gathered.

A few college-age kids walked past—both guys and at least one of the girls obviously checking Mali out. She remained happily oblivious to their attention, her back straight and one foot tucked under her as she finished up her pineapple soft serve.

Every lick caused his shorts to get tighter, and he regretted buying her the cone. Seriously regretted it. Next meal, he was going to be sure she had a knife and a fork, or a spoon—or hell, even chopsticks. Anything but watching her lap up tasty goodness from the corner of his eye. He wanted to pounce on her and do all sorts of things with that tongue of hers. Problem was, his best friend was going to kill him if he didn't keep his distance. Even if Arin didn't kill him, Mali was a good woman. And he was not a good man. He'd watch out for her until her big sister got back from her mission, but then it'd be better for him to just concentrate on his new duties with Search and Protect.

"Don't turn around." He smiled slightly when she froze mid-lick, her tongue touching her frozen dessert, mouth open, eyes wide. There was an image to tuck away for later. "Keep eating. Talk to me. If your contact can pull it together and come to us, we greet her like she was with us all along. Okay? Stay loose."

The woman in question was dressed in a long-sleeved blouse of airy material and slashed shorts. She had shapely legs and tanned brown skin without the gold undertone Mali had. The woman wore a practical straw hat, ostensibly to protect her head from the sun, and big sunglasses. She looked stylish. She was also ready to bolt, her face turned toward them and probably staring at Raul.

Well, he was an unexpected extra in this scenario. But it was a good thing as far as he was concerned.

Her stiff pose had caught his attention, plus her hesitant step away before waffling in place. No one else seemed to be watching her, no shady characters in the background. Her grip on her shoulder bag was so tight that her knuckles were turning white.

There was no point in pretending he hadn't seen her. He gave her a friendly smile, letting his own posture remain relaxed and laid back. He didn't call attention to either of them by waving her over. He let her make the choice.

After a long moment, the woman approached with hesitant steps. Once she approached their table, Mali gave her a bright smile. "Hi."

"You aren't where I told you to meet." The other woman's voice was husky.

Maybe some clients thought it was sexy, but he wondered if it was an affectation. Or maybe her husky voice was from rough use of her throat. Many night clubs and bars played loud music. Talking over all the noise, maintaining conversation, and entertaining guests every evening probably wrecked her vocal cords.

"It wasn't a good place for any of us." He kept his tone pleasant. "I'm only here to make sure this conversation is safe for everyone involved and we all get to go our separate ways. Okay?"

The woman's face turned toward him as she studied him. "You don't look like police. Military?"

He shook his head, allowing his mouth to widen in a rueful smile. "Not police. Former military. I'm a friend of her family."

He didn't bother mentioning his recent move to the island. Let the woman think he was a short-term visitor, like Mali was supposed to be.

The woman sat in the third chair at their table, staying perched on the edge of her seat. In response, Mali shifted in her seat so both feet were on the ground. Good thing, too: he didn't want her slowed by a leg fallen asleep due to cut-off circulation.

"You should not go back to your hotel again." The woman turned to Mali.

Okay, so they were going with the no-name route. He was fine with it for now, but Mali probably knew the name the woman went by.

"Why?" Mali kept her voice low to match the other woman's volume. "Where is everyone else? Did they leave earlier? The front desk said they'd checked out."

The other woman's perfect, bow-shaped mouth curved downward in a frown. "No. They never got back to the hotel. They were taken."

Mali's delicate brows drew together. "But the front desk—"

"The message left for you wasn't from them." The woman paused and then continued in a rush. "Those people, they're not small time. They aren't locals like my...boss. They get their girls from overseas, bring them through Waikiki, and then the girls could be sent to the mainland to work more, but they'll never be free. I'm from this island, and my boss keeps me and his other women close, but these people, they are taking over, and my boss is starting to cut business deals with them. I don't want to disappear too, so I talked to you and your people. I want a chance to get out."

Raul maintained his posture, keeping his mouth and facial muscles relaxed. The woman's eyes were darting from

Mali to him to gauge their reactions. Any woman who'd sur-
vived in the business of prostitution would've had to learn to
read body language. Mali was an open book, her attention
completely on the woman. Mali was anxious, concerned,
and completely hooked. It didn't take much to lean forward
and give the woman the same impression about him.

He also kept an eye on the people around them, watching
for the handler who was most certainly with the woman to
ensure her message was passed on to Mali. Whoever it was
had decided to blend in. There were no conspicuous black
suits to be seen this time.

"What do they want?" Mali had placed one hand flat on
the tabletop. The cone in her other hand seemed forgotten,
dripping sticky pineapple down over her knuckles. "The university might be able to pay a ransom."

"This business takes money in exchange for people. Let's
hope your university will have enough." The woman patted
Mali's hand, and it took everything he had to remain relaxed,
and let the woman touch Mali. "You have two days to get it
and deliver it."

Raul stopped listening. There: something out of place. A
man stood yards away, near a family but not taking pictures
of the people posing. The camera lens was pointed toward
the women, at Mali. And the camera was a high-end digital
SLR, too expensive for someone in ripped up, dirty clothes
like this guy's.

Raul surged to his feet. "Hey!"

His shout made the man jump. Even better, the man
backpedaled a few steps and started to run away.

"Taz." Raul pointed. "*Fass*."

His partner shot out from under the table, a black and tan
streak. It didn't matter how quick the target was; Taz was
faster. The GSD got within jumping distance and launched

himself at the man. Taz's jaws closed on the man's shoulder, and the big dog's momentum took them both to the ground.

The woman bolted, heading into the crowd in the opposite direction from the man. Raul wasn't chasing either of them. He was not going to be lured away from the person he was protecting. The entire area was in chaos now, and people were shouting in alarm. It'd be too easy for someone to make a grab for Mali if there were more than just the two people here for her.

"The police are on their way," Raul called out, holding up his smartphone. Not exactly the truth yet, but he'd call after he had Mali safely away from here. In a lower voice, he spoke to her. "Come with me."

He kept her close as he made his way to Taz and the downed man. People were keeping their distance. Taz's service dog vest was the same the K9s wore when they were working with law enforcement on search missions. It gave Taz a measure of protection from the random Good Samaritan who might want to help the attacked person.

"*Aus.*" At Raul's command, Taz immediately let go of his hold on the target's shoulder and stepped back. To the man, Raul said, "Don't move or the dog will attack again."

Onlookers settled into an uneasy silence as they watched Taz stand by, ready to leap back into action.

Raul stepped forward and grabbed the man's arms, securing them behind his back with zip ties. Some people carried duct tape everywhere they went for the odd situation. He carried zip ties. The man cried out in pain but didn't say anything.

He patted the man down, pulling a handgun from the man's waistband and a nasty looking butterfly knife from his front pocket. He left them on the ground near the man but out of reach. There were no doubts now. Raul was relieved the man hadn't tried to use his gun in the crowded area, but there was no telling whether it'd been because of panic or because it'd been his job to lure Raul away from Mali. It was too bad there wasn't time to ask him questions. Raul's priority was to get her away from here.

He took a picture of the man's face with his smartphone—maybe the Search and Protect team could run facial recognition on him and figure out who he was working for—and then he snagged the man's camera from the ground nearby. It took a precious second for him to figure out where the memory card was, but he retrieved it and stuffed it into his back pocket. He leaned down and put the camera back where it had fallen, and then rose, taking Mali's hand. "We're leaving."

She came with him without question, and Taz fell in at his side. He maintained an authoritative expression with his head held high as staff rushed out of the nearby building. He didn't break stride or even slow down. He raised his voice to be heard. "When officers arrive, tell them to have Officer Kokua contact Todd Miller."

Miller's police friend was aware of Mali's situation and would be able to connect the dots between what had happened to her yesterday and this mess today. Hopefully, it'd help mitigate the consequences once they all had time to come back together and address this bigger situation. For now, they were leaving the scene.

No one moved to stop them. He took advantage of the confusion and headed straight back to the car, scanning the crowd for more potential danger. Even once he had Mali in the passenger seat he didn't relax. The windows to the car weren't tinted, and she was too visible.

As he got into the car and started the engine, Mali finally asked a question. "Who was that?"

"Miller's friend will find out. Can you call the police now?" He put the car in drive and headed out of the parking lot as fast as possible, watching the rearview and side-view mirrors for other vehicles pulling out to follow them. "My priority is getting you away from here."

"He had a gun." Mali's voice was beginning to crack.

"He didn't use it." He didn't want to scare her more, but there could've been more people there. Someone else could've had a weapon, too, and they might've been ready to use theirs.

CHAPTER EIGHT

Mali jabbed her smartphone with her thumb, hanging up the call after yet another fruitless voicemail.

"You know, the touch screen isn't going to make a louder noise if you mash that thing harder." He wasn't laughing but Raul was definitely not her favorite person at the moment.

They'd called the police. They'd called Todd. The kennel master hadn't sounded happy at all but he seemed to agree with Raul's plan to continue driving until he was sure they weren't being followed. Mali was freaked out but she tried to get control of herself by doing things, like contacting her university with the information she had so far.

"The mainland is hours ahead of us, and it's too late in the day for most people to be at their offices anymore." She finally looked out the car window at their surroundings. "Where are we going?"

He tilted his head to one side and then the other, stretching his neck. "We've been driving around long enough to be sure we aren't being tailed anymore. I didn't see any vehicles leave the plantation to follow us, but I made it very hard for anyone to tail us at any kind of close distance without being obvious. Once we had enough of a lead, I took a few random turns to lose anyone even if I didn't have eyes on them."

She blinked and swallowed hard, looking into the side-view mirror at the cars behind them. "There's people on the road with us now."

It'd been a while since they'd left the plantation. She'd been so focused on making the calls that she'd lost track of where they were. She hadn't even noticed him making turns. Any acceleration or deceleration she'd assumed to be because of stoplights.

In the silence, he cleared his throat. "Yeah. I came back onto the main highway. The GPS on my phone says there's a popular spot for shaved ice nearby. I figured it'd be good to head over there and find a replacement snack for you before we head back toward the team house. We're being unpredictable, and we don't want to head in the direction anyone would expect us to right away."

"You think it's safe to just stop?" She wasn't sure she had it in her to get out of the car at the moment.

Raul glanced at her. "They have no idea where we went. We're not going where someone might assume we're headed. There's no reason for anyone to be waiting for us there."

Even as he spoke, they'd driven into a small town. Seeing children laughing on the sides of the streets in front of small shops and adults sitting out on lanais, her anxiety eased back a notch. The feel of the town was laid back, with surf shops here and there as they continued to drive along the waterfront.

"This is North Shore." She struggled to recognize a few

of the spots but maybe she remembered another town. "The research team drove up here to check out the beaches when we first arrived, before we got started with our research."

"You've been here, then?" Raul pulled into a parking spot along the roadside. There were shops and even small art galleries on either side of the street.

"Not here exactly." She shook her head. "Our research activity was focused around downtown Honolulu and the Chinatown area. If we came up here, it was for the beach on our time off. I wasn't ever the driver, so I didn't pay much attention to how we got from Point A to Point B."

She waited in the car while he got out, a repeat of the process he'd asked her to follow at the plantation. He came around and opened the door for her first this time.

"So does napping run in the family?"

The question surprised her out of her hesitation. She stared at him and let him help her out of the car. "Sounds like a non sequitur but yes, it does. How did you know?"

He chuckled as he let Taz out of the car and led her to a crosswalk. They escorted her to the other side of the street, where plenty of people were walking in and out of various shops. "Soldiers learn to catch sleep however they can. Could be a few seconds or a minute sitting straight up or even standing. I noticed Arin could do it. Any time we had to sleep, anywhere, she could curl up in the damnedest positions and nap like a cat. I'm guessing you do the same thing in the car when someone else is driving, whether you look like you're sleeping or not. Your brain goes someplace else."

She studied him. He knew her sister well. Even if Mali hadn't believed it from the beginning, it was sinking in now.

"Were you and she a thing?" Because the idea of being with the same guy as her sister was not appealing to her.

He paused his perpetual scanning of the area around them

to glance at her with an upraised brow. "No. We aren't like that. We've let people assume it plenty of times in certain situations, but we've only ever been friends. Serving together, we're both smart enough not to get involved with someone in our own unit."

"Uh huh." It was like claiming a person never dated in the same lab or the same office. It wasn't a good idea, but people acted on bad ideas all the time. She'd done it plenty.

Well, she'd acted on bad ideas, just not dating in the same lab.

Raul snorted. "There wasn't that kind of chemistry between us. Friendship mattered more, and we both needed it. Besides, what happened between you and me will already earn me a beating from Arin in big sister-mode. I'd be about seven different kinds of out of my mind to go from one sister to another sister."

"Was it worth it?" The question popped out before she had a chance to think about it, which was odd for her. She thought about everything, over and over.

He paused and leaned in close. "I'd do it again in a heartbeat."

She froze, caught between laughing and intense awareness of his proximity. He wasn't joking.

She didn't want him to be.

"I shouldn't say that, though." He gave her back her personal space. "I shouldn't even be thinking it."

After a long moment, she thought she might've forgotten something, like air. He glanced down and took her hand in his, tugging her along the walkway. "Out in the open is probably not the wisest choice. Let's get something to cool us both off."

They reached a courtyard area, and the shaved ice shop had a few people forming a line right out the door. They stepped into line and stood in awkward silence for a minute or two.

"Okay, let's agree that there's plenty of potentially complicated situations out there. Relationships are messy." Mali considered her initial issue with their topic of conversation. "The scenarios where it bothers me are when people take siblings or any kind of fantasy and get creepy about it."

He held up his hands. "I wouldn't dare."

It was her turn to shoot an incredulous glance at him.

"Okay. I think every person, man or woman, is going to imagine it if the topic pops up. Power of suggestion." He shook his head. "But I don't go nurturing the fantasy or leering at any women asking them if they're willing to act it out. I mostly try to burn it out of my mind before those kinds of ideas get me into trouble."

A smile tugged at her lips even if she wanted to be irritable. It'd been a long day and her skin was tight, still healing from yesterday's sunburn. A dull headache was becoming more acute. "Confession: I wanted to get mad at you. I can't. You're being honest and reasonable. You're a good guy."

"Thank you for that." He sounded quietly sincere and more serious than she'd intended. "But I'm not."

She didn't know what to say in response. They moved forward in the line into sweet, cool air-conditioning. She started to study the menu.

"I'm human." He shifted to her other side. She guessed it was to have a better view of the interior and the windows, but he was also between her and anyone looking in from outside. His vigilance reassured her. "I try to be a good man. I don't always succeed, but even if I don't, I at least try to be candid. Truth is, I've done too many things, and I can't ever make up for them. Best I can do is try, day by day."

There was a lot of weight in his words. That might've

weirded her out another time, but instead, it steadied her. The silence was comfortable then. Both of them had a small smile. His widened into a grin when she ordered the special.

She was hungry, and the earlier frozen pineapple soft serve hadn't been filling. As they placed a generous scoop of vanilla ice cream into an edible waffle bowl, she rose up on her tiptoes to watch. Fluffy shaved ice was shaped in a ball over the ice cream, and a generous scoop of red, slightly sweet azuki beans was added on the side. They splashed lychee syrup over the top of the shaved ice and then added a healthy drizzle of sweetened condensed milk. A handful of round mochi balls bigger than marbles were added as a final touch.

Raul held his peace until after they made it back outside and sat under the shelter of a large tree. "Which shaved ice was this again?"

Handing him a wooden spoon, she gave him a brilliant smile. "The ichiban special. It roughly translates from Japanese to the 'number one' special. There's a lot of shaved ice served all around the island, in a bunch of different ways, but this has all the elements I love."

"You sure you're not going to pass out from a sugar crash twenty minutes after we eat this?" He sounded dubious, but he dug in and helped her with the huge dessert.

"Maybe." The word came out barely understandable around a mouthful of azuki beans and creamy ice cream. "The azuki beans are a tiny bit of protein."

"You're stretching it there." He narrowed his eyes at her, his shoulder brushing hers as he leaned in for another spoonful. Electric tingles ran across her skin from the contact, across her collarbone and down over her breasts. "These beans aren't too sweet but they're still in a dessert."

She sucked on her lower lip, trying to hide her reaction to

him. They'd just been talking about what a good person he was. He'd been helping her through all of this, at the expense of his own time and business. He had a job to do. She'd taken him away from it. Here they were, sitting and eating as if this was a date. If anyone was leading him astray from being good, she was.

This was another bad idea, and she shouldn't keep tempting them both with it.

"Hey, wherever your brain went, there's still a third of this shaved ice left." His voice broke in on her thoughts.

"Sorry." She scooped up a mochi and concentrated on chewing.

"What is that, anyway?"

"Hmm. Mochi." She swallowed so he could understand her better. "They take sweet rice, or I think some people call it glutinous rice or sticky rice? It's pounded into a paste and shaped into doughy balls. I love them. On the mainland, I've seen stores serve mochi cut into bits to sprinkle over frozen yogurt. It's soft, chewy, and slightly sweet. They also sell mochi ice cream where the mochi is wrapped around balls of ice cream. But I like it best like this, in chewy balls."

He fished for a mochi with his spoon and lost the battle twice chasing the ball around the mostly empty dish before he came up successful. Once he had it, his expression changed to somewhat uncomfortable as he rolled it in his mouth and chewed.

"So?" She was going to laugh at his expression in another second.

"Not bad." He worked his jaw some more. "More chewy than I expected. Really mild flavor once you get to the inside of it. Probably not my favorite thing."

"More for me." She scooped the last mochi and ate it happily. No need to share.

He laughed. "Not a problem. I think we can hit the restrooms, then head back now. We've got some thinking to do."

"About what?" She nibbled at the side of the waffle bowl.

"Your friend." He sighed. "There were too many red flags about her. It's good you made the calls to your university about the ransom but I don't think it's going to be a simple exchange."

She'd been hiding from what happened, if only for a couple of hours. She'd tucked it far back in the corner of her mind, pretending this time with Raul was nothing more than an outing. That couldn't be healthy. Perhaps she'd been mentally protecting herself. But the truth was, she'd been frightened out of her mind by what had happened at the plantation. Who knew what else the man had planned to do? She needed to start to face it.

"The university has us covered by insurance in the event of this sort of thing. We've been trained on what to do." The shaved ice sat cold in her stomach. "There's even a security consulting group that will handle negotiations once I can give them the information they need. They handle any coordination required with local law enforcement or even discreetly if the ransom demands insist police be left out of it."

He nodded but his lips were pressed together, and he looked concerned. "The insurance and training are good things, but negotiations handled by a security consulting group can go a lot of ways depending on how good the resources are. I've been assigned to missions where the situation gets complicated faster than the negotiators can get ahead of the kidnappers. I don't know enough about the consulting group your university is working with to judge, but we'll probably want to look into that group when we get back to the team. Right now, while our talk is fresh in my head, I'm more focused on your contact."

"Why?" She wanted this to be simple. He was like Arin, looking at shadows and what ifs all the time. Arin couldn't walk down a perfectly safe city street without asking Mali if she'd checked the shadows around them.

"Your friend had a rough voice for a woman." He cleared his throat. "And she was wearing a decent amount of makeup. It was blended from her face all the way down her neck and into her collarbone."

"It's makeup. It's supposed to be blended." She argued, not really sure where he was going with this. "She wears it all the time, and she's not going to make the mistake of having it end right at her jawline."

He nodded. "True. But this was heavier makeup, almost the kind models or actresses wear onstage. A lot of women choose to wear it in the kind of lighting clubs and late night bars have but not out in natural light like this. It's too obvious and has got to be uncomfortable with this heat. I'm wondering if there were bruises hidden under the foundation and powder."

Oh. "You have a point." It wouldn't be unusual in her contact's line of work.

"A woman subject to abuse like she might be wouldn't be out on her own." He continued with his logic in a low voice. The gravity of his words took on even more weight as he continued to keep watch on their surroundings. "She had someone there watching her, making sure she made contact and gave you the message you were intended to have. He was definitely not there just to watch over her."

Mali sat up straight, angry on her contact's behalf. "She risked a lot to come meet us. Maybe she didn't know about him."

"How did she get to us? Public transportation? A cab? The plantation was more than an hour out of town." He remained unperturbed, not raising his voice to meet her ire. His tone remained steady as he continued, reasonable and rational. "Someone would've missed her if she was gone for hours. Sure, she could probably talk to you in her comfort zone back in town. A few minutes here and there wouldn't have been as risky. But hours? Someone let her come out here to give you information. They let her lead them to you so they could get a good look at you, gather more intel about you."

It made sense. Still. "You have the SD card from the camera. They don't have what they were looking for and she's not a bad person. Getting into this business wasn't her choice. She wants to get out and help others. She's not one of the bosses. She's a worker against her will, a victim."

He chuckled sadly. "Whether a person is good or bad can't be identified by their job title. People aren't that easy to categorize."

She frowned at him. "What do you mean?"

"Don't trust a person just because you see them as a specific role in a situation." He lifted his chin to indicate the various tourists and locals walking around them. "People automatically put their trust in a doctor because of his vocation. But there are doctors who do awful things in the world. Maybe not things as obvious as conducting horrible experiments. Maybe they just prescribe a less effective medication so they can extend treatment. Maybe they make a mistake in surgery and protect themselves rather than coming clean with the patient and their family."

"That's horrible." She stopped eating her shaved ice, the treat having lost its flavor.

"It is," he agreed. "Doctors, teachers, religious leaders—

they are all vocations with the potential to do a lot of good. That doesn't make those people automatically good people."

"You have a point." She made the admission reluctantly. But her contacts didn't have that sort of power over their situation or the people around them. "And it applies here because...?"

"Don't assume that a person who is a victim is innocent." He tried to keep his words from being harsh. "Some are. But there are a few who created their situation for themselves and would choose to screw you over if they thought they could get what they wanted faster, or they'd do it just out of spite."

She shook her head and then stopped mid-motion. "I believe you. I just...find it hard to understand how a person could be that way."

He shrugged. "Because you're a good person."

"And you're not?"

He turned to look at her directly, his gaze unwavering and somber. "I already told you. I'm not."

Okay. His reply should've been unsettling, but instead she was drawn to him and curious. If anything, his frank admission of the kind of person he thought he was made her want to know more so she could argue with him. He was a better man than he gave himself credit for. She didn't have a lot to support her argument, but she was sure of it.

"So you don't want me to immediately believe everything she said." That was reasonable, too.

He nodded, the hard lines of his jaw softening a tiny bit. "Maybe she didn't realize she was followed. Maybe she thought she was sneaking away, and they let her. We'll know more once the police question that man back there. Hopefully, Officer Kokua will share what they find out with Todd. But I guarantee you, this isn't going to be a simple ransom request for some kidnapped academics. I wish I could encourage you, promise you the cheerful version of the story, but I'm giving you the Grimm fairy tale with the lesson buried in it."

She thought about it for a moment and then slipped her hand into the crook of his arm. "I prefer the Grimm fairy tale version. I want to know what monsters to look out for."

*   *   *

It was late afternoon by the time they made it back to the team house. Miller and Kalea weren't immediately around but there was the ever-present plate of snacks on the kitchen table. This time, it was a mountain of sliders stacked on a plate. Raul lifted the net dome protecting the goodies and snagged one of the small sandwiches. Juicy pulled pork was piled high in each, the savory goodness complemented by the airy softness of the Hawaiian sweet rolls.

"Oh, protein." Mali nipped one, too. "Mmm."

Okay, maybe he should've made sure she had a more balanced set of meals while they'd been out. It wasn't exactly the best idea to keep her in various stages of sugar highs throughout the day. Of course, there'd been at least one serious hit of adrenaline, too. If she was this calm now, he'd let her stay that way until the rest of the team returned. Then it'd be time for serious discussion. This wasn't going to be resolved as simply as a paid ransom and return of her coworkers, and he shouldn't let her keep thinking it would.

"I'm thinking about looking for a good poke place nearby." Couldn't get much more protein focused than good raw tuna marinated in one of any number of flavor combinations. "Would you like me to bring you back a poke bowl, too?"

Mali nodded, nibbling at her pork slider. "'S'good idea."

He chuckled. "Are you even awake? You fell asleep in the car."

She wrinkled her nose but didn't argue, instead heading for the refrigerator and grabbing a bottled water. He'd driven a long while, taking a circuitous route back from North Shore. Part of it had been to ensure they weren't being tailed. Another was the desire to get to know the island better now that it was going to be his home and not just a vacation destination. Mali hadn't seemed to be in any rush, and she'd been a comfortable road trip companion. Even napping, her presence had been pleasant. Without her, it would've been just him and Taz.

Taz was good company, of course. But he wasn't as easy on the eyes sleeping curled up in the passenger seat with a hip turned up to the sky.

"What are you going to do now?" Mali stood in the kitchen, scratching Taz behind the ears.

The big dog leaned his head against her hip, jaws parting in a broad grin as his tongue lolled out to one side.

"There's always more cleanup downstairs with kennels." Raul wasn't looking forward to it but it had to be done, and it seemed there was an ongoing battle with humidity on the island. Keeping away mildew was an epic challenge. "You can keep Taz here with you, if you like. Otherwise, I'll probably take him out back for some ad hoc training."

She glanced around her, uncertain. "I have data to analyze and notes to record, now that I've got my laptop. I don't want to be in the way out here, though."

"You could always work in Arin's room." There was a small desk in there.

"Mmm." Mali headed out of the kitchen and down the hall toward the room in question. He and Taz both followed for the moment, pulled along in her wake. As much as he did have other things to do, he was loath to leave her company just yet. "It's not her room, really. Her stuff is here for now, but she told me she's looking for a place of her own. She's been really picky, though."

"I hope it doesn't take me long to find a place." He considered the possibility with some trepidation. "Hotels can get pricey. Plus, it'd be good to get a place where Taz can stay with me."

He and Taz were partnered well. It'd only strengthen their bond to have a common place to go home together.

Mali entered the room Arin—and she—were currently using. "I think women take certain factors into consideration that men may not prioritize as much."

Danger. Red flag.

He studied Mali. She stood there, slightly rumpled and adorably hot. He was glad he knew her age because her petite height and the slight roundness of her cheeks made her look on the young side. But inside that beautiful head of hers was a sharp, PhD-level mind.

"Most people do their best to balance cost of rent with commute time when it comes to where they live. A majority of my undergrad and graduate-level friends were looking for places to live off-campus through the years, and for the men, those two things were the highest priorities. But crime rate was something I gave equal consideration." Her eyes held an awareness and a fatigue that went beyond the last twenty-four hours. "There are plenty of gender studies out there illustrating the differences in worry or fear between men and women. All it takes is a sudden moment and your sense of personal safety is shattered forever. I'm betting you and my sister have seen awful things so, intellectually, you know they happen. I'm also certain she absorbed those lessons in a different way and will create her private place taking those things into account."

He was sure she was right, and he didn't want to take away from her stance on the subject so he chose his next words carefully. "We all have different priorities. I'm sure Arin is going to choose the right place for her, the kind of place she feels is safe and has the atmosphere she wants."

The corner of Mali's mouth quirked upward. "Glad you acknowledge it's not an easy thing."

He leaned against the doorframe. "A place to call home isn't easy to find."

She nodded and took a step or two closer to him, leaning against the edge of the doorframe, too. "Not all of us are looking for a stationary home. Our definitions of home could be a lot of things. Could be a person or group of people, a particular travel bag, or an actual building. Hard to say what each person needs as a center of their world."

He chuckled. "I hadn't ever thought about it that way. It's an interesting perspective."

She was inches away, her head tilted as she looked up at him. All he had to do was bend his head and taste her lips. He very much wanted to.

She smiled. "I'm glad you like the way I see the world."

"I like the way you taste the world, too." He wanted to tease her a little, considering how much she was tempting him right now. "You don't ever seem too full to try something new."

Her mouth formed a surprised O as her eyes widened. "Like you weren't eating everything in sight right along with me."

He shrugged, tipping forward until his forehead touched hers. "True. You make it fun."

She bit her lower lip, her lashes dropping to hide her eyes

as her gaze left his and settled somewhere around the region of his mouth. He gave her a slow smile. "It's been interesting being around you, wondering what you're thinking. It's like I can see wheels turning inside your head."

"Yeah?" She sounded maybe a little disgruntled.

"Yeah." He let his voice drop lower. "I don't know if I get to find out what's going on inside your mind, but I sure hope you're going to let me know."

Her hands came up, taking his shirt in her fists as she tugged him to her and around the edge of the doorframe. Their lips met in a clash of teeth and tongue and hungry kisses. Blindly, he reached out and closed the door to the room to give them some privacy. It wasn't as if anyone was going to think he was anywhere else with Taz waiting out in the hall.

Whatever. Not the top thought in his mind at the moment.

Mali's hands released his shirt, smoothing the fabric as she reached up and around his neck. He wasn't idle with his hands either. He encouraged her to mold herself against him, enjoying the press of her hips.

Hungry to taste more of her, he released her mouth and trailed kisses down her neck and over her collarbone. She gasped and held onto his shoulders, leaning back and to the side to give him better access. The two of them stumbled away from the wall, maybe in the direction of the bed.

He buried his face in the hollow of her shoulder, breathing in her subtle scent. He coasted his hands up the sides of her rib cage until he was framing her breasts. They fit perfectly in his palms, and he found the firm nubs of her nipples through the fabric of her shirt.

A tiny mew of pleasure escaped her throat.

He lifted his head to chuckle softly in her ear, grazing the shell of it with his teeth. "Like that? I want to lick these. Suck. I want to taste you."

Please say yes. He wouldn't move unless she did. It couldn't be implicit in her actions. He needed to hear the words. And even then, a tiny part of his brain still warned him that her older sister was going to kill him.

Worth it.

Mali clung to him, nipping at his jaw. She dragged in a breath of air. "Y—"

A door somewhere in the house banged open. "Mali?"

Arin was back.

CHAPTER NINE

Mali?"

At the sound of her sister's voice calling a second time, Mali stepped back from Raul quickly—maybe a little too quickly. She lost her balance and stumbled. She probably would've fallen but Raul reached out and caught her, grabbing her by the upper arms. His grip was firm, sure, and pulled the attraction between them taut with vibrating tension. His dark gaze clashed with hers, and she wanted to wrap herself around him.

Of course, her sister came barreling into the room so that was a bad idea. Arin paused, narrowed her eyes and then focused on Raul. "Explain."

To Mali's relief, Raul didn't let her go immediately. He steadied her on her feet and kept his hands loosely gripping her upper arms until he was sure she wasn't going to tip over. A perverse relief rushed through her as she realized he was more concerned about her well-being than incurring her sister's wrath. Which was formidable.

They both turned to Arin and started talking at the same time.

"She was falling…"

"He caught me…"

Arin held up her hand. "Okay. Obviously, you two have gotten to know each other. Let's not talk about how well just yet. I don't think I'm ready."

Raul took a step forward but Arin shook her head. Instead she turned toward Mali and opened her arms.

Mali had been safe. She'd been safe this entire time with Raul. Still, the sight of her big sister unwound an inexplicable knot of anxiety deep in her chest. It was like suddenly being able to draw on a huge breath of fresh, clean air. Mali dove into Arin's arms and wrapped her own around her big sister's waist. She'd called for her, and maybe Arin hadn't been the first to come, but she was here now.

"I was worried when they told me you called for help." Arin's voice was rough, the way it was when she'd been working too hard or hadn't gotten enough sleep. "We wrapped up as quickly as possible and headed straight back."

Truth was, Arin probably hadn't slept. There were nights from their childhood that Mali could remember when her sister had sat up all night at her bedside when Mali had been sick or too stressed about an upcoming test to be able to do anything but shake herself to pieces. The next morning, this is what her big sister's voice had sounded like.

"I'm okay now." Mali spoke into her sister's shoulder, her voice muffled, but she was sure her sister could hear her. "Raul came to get me."

Arin's arms tightened around Mali for a long moment, and then her big sister released her and stepped back.

"He got you, brought you here where you were supposed

to stay put, and took you back out into danger again." Arin's tone had turned hard with an edge to it. "I called, and Miller filled me in on the situation."

Mali froze. This was a different voice, not one she remembered from their childhood. Her sister's face had gone blank, a cold mask, and she was suddenly a stranger. Arin's lips were pressed in a hard line, and she leveled a cold gaze at Raul.

Mali opened her mouth to respond but Raul placed a hand on her shoulder. "She's here safe. We've also got information about the rest of her research team and why they're still missing. It's already been more than twenty-four hours. You can take the rest out of my hide later."

He'd been short, concise, and Mali watched in shock as her big sister came back in place of the hardened professional who'd been standing there a moment earlier. There and gone again, that glimpse of the person her sister had become, and Mali wasn't sure she'd really seen anything.

Sadness flooded Arin's eyes, and the line of her mouth softened as the corners turned down. "My family has never needed this part of who I am. This happened, and I wasn't here." Arin's voice was strained, tired, defeated.

Her sister had tried to explain over the years. Arin was a different person than the family had known, she'd said. No examples or explanations. She'd always seemed the same. They'd all nodded wisely and assured her they understood but they hadn't. Not really. Perhaps this was just the beginning of grasping the reality.

Mali trembled. Maybe she was thinking too hard. Or perhaps she was seeing things. The strain of the last day or so hit her hard. This was her fault. She was bringing out this part of her sister through her actions, from being here. Arin had never wanted this for her family.

"Whoa." Raul looked from one to the other of them with growing panic in his eyes. He raised his hands. "I can definitely see the family resemblance here. Both of you need to quit beating yourselves up. Right now. We've got a situation to handle."

Silence. Neither Mali nor Arin responded. Mali stared at him and then glanced at her sister, just in time to meet her sister's startled gaze. Then both of them looked back at Raul.

Arin nodded. "You have a point. Let's get some coffee for Mali, and we'll go over what happened and what you two know."

Mali blinked and sucked in a quick breath. That fast and her sister had recovered, pulled herself together, and was moving forward. Old resentment soured her mouth. "Just like that. Easy peasy."

"Here we go." Arin met her gaze, and there Mali saw a tired resignation. "It's not simple, and it's never been easy. A lot of people think it means I don't care much if I can just move on this way. They're wrong. I do care. That's why I'm acting, now, to make as much of a difference as possible before it's too late to help anyone."

A lot of people. Arin meant Mali and the family, and she was right. Mali didn't know what to do. She wanted her sister here, but Arin's presence confounded her logic. It'd been simpler, more straightforward, when it'd been just her and Raul deciding what steps they'd take next. Mali was sure her sister was going to take charge. It was what Arin always did. Most times, it'd been a relief not to have to worry about all the decisions.

Now Mali wasn't sure she was going to be okay with what Arin decided. Her stomach churned with the conflicting thoughts racing through her head.

Raul's voice broke through the cacophony in her head. "Let's head to the kitchen and work out the rest as we go."

* * *

Getting the two sisters down the hallway and into the kitchen was harder than herding a pair of feral cats. Raul figured that dealing with actual cats likely to bolt or rip him to shreds might be safer.

Arin was calm for now, but he had recognized her serious look earlier. She'd set it aside for her sister but there would be a reckoning later. He didn't blame her. This was Arin's little sister. They'd sat out long nights on watch, and Arin had told him all about her brilliant, bright little sister. He had a crap memory so a lot of those talks blurred together to impressions of a young kid in school, at odds with the adult here now.

Mali was beginning to tremble—she wrapped her arms around herself even as she walked—and he wondered if she might come apart. He'd worried when it started but he'd also caught the obvious relief on her face when Arin arrived. Mali had barely been holding her shit together, and now that her sister was here she felt comfortable enough to let down the brittle walls and feel for real.

It was an honesty with oneself he admired about Mali. He and Arin could both learn something from her. He admired the earnest way she thought the best of everyone and wished this entire situation wasn't showing her how awful people could be. She was doing her research because she believed people were worth saving. He'd spent the better part of his last assignment proving to people that there was a hell, and it didn't take demons to send them there.

As they entered the kitchen Kalea was just removing

a glass pan from the oven. The rich smell of butter and toasted coconut permeated the space. Somebody's stomach growled, and Raul glanced to his side. Arin's face was blank, and Mali's eyes were wide and blinking with feigned innocence.

He halted.

Usually he could read Arin. Right now, he wasn't sure if Arin's stomach had gone audible and Mali was blinking in surprise or if Mali's belly was about to jump up to eat them and Arin had gone blank to avoid giving her little sister away. Being around them both was going to break his brain.

"Since we have a family reunion going on, I made a batch of butter mochi." Kalea reached for a plate stacked high with golden bars and placed it in the center of the kitchen table. The bars smelled of toasted coconut and butter. "I'll be making loco moco for dinner in a few hours, too, so keep that in mind."

He had no idea what butter mochi was.

Arin crossed the kitchen and placed her hand on Kalea's shoulder, giving the big woman a quick kiss on the cheek. "Mahalo."

Kalea smiled and leaned into Arin momentarily. "You always appreciate good food. I like making your favorites."

Arin chuckled. "Zu's going to appreciate the loco moco, too."

Note to self, Zu's favorite dinner was loco moco. Raul glanced at the kitchen table. Mali had seated herself with her back to the entrance and him, leaving the other seats, with a better view of the room, to him and Arin. He wondered if she'd just taken the nearest chair or if Arin had taught her to make the choice. Either way, he prudently opted to walk around her and the table to seat himself opposite her, leaving a chair between them for Arin.

"I'll look forward to dinner then." A deep voice preceded the man who stepped through the doorway.

Raul was back on his feet without a thought. He managed to remain relaxed once he was standing, instead of stiff at the position of attention. He didn't usually have this kind of reaction, even when he'd been active duty, but Zu Anyanwu elicited strong reactions from people, and Raul's former military habits had been riding him hard over the last day or so. Zu wore a natural air of leadership like a mantle and inspired confidence. Even if Arin hadn't recommended Raul to this team, Raul would've signed up if he'd met Zu first.

"Speak of the devil." Arin, on the other hand, had no such response. She turned from Kalea and flipped one of the kitchen chairs around to sit on it backward, then reached for a piece of the snack food. When she took a bite out of the treat her eyes fluttered closed, and a look of pure pleasure crossed her face. "You're just in time for heaven. Kalea made us butter mochi."

Zu leaned back against the doorframe and crossed his arms. He was a big man, and even sideways, he almost filled the entryway to the kitchen. "I can see that."

Mali had leaned forward, studying the stack of golden rectangles the way a curious kitten would. One hand was on the table surface, inching forward, as if she was fighting the urge to poke one of those mochi. "What are they? They smell amazing, and I love mochi from Japan, but these look different from any mochi I've ever had."

"Mmm." Arin finished chewing another bite. "They've got all the chewy mochi goodness with the added bonus of butter and the coconut flakes rise to the top during baking to give them a sort of macaroon browned crust on top."

Mali finally chose a golden bar and took a big bite, obviously trusting her older sister's assessment. Mali's

lashes came down to half-mast, and she uttered a word-
less groan.

Raul panicked and looked at the ceiling, the wall, even
the kitchen sink as he tried to squelch his reaction to the
sight of the pleasure on Mali's face and the sound he was
wishing he'd caused her to make in a completely different
situation. Between Arin and Zu, he was a dead man. Hell, Zu
had the exit blocked. And Arin was totally capable of elimi-
nating Raul all by herself.

Arin grinned at Mali and waited until her little sister finished chewing and came back to the world. "You remember
Zu?"

Mali blushed and turned in her chair, waving the butter
mochi in her hand by way of greeting.

Zu gave her an easy smile, bright white teeth flashing in
contrast against the intense black of his skin. It was warm
and friendly, a smile Raul hadn't seen before in his brief experience with Zu. Then again, he'd only had a few phone
interviews and a single face-to-face back on the mainland.
He'd seen enough to know this was a team he wanted to join
but he hadn't gotten to know Zu well yet.

Zu approached now that Mali had said hello and gone
back to devouring her treat, and he reached over her to snag
a piece of his own. He towered over Mali, and Raul pon-
dered whether Zu's thigh might be bigger in circumference
than Mali's waist. She was a waif next to a man with a warrior build like Zu. "Good to see you back here in one piece.
We had a moment when we heard you'd gone out again."

Raul wondered if he could die of a glare as both Zu and
Arin pinned him with dark looks.

Mali sat cross-legged in her chair and braced her palm
against the table edge. "There were good reasons, and I had
the presence of mind to take an excellent buddy with me."

Granted, he was glad she was taking the accountability for their outing, but he intensely disliked being referred to as a buddy. They weren't kids headed out on a field trip.

He wasn't going to let her take all the heat though. "I made the call to take her back to her hotel."

"I was going with or without you." Mali shot at him, sitting straighter in her chair.

He fought the urge to grin. He liked getting her amped up. "I figured it was better to go along then and follow some safety precautions instead of letting her try to sneak out of here."

Mali relaxed back into her chair, somewhat mollified, but she was still giving him serious side eye. In a few short sentences, she gave them a terse summary of her reasoning and their adventures for the day.

Raul kept his gaze locked on Zu's throughout. As Mali mentioned the trip to the pineapple plantation and the meeting with her contact, Zu's eyebrow rose. Meanwhile, Raul thought he could feel Arin's stare burning a hole in the side of his skull. He didn't dare look at her yet.

"I'm waiting to hear back from the university about the ransom." Mali reached for another butter mochi as she finished her update. "I figure I'll be the one to make the exchange since I'm the only university representative here on the island."

"No." Arin's voice was quiet and cold enough to freeze the tabletop.

Both Raul and Zu looked at Arin. It'd be stupid not to be watching her when she had that dangerous tone and deadly calm.

Taz whined at Raul's side, and Raul dropped a hand to his partner's shoulder to give him a reassuring pat.

"This is my job." Mali hunched her shoulders, studying her butter mochi without taking a bite.

"A ransom exchange is complicated." Arin frowned. "We need to know more about who took your research team."

"What, money isn't enough?" Mali glanced up and took a bite out of her treat.

Interesting. Raul focused on the exchange. Maybe Mali had been bracing for a fight. With Arin calm, Mali was more ready to look up and talk. They might not even be aware of the strain in the dynamic between them.

"Money is always a good enough reason. Most people don't look deeper." Arin rolled her shoulders. "That's how they end up captured themselves. They bring the money, the kidnappers take them, too."

Mali paled under her tan. "For more ransom."

"Depends." Arin hesitated. "Sometimes the kidnapped could identify their captors. You said the men after you didn't make any attempt to hide their faces."

Mali connected the dots. "They want the money but they aren't going to let anyone go."

Or live.

It hung in the air, a hard truth. All of them understood. No one wanted to lay it out there just to drive it home.

After a moment, Mali nodded. "So following instructions is out of the question. What are our other options?"

Raul looked at her with respect.

Zu stepped around to lean his hip on the counter behind Arin so Mali could see him without twisting in her seat. He still stayed a healthy distance out of Kalea's way at the stove. "You're willing to deviate from your university's policies on these situations?"

Mali's gaze darted to Zu, to her sister, and then back to

Zu. "What you're saying makes sense, and I don't want to be a walking victim."

Arin let out a sigh. "That's settled then."

"But I am not going to give up on my research team." Mali's voice hardened with conviction. "We have the ransom money coming from my university for this situation. You are professionals who specialize in finding lost people. I'll hire you with it."

"That's not what I was getting at here." Arin shook her head. "Contrary to what you might think about private contract organizations—"

"Mercenaries," Mali pressed.

Raul winced. They were professionals. The word "mercenary" was almost always hurled in their direction as an insult.

Arin gave her sister a tight-lipped smile. "This is not about getting that money. To be honest, our current contracts are more profitable."

Mali wilted. "I'm not giving up on my colleagues." She hesitated, and her tone took on a much more human, vulnerable pitch. "They're my friends."

Those words, that tone...it was like taking a shot to the chest. *Ouch*.

"I'll help you." The words tumbled out of his mouth, and he didn't even want to take them back.

Both Zu and Arin glared at him.

"You don't know this island."

"You're new to this line of work."

They both started and stopped at the same time. Zu cleared his throat, and after a tense moment, Arin leaned back on the chair until it balanced on two of its four legs as she held onto the back for balance.

Zu gave Raul a hard stare. "You just reported in for this

position. You don't know how we work yet, but I told you when you interviewed: this is a team. We don't do solo work."

It wouldn't be wise to point out, at the moment, that none of them worked alone. They each had their canine partners. Taz's head pressed against the side of his knee was a comfort and silent support.

"You also chose me for your team because I chose to do the right thing." Raul might be alienating himself from his team or even getting himself fired. But a research team taken right off the streets sounded like people who weren't concerned about local law enforcement.

"I do not want you exposed to any more danger." Arin drew the statement out word by word. Her gaze settled on Mali, but it wasn't harsh or angry. It was intense.

"I wouldn't be anyone you respect if I hid away or went back to the mainland while the rest of my team was in danger." Mali met her sister's gaze. "I'll listen to you all. I'll follow your procedures. But I'm going to help you every step of the way."

Arin stared at Mali for what seemed like a long time. Everyone in the room seemed to be holding their breath, and even Kalea's cooking had gone silent. Then Arin set her chair back down on all four legs. "If we leave you here, you'll climb out a window. It's safer if you're with us."

Zu nodded. "I'll put a call in to Pua and Kai. Pua'll need to put a hold on our schedule. Kai will get set up to be our communications coordinator. We'll need him to get started on as much research as possible while we go for more unconventional intel."

Raul looked at them in surprise. They'd given in, fast. "We have some data to get them started."

He quickly told them about the situation with the man

taking pictures. Apparently, Todd hadn't had a chance to talk to either Zu or Arin yet. They'd all need to catch up with him to find out what Officer Kokua might've learned from the man when he'd been taken into custody.

Raul had looked briefly once they'd finished up their shaved ice treat and returned to the car. It'd been a temporary moment of safety and Mali had been calm. He hadn't wanted to wait any longer to know what pictures were taken. There were definitely images captured of Mali, so those at least established why Raul had stopped the man. At a quick glance, he'd found other, more damning images on the storage card.

The bastard was definitely going to be held accountable for those. With luck, it would be enough to overshadow any questions about Taz's part in apprehending the man.

"Do you want this card to go to your people or your unconventional source? Miller mentioned you had one," Raul asked.

Zu considered for a moment. "We'll leave it here for Todd to turn over to the police as soon as possible, but we'll make a copy to take to our source."

Raul nodded.

Zu shook his head. "It's good that Todd has such a strong relationship with local law enforcement. None of us can do this kind of thing in the future. We want the law on our side, not watching over our shoulders, expecting us to go rogue."

"Understood." Raul met his new team leader's gaze. "It won't happen again."

"See that it doesn't." Zu let the discussion drop.

Raul looked at Taz and then Mali. It'd been worth it, and the best action he could think of in the moment. He had no regrets, but he'd expected more resistance and definitely a reprimand for his actions.

Arin gave him a sharp glance. "We're still having a serious discussion when the clock isn't running, and I might rip you a new one in the meantime, once we're on the move."

Well, that felt more normal.

CHAPTER TEN

Seriously?" Arin's face was dark with barely contained anger. "You took her back to her hotel."

Well, that hadn't taken long.

Raul watched Arin step into the house's small office with him and shut both their dogs out in the hallway. They were about to go head to head, and it made sense not to risk their dogs responding to their tempers. It wasn't likely, but better not to expose the dogs to it. For the moment, he opted to keep his responses short and let her have her say.

"Yes." It was a fact. He wasn't going to deny it.

"Then you took her all over the island like you two were sightseeing." Arin's voice turned incredulous. "It must've been a lovely date. Let's not worry at all about people trying to kidnap her yesterday or the same people contacting her today." She paused, nostrils flaring as she breathed in and let the air out in a slow, measured breath. "If they could take pictures of her like they did, they could've shot and killed her before you could get her to cover."

"They didn't." It wasn't much of a defense, but it was all he could say.

"You exposed her!" Arin had barely raised her voice, but the intensity of it lifted the hairs on the back of his neck. "She would've been safe here, and you took her where they could find her."

"Which was why I got her out of harm's way and stopped for the damned shaved ice." He raised his hands, trying not to escalate into arguing. "We lost anyone following us from the plantation. It was a risk, but it worked. She's here in one piece and happy to see you. That's what matters."

"They could've gotten their hands on her." Arin wasn't satisfied. "They could've decided it wasn't worth taking her, and they could've tried to kill her instead."

"She could've been out there by herself," he countered. "She's an adult, and it wasn't like we could sedate or restrain her to keep her here."

Arin didn't answer, but the look on her face seemed like she was considering whether they could've kept Mali against her will.

"She was going to go to the hotel on her own. Then she would've been grabbed there or would've gone to the plantation with no one to look out for her." Raul continued rationally. "We can't guess at what could've happened. It didn't."

Arin curled her hands into fists and released them. "That's my sister."

"Trust me. I've had that at the top of my mind." Raul lifted his hands, palms out, in a sign of surrender. "But I seem to be the only one remembering she's an adult here. Want to tell me what's going on?"

For a second, he thought Arin was going to blow up in his face, but then her shoulders slumped. "She's my kid sister.

No matter how old we get, that's not going to change. I look at her now and I remember how much she struggled when we were children."

He drew his brows together. "What do you mean?"

Arin leaned against a nearby desk. "She was a prime target for bullies as a kid, small for her age, quiet, and studious."

He could picture a tiny version of Mali. She'd have been a cute child. He dismissed the image quickly though, because the child grew in his mind's eye into the adult he'd met and held in his hands. He was very fixated on the adult Mali. "She's very smart."

"She's brilliant. Our parents did everything they could to provide for us so she could concentrate on her studies. I did everything possible to make sure bullies left her alone." Arin sighed. "Maybe I didn't do her any favors."

"How so?"

"Most times, I took care of things before the bullies got to her. It only took a couple of minutes to discourage them. They weren't really going after her, just looking for easy prey. But a couple of times, I jumped on a bully right in front of her." Arin barked out a laugh, but the sound was sad. "There I was, barely ten. I was wearing a party dress, lace stockings, and patent leather shoes, sitting on top of some boy's chest and punching him in the face. As little as we were, the violence scared her. I made her afraid."

Raul wanted to grin at the thought of a young Arin in a frilly dress, but the memory was obviously hurting her. Where he respected and liked her, his best friend hated parts of herself. He didn't know how to help her. "You were defending Mali."

Arin nodded. "And as an adult, she knows that. But deep

inside, we're both still those kids and she's still afraid of what I can do."

Raul remained silent. Everyone struggled with their own issues. Some of them came from childhood, like Arin's. His had happened more recently. They each had to battle their own demons and live with the scars. The best he could do for her was listen, try to understand, and accept her for who she was. She'd done the same for him. Besides, if Mali was afraid of Arin based on childhood memories, how would Mali feel about him once she learned about what he'd done as an adult?

"All our lives, I've done everything I could to protect her, even from me." Arin shook her head. "I kept my distance and didn't give her details of what I did. She didn't need to know I'm still a monster, but she's going to remember again."

There it was. Raul finally realized where Arin was going with all of this. "You're not protecting her from these people on your own."

There was a deep sadness in Arin's eyes. "I'll do what I have to do."

He took a step toward her, angry now. "Not alone. Don't fool yourself. If you try to take these people out single-handedly, you'll fail and you'll leave your sister even more vulnerable. That's unacceptable." His voice came harsh, almost a growl, and Arin snapped out of her melancholy in response to his aggression. He continued, carried on the heat of his own temper. "If Taz and I weren't enough in your opinion, then with what we know after today, you and King aren't enough in mine. The best way to keep her safe is to do this as part of the team. We're going to protect her as a unit."

Arin stared at him, and he held her gaze. He wasn't backing down. After a long minute, she nodded. "You're right."

Just like that, his best friend was back. She was a little subdued, her ghosts still haunting her, but she wasn't thinking stupid things anymore. She also wasn't about to rip him a new one anymore. Her gaze was clear and she held herself with an air of purpose again.

Raul dragged his fingers through his hair. "Good. I didn't want to get to a point where we really tried to kick each other's asses."

CHAPTER ELEVEN

It was dark on the island, really dark. Mali peered out the car window trying to see beyond the road and into the heavy black on either side.

"We're headed back up to North Shore again?" She still wasn't clear on the thought process for this evening's foray out on the island. "It's after sunset, and don't most businesses shut down pretty early?"

The first part of the highway had been well lit, but as they'd driven an hour and more, lighting had tapered off. Now there were only streetlights near infrequent intersections, and many were low intensity. The stars shone bright from this part of the island.

"Depends on the business and where you are. I haven't been here long either, but I got the impression only offices close in time to catch sunset." Arin shrugged. She sat relaxed in the driver's seat, but she looked up into the rearview mirror to give Mali a reassuring wink before returning her attention to the road. "There's plenty of places open for dinner. Lots of shops are open into the evening for tourists in town."

Mali frowned. Okay, her sister had answered her question but... "I'm still not clear on why we're headed out to North Shore."

The SUV was full-up. Arin was driving and Zu sat shotgun, theoretically navigating but he'd mostly been silent on the ride. Mali wasn't anxious about that, though. Arin had a tendency to remember how to get to and from a place if she'd been there at least once. Wherever this was, Arin knew how to get there even in the dark. Raul sat next to Mali in the passenger seat of the SUV looking out the window on his side of the vehicle while no less than three dogs were laying in the back.

Mali had been surprised about the dogs coming along. Then again, she'd never seen Raul go anywhere without Taz. In years past, Arin had come home to visit without her working dog partner. Arin had been serving in the US Military back then, not as a private contractor, but Arin's current dog was with them now as well as Zu's. Maybe it was a team policy.

"We need information." It was Zu who finally spoke, his voice deep enough to resonate in her sternum as it filled the small space of the SUV. "Kai is running searches online and in databases we can access, but intel from those sources will take some time."

"They're also a few steps removed from the primary sources," Arin added.

Zu grunted. "We've got a contact who specializes in intel regarding this island, specifically. If anything is going down on Oahu, he'll have some kind of information on it. He's our fastest and most direct source to help your friends."

Arin slowed the SUV and guided it off the road onto

a large shoulder with parking spots. There were no street-lights, but the moon was rising in the sky. Mali's eyes adjusted enough to see a little once Arin switched off the headlights. There were no buildings for several yards, but they'd passed some residences set back from the road and mostly hidden by trees. "This contact is out here in the middle of nowhere?"

She trusted her sister but damn, she was confused as hell, and she didn't like being the one with the least amount of knowledge about what they were doing.

"Our guy is shy." There was a thread of amusement in Arin's voice as she opened her car door. "Let us all get out first, and we'll open the door when it's good for you to step out."

Mali glanced at Raul. He gave her a sympathetic smile but also disembarked from the SUV, leaving her alone inside as Zu took up a position outside the window where Raul had just left and Arin opened the back.

Each of the dogs had come to their feet, but they all waited in response to some quiet command from Arin. One at a time, she had each of them hop out until she, Raul, and Zu all had their dogs. Mali waited impatiently for long minutes as Raul and Taz remained outside the vehicle with her. Arin and Zu took their dogs in two different directions up and down the shoulder and then across the road as well. It felt like a long time, and Mali wondered what they were looking for.

Surely, the people who wanted the ransom money wouldn't be able to find her out here. Her stomach did a flip, and she peered out the windows past Raul and Taz, searching for any movement along the roadside. Raul had been super careful when they'd been out earlier in the day. She'd thought he'd been overly cautious but Arin had taken him aside for a discussion earlier in the afternoon once they'd finished asking Mali everything she knew. No one was as careful about every detail as Arin was, and Raul had come back with the expression of someone who'd caught the sharp edge of one of Arin's serious lectures. Maybe Arin had felt the precautions Raul had taken were insufficient.

Not maybe. Definitely.

Nothing was ever good enough for Arin, ever. In a lot of ways, Arin was too much like their mother for Mali to ever feel completely comfortable. It was why Mali and Arin didn't ever meet up for long on visits. Dinner, maybe an afternoon of chatting, but never more than a weekend together before they started pricking each other's nerves. Mali loved her big sister far better when they had plenty of time to miss each other.

"At least she never says 'I told you so.'" Mali wrapped her arms around her torso, trying to control her growing unease.

Sitting alone in the car, even with Raul and Taz right outside, Mali was left with nothing to do but finally pay attention to the churning thoughts hovering in some other part of her mind. Without something to pay attention to right now, things were sinking in again.

Her colleagues, her friends, weren't safe. They'd never made it back to the hotel. They'd been kidnapped.

She'd been telling herself to stay calm. After notifying the university, the process was started to make arrangements for the ransom. She'd done all the right things. Arin had even said so.

But Raul and Arin and Zu were all being so very careful. She needed to be hidden, protected. She wasn't safe. Which meant her friends weren't safe either, wherever they were.

Her heart rate picked up, and anxiety kicked those

thoughts into repeat inside her head. Hide. Be protected. Not safe.

She squeezed her eyes shut but images of horrible things happening to her friends played out in her mind's eye so she opened her eyes again. The moonlit road stretched out on either side, lined by the dark shadows of trees here and there. It could be beautiful.

At the moment, she felt small. She cowered inside the car as her stomach twisted into knots.

Arin had always been there when they were children. Once her big sister had gone into the military, it'd been a tough adjustment for Mali. Arin had been a steady influence in her life, a source of comfort and confidence. Yes, Mali had made her own way as an established adult, but the last day or so had brought all that rushing back. Even if it was ridiculous to feel this way, Mali couldn't shake off the sense that something bad was going to happen while Arin was away.

Raul shifted his weight, catching her attention. She honed in on his back just outside the window. The tips of Taz's upright ears were just visible from where she huddled inside the vehicle. They were there with her, keeping watch. She stared at Raul's broad back, and the churning in her gut eased. He'd kept her out of danger so far. He was right here, while her big sister was farther off doing whatever it was Arin needed to do. It'd be okay to knock on the window. Right? She wouldn't open the door or get out. She just wanted to interact with him, hear his voice, be constructive.

She scooted closer to the door again and lifted her hand but Raul turned at that moment. She snatched her hand back as he opened the door. "All's clear. They're waiting for us across the street."

His dark eyes were kind as he gave her a quick smile before looking out over the road again. The faint moonlight lit his profile, and she stared, completely distracted. He was a beautiful man.

He faced her again. "Ready?"

She nodded, a blush heating her cheeks. It was probably too dark for him to see her being flustered. Right? "Thanks."

"Sure thing." He held the door open for her as she slipped out.

"I mean thank you for being here." She glanced across the street. The silhouettes of Arin and her dog were visible in the space between two trees. "We wouldn't be here if it weren't for you. I wouldn't be."

His smile faded. "Hey, no. Don't think like that. You acted fast when your research team was taken and you evaded capture. You came looking for the people who could help you and kept yourself safe until we could get to you. Don't go making me out to be a hero inside your head."

Mali shut her mouth with a click of her teeth. She hadn't expected this response. Embarrassment joined the mix of emotions stirred up in her belly.

He held out his hand then, palm upward as if he was helping her out of the car even though she already had both feet safely on the pavement. She considered brushing past him and just going across the street, but there was a steady patience in his gaze. Aside from her discomfort, there was no good reason to blow off his offer of help. She placed her hand in his.

"You're an impressive woman, Mali Siri." He led her across the road. "I'm glad I'm here to help you, too."

His words pinged against her sternum, making her heart skip.

"So I feel guilty having you thank me," he continued, his voice dropping lower as they approached her sister. "Because my intentions aren't entirely altruistic. I would've helped regardless because this is my new team and your sister is my best friend, but I'm also taking every second I can get to get to know you better."

They were close enough to see Arin now, more than a shadow, and her big sister was glaring at Raul. Mali tightened her hand around his. Getting to know each other.

Oh, that could take on so many levels of interesting.

* * *

Raul handed Mali off to Arin. It was the wisest course of action with Arin already staring a hole through his head. Considering Arin's sniper skills, it was a possibility for the near future.

The moon had risen fast in the evening sky, and there was enough light to see by, especially for people trained to find things in the damnedest places. Arin had been waiting for them at the head of a very short trail leading to a beach.

The ocean breeze was cool and balmy. But now the waves crashed very close by. The short rise from beach to roadside and the line of trees had acted as a sound barrier, and he hadn't been sure of what he'd been hearing until they'd crossed the road. There was a small strip of sand along the edge, and Raul could imagine people parking up on the shoulder to just cross over and enjoy their lunch break there during the day.

"Watch your step," Arin murmured to Mali, steadying her younger sister with a hand under Mali's elbow. "The sand is deep."

Raul and Taz fell back into the rear-guard position as they started down onto the beach. Taz handled the uneven sand with ease, ears up as the dog took in the night sounds and smells at easy alert. They stayed in the shadows of the tree line mostly, and Raul's position gave him some perspective.

The two sisters had a lot in common but what he saw now was a stark comparison of basic physique and posture. Mali was more delicate than Arin, not only shorter by a few inches but slighter in build and more slender in bone structure. She stumbled as the beach sand shifted beneath her feet.

Arin was broader through the shoulders and carried more muscle mass. His best friend had better footing than most soldiers and moved with surety over any kind of terrain. Most important, Arin was the support. She held her sister up, caught Mali when she stumbled, and had trouble letting Mali set out on her own again.

But the Mali Siri he'd gotten to know over the last day and a half was stronger than either of them might realize at this point. He'd served through hell and back again with Arin and had serious respect for her capabilities. But maybe neither of them had really seen the other under duress because Arin didn't seem to understand the resourcefulness he'd witnessed from Mali.

"Close now." Arin's murmured reassurance was so faint that he barely heard it carried on the breeze, but there was a whole lot of caring there. Arin would do anything for her family, but his best friend was especially protective of her little sister.

He was in a lot of trouble being anywhere near Mali. Arin had flipped out on him over his actions since retrieving Mali from Waikiki Beach. Her tirade had been focused specifically on Mali's safety and she hadn't even touched on any possible attraction between him and Mali. He hadn't breathed a word about the heat between them, but Arin couldn't have missed it when she'd walked in on him and Mali earlier.

Being near Mali was a bad idea if he wanted to respect his best friend. Problem was, the attraction was impossible to ignore the longer he was around her. He could step back, let Arin and Zu take this situation from here. He'd planned to after tonight. But then Mali had gone and thanked him.

He'd stopped her but he'd gotten the message. Her relief to have him nearby—not anyone else, just him—had been loud and clear. How could he step back and disappear for the rest of the time she was on the island?

He couldn't. He'd be a bastard to try. And he'd told her the truth earlier; he fiercely wanted to get to know her better. The chemistry between them was amazing. But she deserved better than him, and he needed to step back before this became more than amazing chemistry. He'd done too many things, too recently, and he hated himself for them. With as much emotional baggage as he was carrying around, he couldn't be anything but bad for someone like Mali. So he was left with trying to be a good friend and a gentleman. He'd see this through to get her friends back and then see her off to the mainland.

And he'd have some amazing dreams about her for the rest of the foreseeable future.

CHAPTER TWELVE

They'd been moving along the edge of the beach for several minutes before Mali started to give in to frustration. It wasn't the dark or the soft sand rolling under her feet, making her legs ache with every step. She wanted to know who the hell they were trying to meet up with out in the middle of a beach.

A pair of bright eyes appeared ahead of them, reflected light in the eyes of an animal, and Mali stopped in her tracks.

"It's Buck, Zu's partner." Arin's hand squeezed Mali's elbow gently.

Intellectually, Mali had known dogs and other animals had pupils that picked up the light and reflected it back. She just hadn't realized how little light they needed for the effect or how damned creepy it was.

They turned away from the waves and onto a portion of the beach nestled in a thicker patch of trees. Hidden in the brush was a rusty old RV. A small fire was burning in a tiny pit sheltered by a few sheets of metal. Maybe the light of the flames had been what she'd seen reflected in Buck's eyes, but she hadn't even noticed its light until they were right on top of it.

"Arin, lovely lady of doom, howzit?" A genial tenor voice greeted them quietly as a tall man unfolded himself from a squatting position by the fire.

He was tall, way taller than either Mali or Arin. Mali was five feet even, and Arin had a few inches on her so this man had to be six foot three, maybe. He reached out a big hand with long fingers—their mother used to call those piano fingers—and grasped Arin's hand in greeting, pulling her older sister into a loose hug and leaning in to press his forehead against Arin's for a moment.

Mali raised her eyebrows. Arin was not a hugging sort of person.

"Kenny, I'd like to introduce you to my little sister, Mali." Arin turned and held her hand out to Mali.

Mali allowed herself to be pulled in close to her sister, awkwardly giving the man a wave. He had a gentle sort of smile and springy corkscrew coils framing his cheerful face. His skin was a lighter shade than Zu's deep black, more of a copper brown. Where Zu was a wall of intimidation, this man gave off an air of easygoing reassurance. Nothing dangerous here; just enjoying the island life.

Kenny spread his hand over his heart. "Ohana. Arin doesn't introduce her family to just anyone. I'm honored to meet you."

Zu cleared his throat, saving Mali from having to find something to say. "We have new team members, too. Raul and his partner, Taz, joined us this week."

"Right on." Kenny took the introductions in stride, reaching out to shake hands with Raul.

Taz sniffed the man as he stood relaxed, his long arms

loose at his sides. Then the big dog's attention zeroed in on something on the other side of the fire. Taz leaned forward, almost trembling with eagerness.

Mali followed Taz's gaze and noticed both Arin's King and Zu's Buck were looking, too. A small pig wandered out from the shadows.

A pig. Dressed in a T-shirt.

DON'T EAT ME was printed across the back.

"Zu, brah, I know your dogs are smart." Kenny rubbed his palms against the sides of his shorts. "But can they read?"

The pig strolled right past King and Buck to sit next to Kenny's feet. Obviously, the pig had no worries.

Mali covered her mouth to stifle a giggle. This could all turn very bad in a split second. These dogs were fast. She was sure of it. But she'd also watched Taz pick up a piece of fruit and place it back on a plate.

"Laki is safe." Zu's tone was dry. Neither he nor Arin or Raul seemed worried at all. "Give that pig some time and he's going to be as big as our dogs."

"He's good company." Kenny grinned. "Come, sit. How can I help you?"

Mali sat gingerly on a woven grass mat several feet from the small fire as Kenny crouched and turned a fish grilling over the tiny flames.

Zu gave Kenny the summary of recent events. "We need to know who is active on the island. Someone who doesn't care how identifiable their men are. We sent you images from a camera, too. Were there hits on any of the faces of the armed men in those photos?"

Kenny's eyebrows lifted at the mention of them, and he glanced her way before turning his attention back to Zu.

"Ballsy." Kenny nodded once Zu wrapped up the overview, feeding the fire with twigs. "No hits on the facial recognition yet. Those queries take time to run, but while we're waiting, a few names come to mind. Some of those images showed some heinous deeds. What kind of research were you conducting again?"

"Human trafficking." Mali bit out the two words, putting some punch behind them to see if this information specialist had any kind of reaction to possibly the worst thing a human could do to another human.

Arin gave her a sharp look. Raul looked from her sister to her and cleared his throat.

Mali doggedly kept eye contact with Kenny.

Okay. Minor miscalculation. She'd been so intent on inciting a reaction in the laid-back man with no cares that she'd forgotten to anticipate how upset Arin was likely to be. So maybe Mali hadn't told her sister exactly what research had brought her to Oahu. She hadn't lied. In fact, her big sister was the master of misinformation by omission. When their brother had been with them, their mother had called the three of them See No Evil, Hear No Evil, Speak No Evil.

Under duress, Arin never gave up anything, not even when she'd be the one punished.

Mali had never been one to endure listening to any negative commentary, not about her and not about the people for which she cared. But she'd learned from her big sister over the years. She could leave a few things out of a conversation, too.

Oblivious or maybe too polite to pause, Kenny patted his pet pig and considered the topic at hand. "This is the portal to the mainland from many points overseas. Sadly, there's more than one organization dealing in flesh, and one is already too many."

Mali sat forward, wanting to prompt the man to think harder, but Kenny held up a hand to stall her.

He reached over the pig and pulled a ukelele off the step of the RV and began to strum a few light chords. "One guy comes to mind, though. He stands out from the crowd. Created space for himself here a few years ago. Not easy with the local elements. Takes a special kind of ruthless with the financial backing to supply him with more firepower than the established organizations could counter right away. He's a haole with an estate up here around North Shore. Hand picks his own estate workers from the flesh he's shipping in from East and Southeast Asia."

"Haole?" Raul tossed the term back as a question.

"Just about anyone who isn't from Hawaii," Mali explained absentmindedly, never taking her eyes off Kenny. There were specific slang or pidgin terms for people of color who'd grown up on the mainland. But there was no need to get into that here. "We were focused on women forced into the sex trade. We didn't gather metrics on other types of human trafficking."

Kenny nodded, switching to minor chords. "Nasty business. No doubt. This guy, though, he brings in men and women, whole families. Splits them up. Some go into the sex work in a few businesses he has here on Oahu. Others go into forced labor on farms over on the Big Island and elsewhere. Eventually, a lot of them trickle onto the mainland or up to Alaska. They get to the place they've dreamed of as better but it's not the future they risked their lives to have."

There was a long silence.

"You." Kenny stopped playing. His eyes held a melancholy knowing. "You are lucky he didn't get a hold of you. Pretty little thing. Oh no." He resumed playing.

Goose bumps rose on her skin. Mali had considered the risk intellectually and had been warned, of course. But her research had been specifically about the ways a young person could find themselves trapped in the sex trade. She figured she'd recognize the danger before she could be sucked in.

"We were careful." She defended the entire team. "Most of the girls we interviewed were approached in public places like the mall. Some guy had told them they could be models or actresses and asked them to show up at some hotel for a test shoot. The girls were lured in or maybe even thought they were dating the man that'd eventually become their pimp. Once they thought they were in love, they'd be asked to do some favor to save their boyfriend. In other cases, their family would be threatened if they didn't sell themselves."

She balled her hands into fists as Kenny listened to her politely, with too much kindness in his eyes.

The possibility of being pulled in herself hadn't been a real danger in her mind. Now? She cursed herself for assuming being a US citizen and affiliated with the university protected her. Her entire research team had assumed they were secure in their status.

"Those are some of the stories, yes." Kenny's confirmation was sad and infuriatingly matter-of-fact. There wasn't anything normal about the awful reality of the situations these girls found themselves in.

Kenny kept strumming his stupid ukulele. "You spoke to the girls allowed on the street. They have the most freedom to be away from the business because they've lost the will to leave on their own. Sure, they talked to you, but most of them won't take the chance to save themselves even if you offered it to them. Despite recent legislation improvements, the law mostly punishes the victims as much as the people who trapped them in that way of life. There are some people who will always be afraid enough to stay in the hell they know."

Hell, in Paradise. There were government and private nonprofit organizations to help people start over. But they were far away from the mainland. Mali was working with a team of mercenaries to handle what local law enforcement wouldn't even acknowledge as a situation here.

Tears welled up in Mali's eyes, and she blinked rapidly before someone thought she was melting into frivolous panic. She was angry and frustrated. This wasn't what tears were for as far as she was concerned.

"He's a frugal kind of businessman," Kenny continued. "Waste not. If he took your research team off the streets, he'll take the ransom for them, and they'll still disappear. You don't have much time to find them."

"How much time?" Mali asked, jumping to her feet. She'd assumed her colleagues would be safe if there was a ransom demand, that their captor would have the ransom as incentive to keep them in good health. Now it was becoming clear she'd been naïve to assume their well-being. Damn. It'd been more than twenty-four hours at this point.

Statistics on kidnappings and the chances of finding the victims zipped through her head with rapid calculations on the time of disappearance. Facts, data, quantifiable information—she could absorb those and make sense of them. The events of the past two days had been action and reaction. They'd thrown her off her stride, and she wanted to get back to what she was good at doing.

Zu shifted his stance. Mali looked up, startled. The big man had moved around the fire until he'd blended into the shadows on the other side. He wasn't facing them. Instead, he was looking out into the trees. "The island makes it hard for this man's victims to escape. He's just as trapped. There aren't many places he'll keep his assets, and he isn't hiding."

"True," Kenny agreed. "Given some time, I can give

you details on his estate and warehouses at the shipping yards. Probably can dig up a list of his current businesses in Chinatown and on the east side of the island, too—for appropriate compensation, of course."

Zu snorted, keeping his words directed at Kenny. "You do that. We'll send our standard gratuity."

Kenny smiled and nodded, shifting to major chords. "Rock on. I'll keep watch for a hit on facial recognition and look closer at his business transactions and see if there's patterns. I'll have something for you tomorrow after Laki's surfing lesson."

"Tomorr—" Mali choked as his words sank in. "Laki surfs?"

"Oh yeah." Kenny gave her a broad smile.

* * *

Raul winced at the incredulous look on Mali's face. He was caught between how cute he found her expressions and how much he wanted to react on her behalf. This was a serious situation, and it didn't seem that Mali had experienced the grim sense of humor Arin and Raul had developed from being in too many dire moments. The levity they used to keep themselves on an even keel might leave Mali puzzled, even hurtfully confused. He didn't want it for her but also didn't have a way to help her immediately.

Instead, he glanced at Arin. Was this guy for real?

Arin was wearing her relaxed look. Interesting thing he'd learned about her over the years was how rarely her face revealed her actual train of thought. Plenty of people adopted the blank mask when they didn't want to betray their thoughts, but lack of emotion could be just as much of a giveaway. Ninety-nine percent of the time, Arin's expression was a deliberate affectation and in no way indicative of what she was actually thinking or feeling. It was one of the skill sets that made her an incredibly adaptable asset on a team.

Right now, all he could guess about her opinion of Kenny was that she was willing to let this play out. Mali had the man's attention, and they'd learn more reading his reactions to her than if the man spoke directly to them.

"Maybe it's best to be clear." Kenny continued to strum but looked at Arin and Raul. "Zu and Arin have worked with me before but we're all still getting to know one another. I'll be starting to send out feelers tonight. Searches take some time. We don't get hits as fast as they show on television, after all."

Mali's eyebrows drew together, and she started to say something, but changed her mind and paused. After a moment, she tried again. "Fine. I get that queries might not turn up immediate hits, but you're making it clear to me that time is critical. Is this the best we can do? Is there anything else we can be doing in the meantime to find my colleagues?"

Raul liked that about her. She was a person of strong emotions, and she balanced her reactions with logic and rationale. While she may have been intellectually prepared for the eventuality of a kidnapping or similar circumstance as part of field research, the reality of it was hitting, and she was adapting quickly. He wouldn't have judged her for running to the police and letting them take over. It wouldn't have made things better but it would've been easier. She'd have had someone else to blame if it didn't end well. But here she was, taking on accountability and doing everything she could to contribute to bringing her coworkers back.

"Do we meet you here tomorrow then?" Raul asked. "We

can regroup in the meantime and check into actions we can take in parallel."

"Could be." Kenny smiled. "We go by the tides here. I try not to look at the time in any particular time zone if I don't have to. We'll catch waves before we move on. If you come after, you should be able to find me on some beach or other."

"This is time sensitive, as you said." Zu's quiet statement carried weight, and the light strains from the ukulele stopped.

"Right on." Kenny set his ukulele aside. "I'll keep an eye on the message boards then. Put up a post, and I'll let you know where you can find me."

"You don't have a phone?" There wasn't any anger in Mali's voice, just sheer puzzlement.

Kenny gave her a quiet chuckle. "I've been in a lot of bad places. I've been too curious, too many times, and I am very good at working the magic in information systems. Best way to stay out of harm's way is to stay off the grid unless I absolutely have to be on it. So no phone. If I ever need one, I can always buy a burner. I'll check in often enough to help you find me when I have the intel you need. That's a promise."

The man did come across a few marbles short, but he also seemed honest. Raul would wait to see what kind of intel the man turned up before judging any further.

Maybe Mali had decided the same because she rose to her feet and brushed sand off herself here and there, staying careful of the backs of her legs and arms. Her skin must still be feeling tender. She would probably need more aloe before the night was over.

The thought of smoothing cool aloe over her hot skin caught and replayed in his mind. The idea of bringing relief to her with his touch was both incredibly tempting and stupid. Mali was likely sharing Arin's room tonight, and he ought to be headed back to his hotel room, alone. Trying to have any one-on-one time with Mali would be basically impossible.

He also shouldn't be trying. He'd decided he wasn't going to. He needed to quit thinking those thoughts. Anything from here on out should be strictly platonic.

Should.

He was either going to prove himself a saint or go to hell for lying to himself.

CHAPTER THIRTEEN

Frustration welled up in Mali until she thought she might throw up or scream or cry. She didn't want to do any of those things so she started walking. The breeze cooled her skin and filled her aching lungs.

"If there isn't anything more we can do here, I'll head to the car." She figured they could go back. Maybe they'd talk more. But she wouldn't feel better until they were taking action, and at least walking to where they'd parked was something, however small. Motion from point A to point B relieved at least a small portion of the anxiety she had coiled in her chest.

"Mali—" Arin started to come after her.

"I am capable of finding my way at least that far." Mali heard the bitterness in her clipped tones and couldn't dredge up any kind of regret for lashing out at her sister. Since Arin had arrived, it'd been more about keeping Mali pent-up and wrapped in bubble wrap than about what really mattered: finding her colleagues who could be in trouble.

Once she was away from the small campfire and beyond the tiny shelter Kenny had erected around it, there really wasn't any residual light. Even if police patrolled the beaches for vagrants, they wouldn't come upon his camp unless they stumbled directly on it. The team, her sister, and especially Kenny were so secretive, skirting the edges of what was strictly legal.

Mali appreciated the help, from all of them, but she was also wrestling with resentment. They weren't just protecting Mali from danger; they were also keeping her sheltered from the questionable aspects of their operation. She didn't know if she wanted the respect of full disclosure, or if she was naïve for thinking things were always clear-cut with a right and a wrong approach, and thus shouldn't need to be hidden from her.

She'd been in a constant state of caution, too, since Raul had come to help her evade those men in suits. She couldn't help but look back on the situation with a weird blend of fear and a sense of the ridiculous. Part of the reason she preferred academia was the way she could shed light on harsh realities while still maintaining a certain objective distance. The current situation didn't allow for it, and she wanted desperately to be able to function, be useful, help.

She strode carefully across the sand, trying to walk along the same path they'd created on the way here. It was dark, but there was moonlight to see by. If she proceeded with caution, she could avoid tripping or stumbling or doing something else to bring her sister running and embarrassing herself.

"Give her space. A few meters will be okay." Zu's deep voice carried, and she assumed his comment was in reference to her.

Grateful, she kept going. Mali had a modicum of outward

calm established, and talking to her sister would only crack the façade and bring her frustration bubbling up to the surface where it wouldn't be helpful at all. Raul would be better but Mali didn't want to grow to rely on him either.

Waves crashed in the night. Her sister loved the ocean and Mali enjoyed it, too, when she could quiet her constant thought process enough to listen. It would be fine to walk ahead. She was just going back the way they'd come. Besides, there were three dogs beside them with superior senses of sight, hearing, and smell.

I'm just going to the car.

She put one foot in front of the other, concentrating on placing her feet on the shifting sand without turning her ankle or losing her balance. It was more effort to walk across loose, deep sand on a beach. When she'd had time to enjoy the ocean earlier in the trip, she'd chosen to walk along the area where the waves ran up on the shore. The sand was firm there and she could enjoy the cool kiss of water as the sea washed around her toes. Not this time.

As she stepped down her foot contacted an odd-shaped root or stick in the sand and she stumbled. Cursing, she put out her hands to catch herself.

Fwwp. Something hit the sand next to her.

"Mali!" A man's shout came from behind her. How closely had he been following? She hadn't heard him as she'd been walking. "Down!"

A sudden weight pressed her flat on the sand; one knee caught awkwardly under her. She struggled instinctively, heart pounding.

A hand covered her head and pulled her in closer to a hard chest. "Shh. It's me. Stay with me. I've got you." Raul.

A warm, furry body pressed along her side. Taz.

Mali tried to look around as best she could, covered as

she was by Raul's entire body. Through the tiny space under his armpit, she saw a knee come down on the sand beside them and heard an odd click.

"I'm here too, Mali." Arin's voice was pitched in the old tone she remembered from childhood, on the nights she'd woken from nightmares to find her sister at her bedside.

Heavy steps scrambled up beside them: probably Zu.

"Where did the shot come from?" Zu's words were quiet. "Any idea?"

Arin answered, and Mali strained to listen as her own heartbeat pounded in her ears. "Not a lot of possibilities. It wasn't from close by. None of the dogs were alerted to the presence of a stranger. Pig wasn't spooked either. Has to be a sniper, and I won't find them unless they get another shot off. We need to move."

"It's going to be okay." Raul's mouth was so close that his lips brushed her ear. "Move with me. We're going to need to try to get back to the SUV. I'll keep you covered."

If he did and the attacker shot again, he could be hurt instead of her. "No."

"Yes." Raul didn't raise his voice but his tone grew hard. "This is what we do, our expertise. The more you cooperate, the better chance we all have of coming out of this together. You don't work with us and someone is going to get seriously injured trying to keep you safe. Understand?"

Mali swallowed hard and nodded. She didn't want anyone to be hurt for her sake.

An engine started up somewhere behind them and fresh fear spiked through her.

"It's Kenny." Zu's statement was almost incredulous.

"How is that vehicle moving on this terrain?" Raul asked. No one answered him.

The rusty little RV? It'd seemed like a battered piece of

junk, as if it'd been there sheltered in the copse of trees for years. It could really drive, over sand. Mali had no idea how that was even possible.

The engine sound changed as it pulled up beside them.

"Maybe we want to surf at a different beach after all." Kenny still sounded relaxed and even cheerful. "I'm guessing you'd appreciate an assist?"

A second shot hit the sand with the muffled thud she'd heard earlier. *Oh god.*

People scrambled around her, creating a wall of humans—and dogs—to keep her from being exposed as Raul pulled her to her feet crouching and stumbling. His hands were gentle but firm as he urged her to board the RV, and she did, glad somehow that he hadn't had to pick her up to get her out of harm's way fast enough. Once aboard, she slipped as far out of the way as she could and tucked up onto a bench to make room for everyone else.

She watched as each of them boarded, human and dog, counting each and whispering their names. All of them, there with her and unharmed. A hot tear escaped and rolled down the side of her cheek.

None of this made sense.

* * *

Raul darted into the vehicle and barreled past Mali, giving her a quick visual check as he moved by to clear space for the rest of the team to climb into Kenny's RV. He pushed aside hanging blue curtains and let out a low whistle as he continued to the back of the tight space.

The back half of the RV contrasted starkly with its exterior and suddenly a whole lot of things made sense to him. Wall to wall, floor to ceiling, the area was packed full of high-tech computer equipment. The space was immaculately clean, and the cool whisper of air-conditioning almost froze the sweat on Raul's forehead. Damn, but Kenny had everything and anything he needed in here to tap into the wide world of information technology whenever the man chose to log in.

Taz pressed up against the back of Raul's knees, and Raul dropped his hand down to rub around the base of the dog's ears. "*So ist brav.*" Taz had been great, and Raul didn't hesitate to tell him how good he was.

It'd been a split-second reaction when he'd heard the initial shot hit the sand, and Raul had taken Mali down to the sand without a thought. He hadn't issued a command to Taz. The big dog hadn't worked with Raul before on this kind of positioning but the GSD had placed himself alongside Mali protectively in perfect coordination with Raul. It blew his mind. Dogs weren't telepathic, but over and over again, Raul had learned some dogs were not only sharply intelligent but amazingly intuitive, too. Taz was one in a million, even among working dogs.

Looking back up the aisle to where Mali sat curled on a bench in the "living" portion of the RV, Raul had a sharp moment of gratitude for Taz. She might've panicked covered by Raul if he'd been alone, and she hadn't. Part of it, Raul was sure, was due to surprise but also because Taz had been pressed up against her side. The big dog's presence had given her pause and let her get past fight-or-flight mode to listen to Raul's instructions.

She was a civilian. Every few hours had brought a shock to her system, psychologically and physically. She was curled up on the bench now, not in hysterics, but taking up the least amount of space possible as Arin and Zu and their dogs barreled inside, too. Mali's eyes were wide with fear but not blind with panic or glazed with shock. Her very agile, flexible mind was still working.

He had so much respect for her in the moment that he leaned back against the counter and was staggered by the relief beating through his chest. It'd been less than forty-eight hours. She was alive and whole and everything to him. It wasn't something a man came to terms with very often. But there it was.

"Try not to fall on anything." Kenny put the RV into gear and drove forward. Laki grunted from the passenger seat in the front cab. Pig didn't seem fazed at all. "No worries about the windows. They're designed for bullet and blast resistance. The whole vehicle is."

Arin slid into the seat next to Mali, blocking his view. King slipped under the table and rested his head on Arin's lap. Raul shifted over to get at least a partial view of Mali in time to see her give her big sister a tremulous smile and a nod. With Arin right next to her, there wasn't room for Raul, and he wasn't about to presume to push between the sisters. Instead, he looked down at Taz. The big dog turned his dark face up toward Raul.

"Taz, *such* Mali." Raul punctuated the command with a hand gesture, sweeping his hand out toward her.

Taz paused, the dog's body trembling with eagerness to obey as he worked through the nuance of the command to figure out what Raul wanted. Mali wasn't out of sight or hiding. She wasn't lost, so the dog didn't need to search for her. After another moment, the GSD moved out and found his way down the narrow aisle to the table. He slipped past King under the table and placed his chin on Mali's foot.

Mali looked down and began petting Taz, the strain leaving her face as her nerves calmed. Raul watched and let out a breath he hadn't realized he'd been holding. Dogs had a way of calming the people around them. Taz was the next best comfort he could offer Mali. He was glad she had responded.

Arin turned on the bench to pin Raul with a neutral look. Raul returned her gaze as calmly as possible. Oh, they were going to have another discussion. Since Raul had been flip-flopping through the night about what he was going to do about the situation, he was glad it'd be a while before they stepped aside to address the elephant in the room. Adrenaline was working through his system and fading away, leaving his nerves jangling and his body tired. They weren't in the clear yet, but being on the move was a significant improvement.

"This changes things." Zu leaned against the tiny kitchen counter area, filling the space with his bulk. "They were definitely following, which means they know where the team house is and had a good, long time to get a look at each of us."

Raul frowned. He'd been careful to lose any tail when he'd brought Mali back from their trip up to North Shore the day before. If they'd been followed anyway, then he was going to have to seriously work on retraining himself on his skill sets.

"Maybe. This vehicle is easy to keep following, too." Arin crossed her arms and leaned forward on the table next to the bench.

"I was planning to give the outside a makeover anyway," Kenny called back over his shoulder. "Happy to send you the tab."

Zu grunted. "If you were going to do it anyway, the tab better be for part of the cost, not total."

"'Course." Kenny chuckled. "I'll be getting it taken care of ASAP, though. I'll drop you all first. How's your HQ in town sound?"

"Perfect. If they know about the team house they know about the office we have in town, but the office is better constructed to protect against sharpshooters." Zu widened his stance as the RV rolled up and over the edge of the beach onto the road. Next to him, Buck did the same. The Rhodesian Ridgeback remained standing through the rough transition and let his tongue loll out in a relaxed doggie grin as the RV began driving over the smoother road surface.

"Well, my name and face was going to come up in their research if they did a background check on Mali anyway." Arin sighed. "We can't be sure they followed Raul and Mali from their little excursion. It's just as likely that they made the family connection and had the team house under surveillance anyway."

It was a possibility. Raul was tired of scrambling to react to the situations as they developed, though. They needed to get ahead of this and take control. "When we get to HQ, let's get a plan of action together."

Zu nodded. "It's past time."

"What about Kenny?" Mali spoke up. "You can't just drive away and expect to disappear. Someone was watching us."

"Does my heart good to have someone worry." The gravity in Kenny's words kept his statement from becoming flippant. "Have faith. I have long years of practice disappearing. I'll be in touch, and next we meet, we'll be on another beach somewhere, Laki and me. Our home may change or it might just look different on the outside. Who knows? It will be a surprise for all of us."

Mali looked skeptical. Raul glanced from Arin to Zu and decided to believe they'd see the man again. People in their line of work learned to go off the grid all the time. If Raul needed to, he could. It might seem surreal to Mali but it was their reality.

There was a pause and then Kenny looked up into the rearview mirror at Mali. He gave her a kind wink, an old soul peering out of those weary eyes. "I'm not from this island. I probably won't be on this island forever either. But tonight, I was here when you were here, and I'll call that fortuitous. It was a pleasure to meet you, Mali Siri, researcher and younger sister of Arin Siri. I'll look forward to meeting you again."

* * *

The offices of Search and Protect were designed to be a headquarters for round-the-clock activity when needed. It was Raul's first visit to the corporate complex where they were located and he appreciated the security measures provided by the facilities. They weren't bad for a first line of defense and a bit better than standard for normal business requirements.

Once their weary group stepped off the elevator onto the specific floor occupied by Search and Protect, there were discreet signs of heightened surveillance. Vibration sensors were distributed to supplement the visual security cameras. Glass walls and doors with security badge access provided physical barriers to entry into the office area from the elevator lobby, stairs, and public bathrooms. He was betting the glass was ballistic—commonly considered bulletproof—but he was surprised by the stylish graphic patterns printed on the glass to provide a modicum of privacy for the offices while still allowing for judicious line of sight at certain heights. The effect was sleek and professional, very corporate yet practical for the defense-minded.

As they all entered, there was a stand with water bowls to one side of reception supplying fresh, circulating water for the dogs. Buck, King, and his Taz each waited to be released to go enjoy a much-needed drink. The seating in the reception area could've accommodated a few guests but wasn't designed for a large influx of visitors. Raul guessed the sort of clients they had didn't come in big groups.

"Hey boss, was surprised to get your call. Everyone okay?" A man came striding toward them along a short hallway. He looked younger than Raul by a couple of years, probably in his mid-twenties, and in fairly good shape. His white dress shirt was a contrast against his rich brown skin, and his sleeves were rolled up to reveal reasonably muscled forearms. The guy worked out, maybe did some outdoor activities like surfing, but he didn't have the efficiency of motion or the carriage of someone with combat experience. This man was a civilian.

"We're good." Zu clapped a hand on the younger man's shoulder and turned to Raul and Mali. "This is Kai Pukui, the face of our organization. He handles contract negotiations and communications. I asked him to lend a hand while we regroup."

There were handshakes and introductions for Raul and Mali, but Raul watched her with growing concern. She'd held up well on the drive back from North Shore but she'd been hyperaware and jumpy. The couple of times he'd driven anywhere with her previously, she'd dozed off in the car five minutes into the ride. She was obviously too stressed, and maybe still afraid, to get any kind of rest.

"We've got offices for each of the team members." Kai stood next to Raul as Arin ushered Mali farther down the hallway to a small kitchenette area. "Yours is closest to the front, here. It's got a couch in it, in case you need to catch a strategic nap."

Raul chuckled. "All of us have couches?"

Kai lifted his hands. "Hey, I haven't known Arin long but she seems to be the ninja master of cat naps. She's also way more fun to work with when she's had good sleep and good coffee in equal portions. We've got a high-quality coffeemaker in the kitchen. Couches in the offices sounded like a good idea."

The offices sounded luxurious. Raul briefly considered the chance of rest and then decided against it. His first priority was to see to Mali's well-being. Then he and the team had work to do. He shook his head. "We're on a clock right now. Maybe another time."

"Gotcha. Here's your badge to get into the office. Anytime entry." Kai handed Raul a slim white card, innocuous and unremarkable. If Raul dropped it someplace, it wasn't likely a random stranger could pick it up and figure out what access it provided just by looking at it. "I'm headed out to retrieve the SUV. We can do the whole getting-to-know-you thing another day."

Raul nodded.

Kai gave him a friendly grin and a jaunty wave before heading out. Nice guy. There'd been a friendly openness about him, a contrast to Miller and Kalea's gruff affection, but somehow carrying the same sincere quality to it. Raul looked forward to getting to know the guy better.

"Getting introduced to the team a person at a time, huh?" Arin stepped up next to him. "Wasn't exactly what Zu and I had in mind but maybe it's a good way to make sure you're not overwhelmed."

Raul chuckled. "You worried I'd spook?"

Arin shrugged. "You've got reason not to be particularly happy in a crowded working environment."

She would know. She'd been there when their team had splintered. Instead of an organized retreat, watching each other's backs in a mission gone bad, what had been left of their unit had scrambled out in twos and threes. Some of them had gone it alone. When they'd gotten back to safe territory—and "safe" was a relative term—none of them had been able to tolerate each other. Their trust had been blown into atoms.

"How is Mali?" He put his memories on a mental shelf in favor of the situation at hand.

Arin didn't miss a beat. She probably didn't want to linger on the topic either. "She's tired and worn out, but all things considered, it could be a whole lot worse. She doesn't have a lot of coping mechanisms for times of crisis or emergency."

Raul paused and straightened, looking his best friend in the eye. "Maybe she didn't need to as a kid with you there watching over her, and that's what older siblings do. But here and now, maybe you should take the time to reassess her as an adult. From where I'm standing she's been handling a whole lot of crises very effectively."

Arin glared back at him, silent for a long moment. He wasn't sure if she was going to snap back at him verbally or physically. Arin had a wicked right jab and one hell of a left cross. She was generally not violent without cause, but when family or close friends were involved, she could be explosive in her responses. But she was also one of the clearest thinking individuals he'd ever met. It was hard to predict which way she'd go in this kind of situation, when someone had just tried to eliminate her little sister.

But Arin sighed, the tension going out of her. "Mali did manage really well under the circumstances. And you were there for her, too. I owe you."

"You would do the same for me or mine." Raul crossed the hall to his new office to reconsider the couch. Maybe he could convince Mali to take a nap.

Thing was, his family was all a step removed. He didn't have siblings, no dependents. Raul had the freedom to serve his country because there hadn't been anyone who'd needed him at home. Even if he'd wanted to build a civilian life for himself, there hadn't been anyone to come home to.

In the last couple of days, he'd watched over someone. He'd become invested in her welfare. He'd wanted to build on the chemistry between them. He'd wanted more than the structure of a team. He'd tried to keep his distance because he didn't deserve her, but he couldn't resist.

Maybe it wasn't the best idea to take the discussion further but one of the things that made his friendship with Arin work was being upfront with each other. "She's an amazing woman."

Arin stared at him.

He didn't waver. "I'm interested in her intellect and much more."

CHAPTER FOURTEEN

I don't like it." Arin set her jaw. "But as you so clearly pointed out, Mali is an adult. For the moment, my best option is to give you the obvious warning that I will take it out of your hide if you hurt her."

Raul did a double take and studied his friend. He'd been expecting a burst of protective anger, opposition, possibly fighting for his life. This was better than the best-case scenario he could've imagined. "I'm not sure where this is going, but whatever this is, I want to explore the possibilities as long as she does. It's not a passing thing."

Arin nodded. "Either way, the immediate future is about figuring out what is going on with Mali's coworkers. The clock has already run out in the case of the standard textbook kidnapping scenario."

Raul gritted his teeth as red flashed across his vision. He indulged his emotions because he wasn't out in the field, letting the anger and frustration burn through him instead of exerting control and calm. "We've seen human trafficking before in a few places around the world. It's despicable, and it never gets easier to see."

It was a hard reality, one most people were only tangentially aware of from action movies and suspense fiction. Modern entertainment had replaced fairy tales these days, but it was like his conversation with Mali about the darker fairy tales. There was a lesson buried in most of those pieces of fiction.

"A lot of people think of Hawaii as a paradise." Arin tapped her fingertips against the doorjamb of his office. "But every wonderful place has its darkness. It's a stark contrast, and it's in these places where we can have purpose."

He scowled at her. "You're saying we only belong in dark places."

She shrugged. "It's a dramatic point of view but who better to deal with what's in these places? This is why we do what we do. Do the right thing when other people can't."

This was why he'd followed Arin. Her conviction was palpable and compelling. It made him believe.

"We'll make a difference a little at a time, one mission at a time." Arin leaned back slightly and looked down the hall. "Zu is giving us the chance to do more than most."

Okay. She had a point. Zu had presented much the same rationale when Raul had signed on, but Zu had put the focus on the practical aspects of the opportunity for Raul while Arin tended to concentrate more on the team's strong sense of purpose and their ethics.

Raul might not have believed Zu if their team leader had gone into the idealism of what they were doing, but perhaps Zu had known Arin would communicate it in a way Raul could believe despite having become jaded over the years. He and Arin were friends. They got each other.

He lifted his hands, palms up. "People like us, we're not

made for civilian life. What we've seen, what we've done, the skill sets we've developed, and the way our minds work, don't let us go home. Not to a conventional life, anyway. At least working like this lets us choose what missions we take and make a living for ourselves."

Arin smiled. "This is why I asked you to join Search and Protect. This future gives you room to move forward."

He grinned. Gratitude wasn't something they expressed often. It got awkward between them when they tried too hard so he left it at that and didn't try to put it into words.

Then Arin's smile faded. "But I'm not sure what kind of future that offers when someone like Mali gets tangled up with one of us. Keep that in mind. You may not intend to hurt her, and she may not realize how she could hurt you, too, but there's potential for both."

It was a risk. He'd seen romances go badly with any number of military types. It was more than time apart during missions; it was a difference in world views and realities. The reality in which Arin and he lived included a harsh understanding of what people could do to each other, but they also understood better than anyone how important it was to enjoy every moment they had.

He'd tried to talk himself into putting distance between himself and Mali. It hadn't felt right. So he'd seize the moment and worry about the future when they got there.

"Sometimes you gotta take it a step at a time and watch the lay of the land in front of you." He shook his head. There was too much to consider all at once. "None of us is going to get a full night's sleep, and we'll want to get an early start. Are there assigned shifts for us to keep watch?"

Arin glanced back down the hallway. "I'll check with Zu. We'll take turns, of course, but let's try to give Mali as much rest as possible."

"Mali can have my couch." He and Taz could make do with the floor.

Arin snorted. "You're stretching my ability to accept this thing between you two. I'll let her know you made the offer and let her decide."

Raul chose wisdom over wit and kept his mouth shut. Instead he smiled and nodded.

*   *   *

Mali stared into a cup of tea, gaining more comfort from the heat of it in her palms than from the beverage itself. It was a sweet and subtle brew of cinnamon, ginger, and turmeric with green tea, enough caffeine to dispel the hint of a reaction headache she'd had but not enough to keep her up all night.

She laughed to herself. Considering the sheer concentration of caffeine she consumed in the first few waking hours of any day, this tea was nothing. Her own mind was busy enough to keep her from sleeping all on its own. What was she supposed to do next, rest?

Not likely.

A young woman bustled into the kitchen area with an armful of boxes. "Oh!"

Mali stared.

The other woman stared back.

"Pua, what are you doing here?" Arin appeared in the entryway.

"Oh." Pua turned, facing both Arin and Mali. She was slender with a deep brown tan and thick, dark hair hanging in waves around her shoulders. A single plumeria flower clip held one side of her hair away from her round face. Her eyes were almost onyx, they were so dark, with catch lights reflecting in her shining eyes.

Mali realized she was being rude. "Hi."

"Aloha." Pua's gaze tripped from Mali back to Arin and back to Mali again, and her eyes widened. "Oooh!"

There were a lot of "oh"s happening in this conversation.

"You must be Arin's family." Pua carefully placed her armload of boxes down on the counter next to Mali. "Right. I'm catching up. Just need to gather my thoughts. I was monitoring communication to your university. I've got an update for you and the team. Where's Zu?"

Arin had a patient smile and raised her eyebrow at Pua. "He's in your office space on the one console you let any of us access. He's not going to admit he tried to log on to the main computers."

Pua scowled. "He's the boss, I get it. Being around all you headstrong personality types is a challenge but my office is my territory, and if you want the quality of information I provide, then you have to leave my computers to me."

Mali sipped her tea to hide her grin. Honestly, being around her older sister and Zu and even Raul had been a strain. Even the dogs had powerful presences, each and every one of them. It'd been too many big personalities in the small RV on the ride back. Mali thought Kenny had been relieved to unload them all here at the corporate office.

This new woman, Pua, didn't have the *oomph* the others had but she obviously had her own way of dealing with them all. Mali took mental notes because she had no intention of backing down either. If Pua could work with them, Mali could find her own way, too.

"Stay right here." Pua had both hands out, fingers splayed, as she tried to include both Mali and Arin in the gesture. "Please."

Then she was gone.

A few minutes later, Zu and Raul were hustled into the

kitchen area. Zu stood across from Mali with his back to another counter. The big man glowered at Pua but glanced at
Mali and gave her a wink when Pua's back was turned.

It wasn't mocking, Mali decided. There was a warmth in
Zu's expression he didn't show Pua when she was looking
directly at him. Come to think of it, when Mali thought back,
Zu had the same look for each of his team members.

Raul dodged Pua as she turned too fast and almost ran
into him in the now-crowded space. He scooted around her
as she started arranging her pile of boxes and settled safely
next to Mali.

Mali glanced at Arin, and when her sister gave her a
raised eyebrow in return, Mali narrowed her eyes. Arin only
shrugged as if to say, *You're an adult. Your choice if you
want him near you.*

It was.

Mali reached out and touched the back of Raul's neck
with her fingertips, moving up to lightly bury her nails in the
hair at the base of his skull. He tipped his head forward in
response and encouragement so she kneaded the tight muscles she found there. He shifted closer until the outside of
his arm brushed her knee where she sat on the countertop.

"Okay." Pua surveyed the boxes arranged on the table,
doing a silent count. "You're all here. These are all here. Kai
is on his way back but he said not to wait for him. Update
first, then these."

While everyone in the room waited, Mali wondered what
was in the boxes. They were in assorted colors: one white
cardboard and another a light teal, another pink. They were
bakery boxes, perhaps, or takeout of some kind.

Pua turned and faced Zu. "I've been monitoring the university. They received a second ransom demand by phone
today at about ten in the morning, our time, for the research

team. No specifics were provided on how many of them were captured, just the name of the research team's principal investigator and a demand for ten million dollars wired to an account number they'll provide in the next twenty-four hours. The university acknowledged the veracity of the claim based on Mali's earlier report. And there's now a direct negotiation going on."

Zu grunted.

Mali leaned forward. "The university will handle the ransom. We're insured for these kinds of things."

"True. Which is why the amount seems odd." Arin pushed away from the entryway to stand a few steps closer to Mali. "That's a big university, and they've got you each insured for several million dollars apiece."

Pua piped up, lifted a finger as she did. "I pulled the insurance details. Researchers for their department are insured for up to ten million dollars per individual in the case of instances like this."

Arin nodded her thanks and continued. "The amount they're asking for is a statement, not an actual grab for as much money as they could go for."

"And if they want ransom money, they put some value on each member of the research team." Raul leaned closer. "So why would they take a shot at Mali?"

Fresh fear burst into Mali's system and she was suddenly glad of his proximity. Taz appeared in the entryway and sat at the threshold, watchful. Behind him, King and Buck settled in to begin a watch on their humans, too.

She was surrounded by people and dogs exceedingly capable of keeping her safe. In fact, they'd managed to do so for at least the last day and a half. The rest of her team hadn't been so lucky. So she breathed in through her nose and out through her mouth a couple of times, sipped her tea, and focused on the discussion going on around her again. To be of help, she had to be aware.

"It's possible they wanted to make a different kind of point with Mali." Arin's tone had gone flat, controlled, even pleasant. "Once she contacted the university, she did what they wanted. She's a loose end now, and they could've intended to prove they would kill the research team members if the ransom money wasn't provided."

Mali glanced at her older sister in alarm. That tone was never a good sign. It was a lure. People listened and relaxed, thinking Arin wasn't mad, and then her sister exploded.

"They failed." Raul's counter to her sister was equally as concise, but matter-of-fact. "Next move is ours."

Arin regarded Raul and nodded. In a lot of ways, Mali found Raul calming and soothing, and it was almost a boost to her growing trust in him that her sister responded to him, too.

"We'll need more specifics on the ransom and hostage exchange." Zu folded his arms. "Pua, you'll let us know when there's a new call."

"You got it, boss." Pua paused and then tapped one of the boxes. "In the meantime..."

Zu tipped his head to the side. "What's all this?"

"Well, Kai told me you were all here, and I have a few friends who work at a really good bakery. Perfect for today." Pua turned to Mali and Raul, her cheeks flushed with embarrassment. "I know we have a serious situation here. But this kind of work means we'll *always* be dealing with serious situations so it's important to make time for the things that make this a team. This is your welcome party, Raul."

She flipped open the various boxes to reveal a variety of what looked like sugared donuts, golden yellow sweet bread, cream puffs, and cake rolls. The delicate scent of sweet pastries filled the air, and Mali suddenly wondered if the dogs had made their appearance out of true concern or because they'd smelled the pastries before the humans had. It was probably the latter but Mali found it more comforting to believe in the former theory.

Pua flashed them all a broad smile. "The bakeries fire up their ovens as early as two in the morning so these are the freshest anywhere on the island. There's malasadas, Portuguese donuts filled with chocolate or vanilla custard cream. I even got a few with haupia filling for you to try, if you like coconut. The pao doce are light, fluffy sweet breads. So good! The cream puffs have chocolate or vanilla or green tea custard filling, and the cake roll is green tea rolled around chocolate and whipped cream."

Raul cleared his throat. "Wow. I don't know what to say. Um, mahalo."

His words came out awkwardly, and his expression teetered between embarrassed and genuinely happy, his smile somehow shy. It wasn't the same smile he gave her. It was hesitant and unsure. Mali realized Raul was new to the group, and maybe more than she, he was finding his place here.

Raul moved toward the table to sample the pastries, but Mali remained where she was sitting on the counter to give him this moment with his team. They hadn't had much time alone together since her big sister had returned from her mission but he'd been on her mind every minute she'd been awake. Heck, he'd been featured in a lot of her dreams.

He was a different kind of man than she'd thought a mercenary would be. He wasn't all violence and confrontation. She'd imagined mercenaries would be a lot angrier all the time. But he saw the world in a way that she hadn't ever considered. And when he touched her, well, his touch was singularly unique and amazing.

Arin approached and handed Mali a full cup of steaming tea in exchange for Mali's now empty one. "Joining this team means a lot to Raul. I'm glad we're making time for this. It sets the tone for the future."

"It's very nice." Mali didn't try this tea yet because it was still too hot. But she enjoyed the heat of it in her palms.

"He didn't gel well with his previous teams." Arin paused, but instead of leaving it there, she continued. "In our line of work, that can be nerve-wracking."

Mali drew her brows together. "How do you mean?"

Arin shrugged, turning to lean against the counter beside Mali as Pua chatted with Raul about logging in to his account on the team network. "You have to be able to trust the people you're with and understand how they think. If you don't harmonize well with them, you don't work well as a unit. None of us have to be best buddies or anything, but building rapport is essential for survival."

Mali considered that. She'd thought of her sister's time in the military as just another job. A person didn't have to have friends as part of their job but no one Mali knew ever stayed with a particular job for long if their work environment wasn't friendly. But not being able to work with your colleagues as a team had never been a life-or-death issue.

Grim possibilities sprang up in Mali's fertile imagination at the mention of survival, and she stared hard at Arin. "He says you're his best friend."

Raul had a friend in her sister. They'd been there for each other. So it would've been okay. Neither of them would've been in those life-or-death situations Arin was hinting at, right?

"I am." Arin's response was succinct, a fact. "But either

of us could be assigned to separate units depending on the mission. Several military branches have canine handlers but we're often used in conjunction with other units or teams for joint missions involving more than one branch. Sometimes we don't have a lot of time to build trust with the others on those joint efforts. You may not want to believe it, but yes, they were very dangerous missions, and yes, both of us are lucky to be here."

But they'd come out of it fine. They were both here, healthy.

"Well, I'm glad both of you are no longer active military." Mali shook her head and sighed. "I'm not sure I understand why you're doing this kind of work, though."

Why go back to dangerous work like that? Mali didn't get it.

Arin narrowed her eyes. "How so?"

"Well, you work for hire, for the highest bidder." Mali took a sip of her drink. Arin had brought her a ginger tea. It was what they'd both grown up drinking when they'd needed to settle their stomachs. She was calling her sister a mercenary, but her sister was the person who still remembered things like the home cure for an upset tummy. Mali pressed on anyway. "Mercenaries don't exactly have the best reputation for being people of integrity or ethics."

Arin didn't explode the way Mali half-expected her to. Instead, Arin chuckled. There was a mix of bitter and sweet in the sound of it. "There were a lot of questionable things I had to do in active duty, a lot of hard choices I had to make. No one comes out of combat with a pristine conscience. There is nothing about real life that is black and white, right or wrong, and sometimes survival trumps ethics."

Arin stepped away from the counter and turned to face Mali. "At least as a private contractor—mercenary, if you

want to call it that—I can choose what missions I take and
choose to act on what I think is right, without relying on
someone's judgment from the other side of the world. This
team—what Raul and I are doing—gives us the opportunity
to make a good impact on the world. It's not so different
from what you decided to do."

Mali wrinkled her nose, skeptical. "Our research studies, the information I gather, will expose real problems to
people so they recognize there's a real need for change. It's
a well-structured, objective method of gathering data and
testimonials, presenting them with as little bias as possible. No one person is making emotional judgments in the
heat of the moment."

Arin jerked her chin toward Raul and the rest over at the
kitchen table, just a couple of meters away. "We've had to
decide what to do and take action in the split second between one moment and the next. You want to make people
recognize the need for change? We *are* agents of change.
Whatever is going on between the two of you, I think you
should keep that in mind. He deserves your respect as much
as you think you are entitled to his."

Anger flared up in Mali's chest, driving more words out
of her mouth before she could filter them. "You know, call
me crazy, but I thought you'd be warning him away from
me. Me being your baby sister and all."

Arin smiled. "You're not a baby, and you are most definitely not going to be celibate all your life. You can make
your own choices. I admire how driven you are to go out
and find the knowledge you believe is there. You're a great
researcher doing important work here, and I am incredibly
proud."

Mali sat there, her mouth hanging open. It might be the
first time she'd heard Arin express any kind of opinion on

Mali's work. It wasn't that Arin hadn't been caring as they'd been growing up, but Arin hadn't been one to use words to communicate her love.

Arin wasn't finished either. "But take a minute from your intellectual pursuits to remember: once you had the knowledge you sought, who did you go to, to take action?"

Mali had called Arin. She'd asked Raul for help. He'd come right away, having never met her. They'd all mobilized on her word.

CHAPTER FIFTEEN

The informal welcome party caught Raul off guard, and he stood listening to Pua while bemused, happy, and barely absorbing the torrent of information she was giving him in a steady stream of engaging chatter. This new teammate was incredibly knowledgeable and refreshingly...untarnished in a lot of ways. Her friendly acceptance of him warmed him from the inside out. Besides, discussion with Pua was easy, requiring little from him other than the occasional noise or nod to acknowledge her and indicate she could continue. She was a font of knowledgeable tidbits.

He was aware of Arin's discussion with Mali, though the two women were conversing at a volume low enough for him not to be able to make out the actual exchange. Whatever it was, Arin was relaxed based on her posture, and Mali only appeared to be a little more frazzled than she had been earlier.

He couldn't blame Mali for being strung tight. It was either very late or too early in the morning for clear thinking, depending on which perspective a person wanted to take. It wasn't likely she was used to external stressors like the current situation even if she did keep odd hours as a researcher.

"There's a courtyard downstairs for the dogs to do their business," Pua was saying. "There's a disposal station at each corner but we have extra little bags here in the office in case they run out down there. We don't want to give the building administration any ammunition to complain about us."

"Good plan." Raul nodded, his attention shifting as Mali wandered past him and headed out of the kitchen area.

At the entryway, she squeezed past the dogs, and only Taz shifted to let her by. She patted him on the head in a sort of absentminded way as she headed down the hallway. The big GSD watched her for a moment before looking back to Raul.

It was clear that Mali wasn't a dog person by nature. She seemed to like Taz well enough, but she wasn't the type of person who lit up when they encountered dogs nor was she the kind of personality the working dogs would look to as a dominant authority. They responded to her more like a civilian, politely but without particular interest—except Taz. He'd been interacting with her a lot in the last day or two so he was demonstrating a greater degree of friendly engagement.

Actually, Taz's agreeable and friendly nature was another reason Raul had been happy to partner him. Every dog had a personality, same as every human. A standoffish canine partner tended to ward off friendly overtures from other members of a unit who might otherwise have closed the distance to get to know Raul better. His old canine partner had been an excellent working dog with outstanding skills, but he'd been a grumpy and aloof character. Raul loved the old boy, but he was appreciating how Taz's easygoing doggy grin helped break the ice with people they encountered.

"That's about it," Pua finished up with a wave at the office. "If you're anything like Zu and Arin, you probably stored most of that to process for later, but if you need a reminder, just come find me."

Raul met Pua's earnest gaze and smiled in response to her genuine smile. She was a gem of a personality, and he was beginning to get a full appreciation for how carefully Zu had put his team together. "Thank you. Mahalo."

"Oh, you bet." A dusky rose colored her cheeks. "It's what I do."

She reached out and snagged a malasada, lifting it to her lips and biting into it deeply.

He snagged one, too, gave her a parting nod, and headed out into the hallway to track down Mali. It wasn't a big place, just a collection of glass-walled offices and the open reception area. He found her in a corner room along the interior wall, the one office that wasn't basically a fish bowl. Ironically, someone had taken advantage of how protected the space was from natural light and placed a saltwater fish tank in it.

Mali stood there, her face lit by the undulating light from the tank.

"Penny for your thoughts." He pitched his voice to be low but hopefully not a creepy whisper.

Her gaze shot to him, betraying a moment of disquiet, but it passed and she gave him a tired smile. "I was too wound up to nap when we got here so I had tea. Now I'm full of tea but I'm not sure where to nap. I came in here because it seemed like a good place to be out of the way."

As an interior office, it also had no windows, and it would feel more secure. She had good instincts for a civilian, even if she might not be consciously acknowledging her delayed reactions to having been shot at a few hours earlier.

"I can leave if you want privacy." He understood. Sometimes people needed time to themselves to process.

"No." The word popped out quickly. "Stay, if it's not keeping you from your welcome party."

He lifted a shoulder and dropped it in a half-shrug. "We're all quick about the warm and fuzzy stuff. Welcome, have some sugar and caffeine. I'm fine. I can stay."

Her responding smile was hesitant, still fragile.

He put a leash on the intensity he'd been building up since they had been on the beach and tried to make his words reassuring instead. "I want to be near you."

Her smile widened into a happier expression. She glanced around. "There's a couch in here."

Raul closed the office door behind him, headed over to it, and settled comfortably on one side with one arm slung across the back. "I'm told all the offices have couches. Crash space, in case we don't have time to head back to our homes."

"Oh. Good idea." Mali joined him, sitting sideways to face him. "But you all have your own homes?"

"I will, once I get a chance to go looking for the right space." He grinned. "It's been a hectic couple of days."

"What kind of place are you looking for?" She leaned her head to the side, within an inch of his fingertips.

He leaned forward a bit and lifted a silky lock of hair away from her forehead, playing with it. "I hear the island is wicked expensive when it comes to the cost of living. I definitely can't afford to buy a place. Apartments here 'in town,' as Miller would say, are also going to be crazy. I'll probably go through a few military channels to see what's available near base for veterans."

"Oh." Mali's lids were falling heavily over her eyes but her voice was still somewhat alert. Still, she relaxed into his touch as he lightly ran his fingertips through her hair. "Yeah, I guess cost of living is a major thing. A lot of people in Hawaii have two, even three jobs."

"Yep." He quieted his tone a notch. With any luck, she could relax enough to get some much needed sleep. Even a power nap would do her good. "'Course, I saw a tent in a tree on the way back into town tonight. It'd be an interesting solution."

Her eyes popped open so fast that he almost jumped. "In a tree?"

He chuckled. "I kid you not. Seriously, there was a one-man tent all the way up in a big tree by that ramp coming off the highway. Whoever is sleeping in there is balancing on one of the bigger branches at a decent height."

Her mouth dropped open briefly, and she shook her head. "Kenny seemed to be fairly nomadic, too."

Raul nodded. "I could manage the nomad life, if the need arises, but I'd prefer an apartment or condo. It wouldn't have to be big. I don't do much entertaining."

She arched an eyebrow at him. "Not much of a cook?"

He let his head fall back against the back of the couch. "Oh, you know, I can put the effort into a nice dinner when the situation calls for it, but usually it's just me and my dog. It used to be Dugan, but he's retired, so now I've got Taz."

She was studying the office door. "Is that locked?"

He studied her, everything in him coming to attention. "No, but it could be."

She rose and crossed to the door, turning the lock, and then returned. "People would probably knock, but if some-one were to walk right in, I'd jump out of my skin right now."

Down boy, down. Locking the door didn't mean what he was really hoping it meant. Damn, he was an inappropriately horny bastard. Here she was, tired and under duress, recently a target of sniper fire...

Mali didn't return to her seat next to him on the couch. Instead she straddled him, spreading her hands across his pecs. "So how are you at making breakfast?"

Okay, then. He settled his hands on her hips, figuring it was that or spread his palms flat on the couch cushions because he wanted to do a lot more, way too fast. This should go at her pace. "I make fantastic omelets."

Her eyebrows rose. "Tempting. What about pancakes or waffles?"

She shifted her hips, teasing. He was rock hard already, and he was very sure she could tell. "Pancakes are easy. Waffles need a waffle iron, and I'd need to acquire one of those."

"Hmm." She leaned forward, close but not quite close enough for a kiss. Her breath puffed against his lips. "Blueberry pancakes are my favorite."

"Uh huh." Words were quickly running away from him. He didn't bother trying for clever commentary. Instead, he enjoyed the curve of her behind under his hands. He was a patient man, for the moment; he wanted her to come to him.

She did, thank god. Her lips touched his in a slow, easy kiss as her hands continued to coast over his chest. She drew back a fraction of an inch and licked his lower lip, a request. He opened for her, and she came back in for a deeper kiss, her tongue exploring as she pressed herself against him.

He did everything he could to encourage her, running his hands over her hips and up her sides. As he brought his palms down again, he paused and gripped her behind. She rewarded him with a little gasp. Bringing her hands up to either side of his face, she kissed him even harder.

When she let them both up for air, he growled out what-ever warning he could manage. "I want you, Mali. Be sure."

She stared at him for a long moment and then pulled away.

He stayed where he was, drawing in deep breaths through his nose, wrestling with his control. He was going to let her go, even if the case of blue balls he was about to suffer killed him.

But she didn't leave. She stood there within reach and undid her pants. He watched as she pushed them down and stepped mostly out of them, leaving her pants hooked around one ankle. Probably she wanted to be able to get back into them as quickly as possible. He thought maybe he'd tried that once, back when he was young. The back-seat of a car might've been involved.

He grinned. Somehow, right now, that was incredibly hot.

She knelt between his legs and attacked his waist. He bit back a curse, jumping at the suddenness, and then moved to help her undo his pants, too.

"I am not waiting for anyone to interrupt us," she stated with sexy determination.

He laughed quietly and stayed focused on doing exactly what she wanted. Because he wanted her too, badly.

His pants came down, and she trailed kisses along the in-side of his thigh until he buried his hands in her hair, keeping it clear of her face so he could drink in the sight of his cock brushing her cheek. She licked his tip and he groaned.

"We're going to need a condom." She pulled one out of her back pocket.

He choked out a laugh. "You came prepared."

"I'm a responsible kind of woman." She quickly had the condom out of its wrapper and stretched over the length of him. He almost lost his mind at the sensations she sent coursing through him while she did it. Rising up, she practically climbed him until she was perched over him again. "I don't want to play."

He looked up at her, falling into her hot gaze. He reached between them, grasping the base of his cock and pressing the tip of himself into her just a little. She was wet, slick and ready. "Don't, then."

She closed her eyes as she lowered herself onto him. His hand released his cock as he entered her, taking hold of her hips with both hands, instead wondering if he was going to lose it right then and there. The heat of her, tight around him, was almost enough.

He wanted more of her.

She settled on him until he was buried to the hilt inside her. Then she leaned forward and kissed him, tangling her fingers in his hair. She tasted so good.

But she'd said she didn't want to play.

He gripped her hips harder and ground himself into her. She groaned and nipped the corner of his mouth. She moved her hips then, riding him, matching the rhythm he set.

She panted in his ear, losing herself. Good. He picked up the pace, driving harder into her. Her hands settled on his shoulders, and she leaned back, deepening his penetration. Her pert breasts bounced in front of him, tantalizing.

"Raul," she gasped his name, her voice strained with an effort to keep quiet. "Yes, this. Don't stop."

"I won't." It was a promise. He drove into her harder and shifted his grip to her behind, helping her ride him.

She let out a sexy little cry, tensing over him. He didn't stop. He'd promised. Even as she crested, he kept going as her inner muscles milked him. *Yes. Definitely this.* He pulled her close, muffling his own cry in her breasts as he came, too.

It took a few minutes for him to come back to his senses. She was collapsed over him, breathing softly against the nape of his neck. He wrapped his arms around her and hugged her close, his chest tightening with the amount of emotion swirling inside him.

Having her here, in his arms, was this amazing, fragile thing. He didn't know how to keep the tenuous hold he had on it, but he didn't want to let her go.

"Mmm." She murmured something unintelligible, her voice slurred with sleep.

"You can't sleep like this." He pressed a kiss against the side of her neck.

"Can." She snuggled closer, if that was even possible.

"Maybe. But you shouldn't." He shifted her off his lap and helped her wiggle back into her pants.

He left her on the couch and took care of the condom, hiding it with tissues in the bottom of a wastebasket for now. He returned to where she was on the couch and sat beside her for a moment. She sighed and turned on her side, curling around him in her sleep.

He didn't know how long he sat there, listening to her breathe. But for a few minutes, maybe forever, he let her be the center of his world.

CHAPTER SIXTEEN

Raul stepped out of the office and closed the door behind him, making sure to turn the doorknob fully and bring the door closed silently before releasing it. He didn't want the sudden click of the door latch to startle Mali awake from her nap.

Of course, if she slept like Arin, nothing short of an earthquake would wake her unless someone besides her dog physically touched her.

Really, though, he wanted the chance to think about Mali separate from her sister. Arin was his best friend, and he'd been curious about her family for as long as he'd known her. Now that he'd met Mali, he couldn't help but compare and contrast the sisters to a certain extent. But the more he got to know Mali, in every way, the more he wanted to think of her as her own person. She fascinated him, intrigued him, and blew his mind, all at once.

"Sá." Zu's low voice brought Raul's thoughts to the immediate surroundings.

Raul looked down the hallway to see Zu in front of another office at the far end of the hallway, also against the internal wall. Raul headed toward Zu immediately, and Taz fell in beside him as he passed the kitchen area. Buck and King were nowhere to be seen.

"Mali?" Zu asked.

"Sleeping." Raul paused. "Do you want me to wake her?"

Zu shook his head. "No need. We can bring her up to speed later. Rest is more important for her now."

Raul nodded. Zu stepped into the office and motioned for Raul to join.

"Welcome to my realm," Pua stated as he stepped into darkness dimly lit by a pink salt lamp and the light of many, many computer displays. Arin sat at a small table off to one side with King lying at her feet. Kai had returned, seated at the table with Arin, and he lifted his chin in greeting. Zu stood at the relative back of the room with Buck sitting at his side. "Kenny is on the line, and I have him set to speak to the room."

"Hey, brah. Howzit?" Kenny's voice came from small speakers set high on the walls all around the room for surround sound.

"We're mostly here, Kenny." Zu spoke to the open air at normal volume. Apparently there were mics somewhere in the room capable of picking up normal conversational tones. Nice. It was awkward to have to speak up for a mic all the time. "You good?"

Considering Kenny's part in their departure from the beach area, he was at some risk. Based on Zu and Arin's calm—not Kenny's commentary—Raul had assumed the man could handle himself. He was hoping there'd be time to ask Zu how well he knew Kenny, both as a source and as a person.

"Yeah, brah. No worries." Kenny chuckled.

"Mali will be relieved," Arin offered. "She hated the idea of putting other people in danger because of her."

"Very kind. I appreciate her consideration." Raul could almost picture Kenny bowing his head slightly with his hand spread over his chest.

Hell. Guess it didn't take too long to get a feel for a person, especially one with as many idiosyncrasies as Kenny.

"I've got intel for you," Kenny said. "The area of Chinatown the little sistah was workin' is definitely run by the haole I told you about earlier. I also identified a few faces from the images you pulled from the memory card. Not many of his people, but enough to be sure we've got the right boss."

Zu grunted and crossed his arms over his chest.

"This man is more extensively established than I realized." Kenny's voice was tinged with wry surprise. "There's too many paper trails to follow off the island so I zeroed in on the area where the research team was conducting interviews. His major chain of businesses in that area of Chinatown are all connected to a massage parlor, if you know how to look at the data."

"Are we all headed there, then?" Raul asked.

Arin stirred. "Mali will want to go."

Raul frowned but Kai voiced his opinion first. "Not the best idea, right? The massage places there tend to be the kind that offer happy endings as a regular service. It isn't a surprise that they'd be the business front for whatever else this guy has going on. Some of his assets could even be employed in those massage parlors. Your sister may know about human trafficking and forced labor but going into one of these places and confronting the people running it is not her area of expertise, right?"

While Raul agreed, he felt moved to point out the value Mali could add. "She can recognize her research team, though."

Arin flashed him a brief, knowing smile. "You really think she should go?"

Well. There was speaking up for the value of an asset, and there was also strategy. He looked around the room searching for a way to pull together the half-formed thoughts in his head.

"It's where she was almost taken in the first place so I don't think any of us is thrilled to have her out in the open again, especially after the shots fired tonight." His gaze landed on one of Pua's monitors, displaying surveillance feed. He recognized the front entrance of their building and figured she must be tapped into the security surveillance for the complex. "What kind of equipment do we have for surveillance? Could we keep her here and have her on comm with us to advise us remotely based on the camera feed?"

He'd worn cameras in the past during missions. Command staff could observe and provide limited orders as teams infiltrated and carried out strategic actions.

Pua tapped the surface of her workspace. "I have surveillance but it's limited range. We'd have to be outside the building—not right on top of you, but close."

"And I suppose we don't own an unmarked van." Raul was half-joking, but someone would've mentioned a surveillance vehicle by now if they had one.

"Trucks and vans park along those streets all the time," Kenny added helpfully. "You'd blend in with the shadier elements in the area. Just don't look like Feds."

Arin snorted. "As much as I don't believe a woman should stay away from where her male counterparts can go, there is a practical consideration. We're looking to gather intel, and it's likely to be easier to go in casual, as customers, to figure out what we can before we take more aggressive action. The girls in that establishment will react differently to women."

"True," Zu acknowledged.

Raul nodded along with Kai and Pua. For his part, he'd jumped to the more aggressive approaches to confronting the proprietors.

"We're not police, and we want to maintain good relations with them." Arin held up her hands. "The guys go in and they are more likely to meet with less resistance to harmless chatting. They'll get more information, faster, than if we went with them. If they can collect enough evidence for the local authorities to go in for a clean bust shortly thereafter, it's a more significant win than if we just go in there and make a mess."

Zu nodded. "There has to be a finder's fee out there for Mali at this point. If his own men couldn't eliminate her, our head of the house is going to supplement with a word out on the streets for people to let him know when she's spotted again. It's too risky to have her out on the streets, even in a surveillance van."

Raul was inwardly relieved. He didn't think Mali would be pleased, but all of them would be unified in telling her to stay at the corporate headquarters.

But Zu wasn't finished. "I'm not saying we might not use her to our advantage later—her ability to identify the rest of her research team and her knowledge of specifics about each one of them will be key to extracting them later—but the most important thing right now is more intel on this group as quickly as possible."

Fair. More than fair. Raul wasn't sure how he would react

when Mali was out there with them, but for the time being, he could focus on the current actions.

"Let me settle Taz with Mali." Raul figured taking this initiative wasn't out of line. "The dogs won't be an asset on this foray either. He'll keep her company."

Zu nodded briefly. "I'll meet you at the reception area."

Raul stepped out of Pua's office and walked back down the hallway to where he'd left Mali. Taz walked alongside him, the dog's claws clicking quietly on the stone-tiled floor. It was an interesting choice for office space but would hold up better than carpet with dogs coming and going all the time.

He opened the door to the room slowly, careful not to wake Mali with either the sound or a sudden increase of light from the hallway. Listening, he heard her steady breathing. She was still asleep.

"Taz." He studied the GSD's eager face for a moment and then murmured a quiet command for his ears only. The big dog slipped inside the room and settled on the floor by the couch, watching the entryway to the room. Taz would remain on guard while Raul was gone.

* * *

They walked to the Chinatown area. Raul let Zu set the pace, and the two of them made good time through the almost deserted city streets.

"We're just about there." Zu's deep voice was the kind to carry even at a low volume. He had kept his volume low though, for only Raul to hear as they walked. "Chinatown is about fifteen blocks in the city, easy to walk to and not a lot of parking. Wouldn't have made sense to drive."

Raul looked around. "Any easy hints to know you've

crossed into Chinatown? In other cities, there's a classic archway or wall with a mural on it."

"There's an arch, but we're walking in from a different street." Zu lifted his chin in the direction of the upcoming street corner. "The street signs change here. They have a red border and include the Chinese characters with the English street name. That's what you can see twenty-four seven. During the day and around dinnertime, there's regular tourism and foodies looking for authentic Asian cuisine. Around this time? Not going to be much on the streets but the homeless. In a few hours, fresh produce carts and other early morning vendors will be out, but we're here at an odd hour."

"All right. I'll look forward to making a follow-up visit at another time." A calm was settling over him, a familiar steadiness, and he welcomed it. This was the reason he hadn't gone into a civilian career. The only time he had absolute surety, control, and confidence was when he was walking into a mission.

He'd lost that feeling for a time. His confidence in himself and his team had deteriorated down to nothing on the last deployment. They'd all been fragmented, isolated, even heading into a combat situation together. Back then, every one of them wanted out, and it'd felt like every man for himself. He'd been in Hawaii for less than a few days and the gut sense of a real team was back.

He had Arin to thank for it, and Zu. His new lead walked beside him, similarly sliding into a state of readiness. They had an objective. It wasn't combat, but it carried a serious unpredictability factor and a high probability for violence. Raul savored it.

"You came highly recommended," Zu said suddenly. "Arin was adamant you were the kind of asset we were looking for in this organization. From what I've seen so far, I am not disappointed."

Raul scanned the streets for anything out of place. Now that he had a feel for the area, it was easier to look for something that didn't fit. "Thank you, sir."

The last he'd added because it came more comfortably to him in this heightened state of awareness.

"I'm looking forward to seeing what you can do once you're fully on board and actually know how to check in with your teammates." A hint of dry humor colored Zu's tone.

Ah well, Raul figured he wasn't going to be allowed to forget the fact that he'd left without completing kennel duty the first morning. Yes, it'd been for a good reason, but Zu wouldn't be a good leader if he didn't have some kind of conversation about it. It could've been a lot worse. "Yes, sir."

"We're all glad you were there when Mali needed us."

Even though Zu was probably referring to the team, especially Arin, Raul bristled. "Even if I hadn't been a part of this team, if Mali had called needing help and Arin hadn't been available, I'd have gone anyway."

"I know." Zu's response was unruffled, despite the edge Raul's tone had taken. "I'm absolutely certain Arin and Mali both know it, too. Seeing them together adds a lot of context to knowing Arin."

Raul nodded. "That's for sure. Getting to know Mali as a person is completely different from just knowing Arin has a sister. Meeting Mali blew my mind. The two of them in the same space is a lot of personality."

Zu grunted. "Enough to fill a room. They have more in common than they realize, and they're more around each other."

"More?" Raul wasn't sure where Zu was going with that.

"More confident. More charismatic."

"Yeah?" Maybe Zu had a point. Arin did have an extra something with her sister nearby, but Raul had been focused on helping Mali through this insane situation.

"Being around people who believe in you is a great thing." Zu kept them at a steady walk. To any watchers, they were a pair of tourists wandering down deserted streets looking for a place still open for entertainment. This conversation, though, had gone places Raul hadn't anticipated. "I know you haven't had the experience of being a solid part of a team yet. Some of that is on the people around you. But some of it is on you, too. I chose the members of this team to build a family. Family doesn't have to be blood. It can be by choice. Those two women are family both by blood and by choice. They're a good example to follow."

Easier said than done. He'd come here with Taz hoping to make a good start. So far, he'd had awkward icebreaker conversations and ditched kennel duty.

"Communicate." Zu's statement was quiet and serious. Maybe Raul's new team lead had an idea of what was going through Raul's head, maybe not. Zu's advice was good, regardless. "Every other decision you make, we can work through, but you need to give me your word you'll communicate with your teammates. Otherwise, we can't build trust."

Raul swallowed. It was the core of what he'd been looking for, but hearing Zu say it hit him right in the sternum. "Yes sir."

CHAPTER SEVENTEEN

Raul stared at the glass door etched with the word MASSAGE and a phone number. Inside, all he could see was a set of stairs leading up to a second level. "This the place?"

Zu studied the door frame. "Think so."

Raul pushed open the door and stared up the narrow staircase. No one in his line of work liked going up one of these blind. There were too many ways really bad news could hit a person from a position of higher ground. He ascended, listening carefully. A wind chime tinkled. Zu moved a few steps behind him, amazingly quiet for such a big man. Raul catalogued those sounds and put them to the back of his mind. A chair creaked, and there was the quiet tip-tap of someone typing on a keyboard.

At least one person was on the landing at the top of the stairs.

He kept his posture relaxed, his limbs loose and ready to react in case he had to dodge something suddenly. He very much wished they'd have been able to come up with a plausible reason to have at least one of their working dogs with them. His partnership with Taz was still new but he already felt the absence of his GSD partner.

As he cleared the stairs, he took in the change from the nondescript street front and entrance. It was a small room, kept from being claustrophobic by the sliding glass doors open to catch the night breeze. There was a sleek, modern white desk set at the far end, lit from within and casting a soft white light across the rest of the room. A few contemporary-style chairs sat along the wall next to a water cooler. There was even a shoe rack with a few pairs of shoes on it. All of the furniture and decor was European, utilitarian, yet clean and modern-looking.

Judging by the shoes on the shoe rack, they had several male guests ranging from the businessman on a late-night outing to the work boot type. The woman at the desk wore the kind of makeup used for the stage or low-light bars. She had powdered her face and looked pale white in the light cast by the desk.

"Aloha." She didn't seem at all fazed by their arrival. "You here for massage? How long?"

Huh. Apparently, there were no appointments required. The place must also get enough business by word of mouth that strangers weren't an unusual thing.

Raul shrugged. "Maybe an hour."

They'd decided he would do the talking while Zu remained the man of few words. People tended to take in Zu's size and build and then underestimate his intelligence. It could be of benefit to see if different things were said in Raul's presence versus Zu's.

He pulled cash out of his wallet and tossed a few big bills on the desk.

The money disappeared. The woman had quick hands.

She leaned forward to tap a slim laptop with the end of a long nail. The monitor came to life, casting more light on her face. Her penciled-in eyebrows quirked as she studied the display. "We have time for you. No problem. Come, have some water first and take off your shoes so you can be comfortable."

Raul cleared his throat. Taking off his shoes and leaving them here before entering the massage area was new to him even if it was obviously the common practice for other patrons. It seemed impractical if he and Zu had to leave in a hurry.

The woman must've taken his hesitation as a lack of understanding because she came around from behind her desk. Standing next to the shoe rack, she crouched slightly and indicated the other pairs of shoes. "See? Keeps the massage area nice and clean. Please leave your shoes here."

Zu bent and began to pull off his boots so Raul moved to do the same. They both wore tactical boots with side zippers for easy on and off. When they left their boots on the rack, they left each pair far apart from the other so it wasn't as obvious two men wearing tactical boots had arrived together. If Raul had seen that on entering, it would've raised several red flags in his mind.

The hostess didn't seem to care. She'd moved to the water cooler and gotten a glass of water for each of them. "Do you need the restroom before your massage?"

Zu snorted and shook his head.

Raul gave her a sheepish smile. "I don't think so."

She only nodded and stepped back toward her desk to a door just past it. Her movements were quick and unobtrusive, but the door had a keyless lock requiring a proximity key fob to open. Interesting. The question was whether it was to keep unwanted people out or to keep someone inside the inner area.

As she pulled the door open, the woman leaned inside and waved to someone. In moments two petite women emerged, each dressed in a flower-patterned wrap. Each of the girls had long, glossy, dark hair and pale skin. They wore only light makeup, in a style popular in some of the East and South East Asian countries. He'd seen a lot of faces in his travels and his military assignments had included parts of Asia as well as Eastern Europe and the Middle East. If he had to guess, he'd have identified them as coming from South East Asia. Neither spoke.

"The haole and the popolo want hour massages." The woman's tone was definitely different with the employees. Where she'd been brisk with Raul and Zu, her tone had still been deferential. With the two massage girls, the hostess's tone had bite to it.

Each of the women glanced at Raul and Zu and then bobbed their heads either in affirmative or in slight bows. It could've been both.

Satisfied, the hostess turned to Raul and Zu again. "These are Gigi and Kim. They'll take care of anything you need. Enjoy."

Actually, Raul wasn't sure which was Gigi and which was Kim but the ladies stepped forward and split up, one urging Zu to follow her and the other approaching him. They stepped through the door, ducking under a Japanese-style fabric divider slit vertically to allow easy passage through.

The next room was huge, much larger than he'd anticipated. It was easily six to eight times larger than the receiving area and the ceiling rose up above them about two stories. This must be part of a renovated warehouse space. Laminate flooring had been installed for the look and feel of wood floors. Ceiling fans were installed and rose quartz lamps had been placed along the beams to soften the stark look upward. Ambient light was dimmer, the way restaurants turned down the lights at dinnertime for a more intimate setting. The entirety of the room was sectioned off into private areas by more fabric dividers rising about eight feet tall, enough for privacy but not enough to take away from the roomy feel of the high ceilings.

"Please," the woman leading Zu murmured. She indicated they should continue down a corridor formed by the various curtain partitions until they came to a place where the heavy fabric was pulled to one side to reveal a small area. "Here. With Gigi."

The last was said directly to Zu as the other woman, Kim, turned to Raul and indicated he should follow her a bit farther to the next curtained area.

Raul stepped into the privacy of his assigned "room" and turned to face Kim with what he hoped was a friendly smile.

She didn't look up to meet his gaze, instead moving forward to indicate a small table in the corner with a woven basket set on top of it. "Your clothes here, please. Then sit. I come back in a minute."

Raul stayed where he was. If he'd followed her, she'd have had to squeeze past him to get out again. "Okay."

Startled, she glanced up and looked quickly back down to the floor. In moments, she'd slipped past him and was letting the curtain down to give him privacy.

Interesting. He wasn't sure what he'd done to surprise her.

Well, best to keep up with the current flow. Maybe he'd get her to talk when he was lying on the table in a less threatening position. Even standing away from her, he was a foot and even a few inches taller than her. It was an effort not to loom. He stripped down to his boxer briefs and sat on the end of the table as she'd indicated, using a thin sheet to cover up to his waist.

Kim was back in moments, carrying a wooden tub of steaming water. She pulled over a short stool and set the tub on it, positioning it next to his feet. Without speaking, she tapped his ankles to indicate he should put his feet in the bucket.

Okay, then. He'd never had his feet washed before but it'd been a service he'd heard of in several places on his deployments.

Once his feet were in the water, he tried to open up conversation. "So do you always work nights?"

Her eyes flew wide open, and she looked up at him again. She lifted her hands, palms toward him, and waved them side to side in a gesture for him to stop. Then she held one finger to her lips.

Maybe he was too loud. He thought he'd heard the deep rumble of Zu but the curtains actually did a good job of deadening noise from the surrounding areas. He had no idea if someone was on the other side of the space he was in currently. The ceiling fans above provided both air circulation and a low level amount of noise, covering any whispers or low murmurs from other parts of the room. It wasn't specifically generated white noise but it worked for this place.

Kim grabbed pillows from under his table and plumped them behind him, encouraging him to recline. Her whisper was barely audible. "Good?"

Actually, he was propped up enough to still be able to see what was going on around him and really comfortable. "Sure."

She kneeled then, by his feet, and proceeded to wash

them. Her movements were slow, sensual. It was very relax-ing. As her fingers trailed up his ankles and over his calves, she encouraged him to let his knees fall open wide to the sides.

Raul got the distinct impression she could, at any minute, rise up and apply her attentions higher.

He cleared his throat and pitched his voice to a clear whisper. "This is my first visit to Honolulu. I hear it's really expensive to live here. Since you work nights here, do you have a second day job?"

Panic flared in her eyes this time. Her reply was still the barest whisper, her lips pursed with urgency. "We don't talk. Must respect the privacy of other clients." She placed a hand on his knee, starting to rise. "Okay? Shh. I'll take care of you."

Oh boy. This was going places he didn't intend. On one hand, refusing would potentially cut off any remaining chance to get any kind of information from her. He'd have to look elsewhere and hope Zu had better luck with Gigi. It wasn't the most unobtrusive way to find out any of what they wanted to know.

On the other hand, the idea of anyone besides Mali touching him left him cold with a growing anger. He wasn't going to let the ruse take this direction. He couldn't and still go back to her this morning feeling clean.

Another option was to be someone he hadn't been in a long time. The cold anger spread from his gut up and across his chest as he reached for the chill calm he'd been carrying just below the surface.

He sat up and dropped his hand down over hers, squeez-ing her hand hard enough to cause a gasp from her. He didn't let up the pressure until her panicked gaze met his. "I'm paying for your time. I get what I want. I like to get to know my girls. Talk to me."

She swallowed and looked down. "No other job. Just here."

He kept his voice to a very quiet growl. "Look at me."

She did, her eyes wide with fear now. Prey. The dull look of a person going through the motions cleared away by the immediate threat he presented.

"Why only here?"

She shook her head. "Not allowed."

"Not allowed anywhere else?" It followed if this really was a business front for human trafficking.

Her lips formed the word. "No."

He'd eased the pressure on her hand but kept his fingers wrapped around her wrist. Her pulse fluttered against his fingertips.

"What if I wanted to see you again, privately?" He had to keep his questions in line with his role as a horny customer.

"Can find me here." Tears began to glisten and her eyes darted to the side.

"Only here?" He stared hard. She was holding back.

Her words came back thready, almost completely inaudible. "Can talk to boss. He arrange special house calls."

He chuckled, the sound harsh to his own ears. Damn, he was a creepy bastard. "House calls, they call it?"

She didn't answer, only trembled.

Terrorizing her wasn't fun but he'd established himself as an interesting John now. Time to change direction. "I like variety. How often do they get new girls here?"

Her mouth dropped open. Her pulse spiked. He tightened his grip in warning and then loosened up again. She whispered hurriedly, "Don't know. Sometimes every week, sometimes a few days. I don't count."

It was often, though. Very often.

"Are all the girls from the same country as you and Gigi? Like I said, I like my choice from different girls."

She nodded. "China, Thailand, Korea, Japan. Many places. Haole from Russia, too. Some local girls. Lots of choice. Boss can talk to you about any of us."

Her English got better as she went through the options. Hell, she got asked this question enough to have more practice answering. Nausea rolled through his gut.

"You have any new girls come in this week? White girls." Mali had said at least one of her fellow researchers was close to her age and Caucasian.

Kim shook her head again. "Maybe soon. A few here now. I can get for you, maybe."

He gave her a slow, cruel smile. "No need. I'm happy with you for tonight."

Good thing there was no mirror in this little enclosure. If he saw himself, he'd probably destroy the reflection right about now. This woman was living a nightmare being near him.

She licked her lips. "You want me now?"

He released her wrist. "I want a massage, a real one. I want to know how good you are with your hands before I trust you for anything else. You massage only. Then after, we'll talk about what I want next."

She nodded hurriedly, obvious relief in her expression.

Satisfied, he sat back. His foot wash turned into a foot massage. As she worked, he listened, hard. No footsteps. They might as well have been alone. Raul wondered if Zu was employing the same tactics. It didn't matter so long as they got the intel they wanted. They'd compare notes later to look for the truth. Raul thought Kim had been honest, though. She had the look of someone who understood a lie could mean her life.

Raul watched her as she worked. Mali could've ended up like this. No one deserved to be trapped into this.

CHAPTER EIGHTEEN

If you keep pacing, the dogs are going to sleep hard tonight."

Mali stopped in her tracks and turned to glare at her older sister. Arin met her with a steady gaze of her own, as unfazed as ever. Fine. Arin might've had experience waiting for team members to come back from a...thing, whatever this was. But since Mali had woken up an hour earlier, she hadn't known what to do with herself.

Now that she'd stopped, Taz paused by her feet and lay down with a sigh. He'd been following her the length of the office hallway and back for the better part of the hour. She wasn't sure if he was anxious too or just supposed to be following her while Raul was away. The dog had displayed a lot more complexity than she'd ever noticed in other canines. It could be a little bit of both.

Arin sat relaxed on the couch in the reception corner. Her King rested easy beside her with his head between his paws.

Zu's Buck was lying by the entrance, keeping watch for intruders or waiting for Zu or both.

"How can you be calm when we don't know what's happening?" Mali flinched at the sound of her own voice. Her tone had come out strained, sharper than she intended.

Arin's initial response was to raise her eyebrow at Mali. Her sister didn't glare, but she had an unsettling stare. Rather than look away and drop the subject, Mali stayed where she was and waited. She couldn't quite meet Arin stare for stare, but she wanted an answer.

"Pua is monitoring the police and emergency channels." Arin didn't sound angry or irritated. To be fair, Mali wasn't sure why she had braced herself for it. If anything, Mali wrestled with her own churning frustration as Arin seemed unruffled by the waiting. "We'll know if there's any disturbance on the streets. This team wasn't designed for local work. We don't have a van with equipment to maintain visual surveillance. The monitoring will be good enough to let us know if they need us. If we don't hear anything, Zu and Raul have maintained their cover."

As she spoke, Arin reached over the arm of the couch and rested her hand on a backpack tucked away unobtrusively.

"What's in there?" Mali hadn't noticed the backpack at all until Arin brought her attention to it. It seemed compact and durable, with no obvious branding.

Arin shrugged. "They went in unarmed. This has enough for me and for them. If we hear there's an issue on the police or emergency frequencies, I'll head out and meet up with them. Downtown isn't far, and we have a predetermined meet-up spot. They'll make their way to it, and I'll be there with enough firearms to deal with any pursuers."

They'd gone in unarmed. It hadn't seemed so serious to Mali when she'd first thought about it. After all, they were going to a massage parlor so they'd be taking clothes off. Hard to hide a weapon when you were stripping down. But the idea of Arin taking firearms to them, of possible pursuit, was frightening.

She should've thought about it right away. She might have. But Mali was good at focusing on the minutiae. It was what she had experience with and where she might be able to contribute constructively. Here, in these situations, this was all Arin's world.

Mali shifted her weight from one foot to the other, uncomfortable with her self-examination. She could and should do it more. She could do it a little at a time and find her way through the chaos inside her head. Instead, she looked at Arin. "I didn't really ask when we met up for dinner. I never ask. What do you do?"

Surprise flashed in Arin's eyes. "Me specifically, or this team?"

"Both." Mali paused. "I'm curious about the team, but I want to understand your role in it, too."

Arin leaned forward and braced her elbows on her knees. "Okay. The Search and Protect is a private contract organization. We are deployed to locations to search for people and things."

Mali waited but Arin didn't continue. "That seems too simple."

A ghost of a smile hovered around Arin's lips, but her overall expression had gone neutral. "Everything can seem simple. The closer you look, the more complicated it gets."

There was a warning there, and a few days ago Mali would've backed off. She'd have decided she didn't want to know. Funny how a person could change after multiple life-threatening scares. "I'd like to understand in more detail."

Arin shrugged. "We're contracted to find VIPs, high-value targets. Sometimes they're political figures or their family. Sometimes they're very wealthy people. Other times they aren't either but what they do or what they know is of extreme value to various interested parties. Almost always, these are people of influence. It's almost never about ransom."

This was starting to sound like a television show or action movie. But Mali had seen for herself what they did, had bullets hit sand right next to her, and had every one of them surround Mali to protect her. Maybe in six months or a year she could play back the memories like they were an episode in some action drama or police procedural show. The memory of almost dying was too fresh right now.

Arin was watching her closely, and beside her sister, King had risen to a sitting position. He was watching her, too. "We specialize in finding those people, fast, and when we find them, we extract them quietly. Our dogs help us search for them, track them down in a lot of different environments. We go in, we get out. If we do our job right, minimal people even know we were there until they find their kidnapped victim gone."

"And if something goes wrong?" Mali asked.

Even the hint of a smile left Arin's face. There was nothing but a neutral, eerily pleasant mask. "We have the skill sets to force our way out to safety."

Goose bumps rose up on Mali's arms, and she rubbed her forearms to dispel the sensation. "You and Raul and Zu."

"And King, and Taz, and Buck," Arin added.

Mali glanced down at Taz. "These dogs aren't search-and-rescue dogs?"

"Most dogs out there can be trained to varying degrees. How much depends on the dog." Arin placed a hand on King's back, at his shoulders. "Basic obedience is easy for most dogs with the right incentive. Dogs suited for service have high intelligence and a lot of specific traits trainers look for to learn other desired behaviors. Search-and-rescue dogs learn to signal when they detect certain scents. The training gets more specific based on whether the dog shows the knack for trailing or detecting scent on the air."

Mali nodded. Her sister was dropping her guard as she spoke about the dogs. Her tone had warmed, too. A pang of recognition hit Mali in the chest as she recognized the happiness her sister's dog brought her. Mali was happy for her.

"I could go on for a while about scent and search dogs." Arin seemed to have realized she was going on about it. "What matters is that our dogs are more. They each have a specialization in the way they can search and what kinds of terrain they have experience searching in. We go with them, and the path forward can have some resistance. So our combat training comes into play and our dogs have similar training to work with us and defend us."

To defend, sometimes the dogs had to attack. Mali might duck away from the severity of the situation most times, but the obvious was right here with the dogs. She looked at Taz sitting beside her. He was a big dog, and maybe if she'd met him on his own, she'd have been unsure—even afraid—of him. But she'd met him with Raul and he'd been wearing a service vest.

Mali reached behind Taz's ears and gave him a scratch. "Well, it's obvious meeting any of them that they're really smart."

Arin did smile, finally. "They're rare. Not all dogs have the temperament to be working dogs. A smaller subset have the talent for scent. And an even smaller subset can be trained for multiple focuses the way these guys are."

Mali finished scratching and ruffled Taz's ears. His eyes just about rolled back in his head.

"He likes you." Arin's statement was full of warmth.

Mali huffed out a laugh. "You were always better with dogs, though."

"You are better with people," Arin answered immediately.

Mali blinked. She hadn't ever thought she was better at anything when compared with her sister. She'd always thought of them as drastically different. Finding similarities had filled her with frustration. Comparing and contrasting hadn't seemed right. But there was no bitterness or negativity in what Arin said. It was a simple matter of fact.

Arin continued. "You're sensitive to the emotional temperature around you. If you don't feel safe, there is a creep somewhere. If you are comfortable, generally the people around you are good people. You're incredibly accurate, and you don't even have to think about it. You probably shouldn't think about it. Thinking too hard can make you second-guess. You should trust your gut. I've trusted your instincts for a long time."

Tears welled up hot in Mali's eyes. Arin had trusted her, looked to her for her reaction to the world. It was like coming to her for advice, but not in any way Mali had ever recognized. "I didn't realize."

"Now you do." Arin cleared her throat, and this time, she was the one to look away. "I'm not good with people. I do things. I make things happen. I eliminate problems. It bothers you."

So much truth being laid bare.

Mali put words to what they both already knew she thought. "You're violent."

Arin's gaze met hers, steady and calm. "Yes."

And there it was. Her big sister became a cold stranger again. Cut off from the warmth and humanity that made people normal. This time Mali didn't try to brush away the goose bumps. Instead, she wrapped her arms around herself.

But Arin wasn't finished. "You have as much potential to hurt people."

Shock splashed through Mali's veins. "Me? No. How?"

"Raul is new to the island, newer than the rest of us." Arin sat up and returned to leaning back on the couch. "He's still getting used to this place. The transient nature of a tourist area hasn't been impressed upon him yet. You being transient hasn't sunk in for him yet."

Mali sucked in a breath. She hadn't thought about it either.

Arin nodded. "This thing between you two, you do yourselves harm if you pretend it's not more than a fling. What's between you is a lot deeper than that."

Mali shied away from thinking too hard about it. She closed her eyes and shook her head. "It's been a couple of days. That's not enough time to develop a relationship. He has his job. I'll go back to my research. We'll see each other through this, and that'll be a good thing through this experience. But we're not anything to each other."

They couldn't hurt each other.

When she opened her eyes, Arin wasn't looking at her anymore. Raul and Zu stood in the doorway to the office, and Raul was staring at her.

* * *

Not true.

Raul stepped inside so Zu could come in and greet Buck. Taz crossed the space between Mali and Raul, coming around to Raul's left and leaning his shoulder hard into Raul's hip.

Mali remained rooted in place, staring at him with wide eyes.

Well, part of what she said wasn't true. He viewed her as something to him. But no one had to know. In fact, in his line of work, it was better that way.

He glanced at Arin.

She actually looked sad. "We were mid-conversation. This wasn't where I was going with the discussion."

Zu surveyed the room. "It's going to have to wait. We have intel, and we need to plan next steps."

Raul followed Zu down the hallway, pausing as he came even with Mali. He looked into her eyes and saw her quietly panicking. He couldn't help it; he reached out and cupped her face briefly. "We can talk later. Let's concentrate on this for now."

There'd been a lot of different things vying for his attention recently, and he couldn't remember the last time he'd had to make so many choices on what to address first. It had to be the same way for Mali, possibly even more confusing. She was going to feel guilty for what she'd said. He didn't want to think about it until he'd had time to absorb how she felt about this thing between them on his own.

It hurt. Shit, it hurt. But this was not the time to deal with it.

Zu rapped his knuckles on Pua's door. There was a rustle, and Pua popped out of her office faster than a bunny let out of a top hat. "Boss! Glad to see you back in one piece."

Zu grunted, all business and no time for chatter. "We're going to need the latest satellite pictures you can get a hold of for the private farms and estates in the middle of the island."

Before Raul could follow Zu, Mali touched Raul's elbow. He stopped, cursed inwardly, and turned to face her.

Yup. Regret and sorrow were written all over her face. He hadn't wanted to see it.

"What?" Damn. The word came out rough, too.

She winced. "What I said..."

It mattered. He wasn't going to ignore it or pretend he hadn't heard her, but he hadn't told her his feelings yet. Not really. "Look. I don't do one-night stands. I genuinely like you. It might not be logical, but not everything that happens in this world has a logical reason behind it."

She didn't reply, only stared at him.

He shook his head. "Don't try to resolve this now. Don't feel bad over me. I'm not worth the time when there's a higher priority for all of us here."

"You are—"

"No. I'm not." He cut her off, his tone harsh. "You ever wonder what I did in the military? I committed heinous acts. I can't go to sleep at night without seeing the terrified faces of people, some children, I helped hunt down for *questioning*. For those people, I was the bogeyman. It was my job to scare people and I did it well." He closed his eyes and remembered the frightened expression on Kim's face, the woman from the massage parlor. He opened his eyes and looked sadly at Mali. "I came here to start doing some kind of good, but I know there's no redemption for me. Stop thinking of me as a good person."

Mali started to step back from him and stopped herself. She didn't seem to know what to say.

He held his breath for a count of ten and let it out slow. "It's okay. Don't fret. I enjoyed us, but I'm not going to continue if you don't want to, and I'm not going to make it hard on you either. We're going to help your friends. And then you're going to go your own way."

If anything, he was trying to make this easier—okay, he was being a dick—but they needed to get their minds on the task at hand, and she'd already made it clear how she viewed this thing between them. He was short on sleep, and this was all he could muster in the way of taking no for an answer and being open with her about who he really was.

He'd been stupid to get pulled more and more into this attraction he had for her. He should've kept his involvement limited to helping his best friend's sister and getting to know the Search and Protect team. It was his future. It'd given him the chance he needed.

He wasn't sure what he wanted, but it wasn't an option anyway. It'd be the nicest thing he could do to let her get back to her life before all this shit had happened to her.

"Let's get your life back for you."

CHAPTER NINETEEN

Mali didn't know what to say, and obviously, she'd already said way too much. More than she meant. She'd been thinking out loud rather than voicing actual decisions. She hadn't thought it all through and wasn't sure it was actually the conclusion she'd wanted to come to. And now she was seeing a whole new side to Raul, open and raw, and she couldn't get a grip on the mixture of intimidation and concern tangled in her chest.

But Raul turned away before she could put all of that into words. Then her sister was next to her, urging her into the office with the rest of the group. He was right; it was time for finding her research team. The rest, they'd hopefully figure out later.

If he gave her the chance.

"Both of us gained good information from our visit to the massage parlor. Piecing together what each of the attendants knew, we're looking for a privately owned estate with farming on site." Zu was leaning against the L-shaped desk where

Pua's main monitors were. "It won't be too far from town but it'll be far enough away to be out of direct scrutiny by police and away from the military base."

Pua blew out a puff of air, lifting a silken strand of dark hair off her forehead. "There's still a decent amount of island to cover, Boss."

"It's got a long private drive with fields on either side of it and the houses are set far enough back that they're not visible from the main road," Zu continued. "Our target takes some of his newly acquired assets to the property either to work the fields for farm-to-table meals or to provide entertainment for him and his men in the main house. The main house is connected to secondary guesthouses by covered walkways. They form a sort of courtyard. He likes stone gardens."

"Okay, I can work with that." Pua's fingers flew over her keyboard as she brought up images and quickly scanned them for the characteristics described.

"Sounds like a large property." Arin took a seat at the small table at the far end of the room.

"Enough space for privacy." Zu crossed his arms over his chest. "If we can get the satellite pics, we can put together a few options for how we go in there."

"No chance the research team was being held someplace here in town?" Arin didn't sound like she was arguing, only exploring.

"No." Raul leaned against the wall opposite all the computer displays. "According to the woman assigned to me, there've been no new girls in the last couple of days at the massage parlor and no strangers in any of the special back rooms. She said everyone goes through that place, even if they aren't forced into servicing the clients. If the research team had been in town, they'd have been in one of the back rooms. As it was, every back room was open and available for special services."

It was pretty clear what special services might be. Mali wondered if he'd confirmed there hadn't been anyone back there directly.

Raul glanced at Mali but addressed the room in general. "I asked my massage specialist to give me a quick tour so I could decide if I wanted special services next time."

Zu snorted. "I heard you talking to her. You had her intimidated as hell. I'm pretty sure she's hoping you don't come back."

Mali experienced a perverse rush of relief. Sure, they'd gone in undercover for her and her colleagues. She and Raul weren't a couple, especially not after her unfiltered commentary just a few minutes ago. But it still eased a wound-up tension inside her gut to know he'd found a way to get his information without partaking of any special services.

"Found it." Pua transferred an image to her largest monitor. "I think. This courtyard looks about right, and none of the other plantations or estates in the area have an enclosed area like this. Any other properties with a stone garden all have them set up behind a house with a wall bordering the garden."

"We'll want information on the property and who owns it." Zu stepped forward to study the image. "This is going to take a certain amount of risk."

Mali straightened and looked at each of them in turn. "Meaning?"

It was Arin who answered. "It's going to get complicated."

Mali deliberately walked over to the table and sat in the chair next to Arin. "Let's get started then."

Raul and Zu turned to stare at her.

Mali glared right back at them. This, she had to do. "You can't go in and just nab anyone who looks like they're there against their will. That could be a lot of people."

"We could get pictures." Raul glowered at her.

"Pictures from the university are outdated and barely look like any of us. Plus they don't have scent." Mali had been thinking about this at least. "I can go back to the hotel and grab something that belonged to each of them. That'll help the dogs. And I can be with you to identify them by sight. Besides, it'll be way easier to get them to come back out with you if I'm there. Otherwise, you're just a new set of scary people."

"You make good points." Zu didn't sound happy to admit it.

But she was right. It wasn't about rationale or logic. Those were more to convince this group. Deep down, Mali knew this was the best way to identify her colleagues and get them to cooperate.

"I don't like it." Arin and Raul said it at the same time. Stereo.

Mali set her teeth and turned her head to glare at each of them. "It's the most effective solution. How much time is there to come up with something better? What are you going to do about the other people held on that property against their will? What about the massage parlor?"

Arin pursed her lips. "We've a strong enough partnership with the local police. We'd be able to give them enough information for them to go in undercover at the massage parlor to get the evidence they need to bring it down."

"But you didn't think there was time for all that with my colleagues," Mali pressed. "So we don't have time to convince the police or go through proper channels or even wait for a ransom payout from the insurance. If you're going to act fast, you need to do everything you can to mitigate potential risks. Having me with you does that."

"And opens up more." There was enough of a growl to Raul's voice that every one of the dogs sat up and looked at him. "You'll be in danger. Or don't you remember what it felt like to be shot at last night?"

Fear leeched the warmth from her skin but Mali breathed deeply to steady herself. "I didn't forget. But I trust all of you. We can all go in together. I'll be safe with you."

The last she meant for Raul specifically. She stared at him, putting her conviction into her words and her eyes. He'd kept her safe through everything so far. He could protect her through this as well.

"I don't like this either." Zu's statement dropped into her belly, heavy and cold.

He sighed and stepped away from the desk, looking from Arin to Raul. "But she's right. We don't have time to find a more effective way to stack our deck. Having her with us increases chance of success. It's decided. So let's work on options to make this happen."

CHAPTER TWENTY

Broad daylight." Mali stared out at the panoramic view of lush green trees and wide open fields. "You can be stealthy in the middle of the day?"

From the driver's seat, Zu looked up into the rearview mirror to see her. "In the right situation, it works."

They'd spent the morning planning. Each of them had taken turns grabbing a short hour-and-a-half nap while the others continued preparations. Kai had returned with the SUV, fully refueled and license plate changed. By the time the sun was high in the sky they'd loaded into the vehicle and headed out of town, toward the middle of the island. Well, most of them had. Arin hadn't ridden with them, leaving Mali with Zu and Raul. It was part of the plan for Arin to have her own transportation, and she'd even left King to ride with the rest of them. Without Arin, Mali had thought she'd be more on edge, but so far she was riding a high of anticipation and fear was only a prickle at the edge of her mind.

Somehow she'd envisioned a nighttime raid, where all

of them wore black. It would've been catastrophic for her, she realized. She had no training, and it wasn't as if she'd be able to suddenly use night vision gear with ease even if they'd given it to her. She was randomly clumsy at the best of times. Trying to sneak around in the dark would've made her an even worse liability than she already was.

Instead, they were all dressed in varying shades of brown and tan. Long sleeves, long pants—the clothing was all light fabric. Arin had loaned Mali a fresh set of clothes. Even though it'd all been a size or two too big, the fit had been adjusted with rolled sleeves and pants legs plus a belt. Now that she saw the landscape, the browns blended with the varying shades of dirt in the fields and the trunks of cultured banana trees. Wearing black would've been a stark contrast against such surroundings.

"Stay close to me and the rest will all be action, reaction." Raul gave her the advice in a quiet, calming tone. "Just follow my lead."

He'd ridden in the SUV next to her without fidgeting the entire ride. In fact, he'd withdrawn, not touching her at all, not even a reassuring touch of his hand. She missed his touch. There was a huge space between them; it was more than physical, maybe more than if they'd been simple strangers. She couldn't blame him, not with her statements about the attraction between them being temporary. But this was more. It was like the warmth and friendliness, his magnetic personality, had been taken and stuffed somewhere deep inside him. The man looking at her wore a mask, like her sister's. He was about to go to work.

"We're here." Zu put the SUV in park and got out.

Mali waited until they'd all stepped out, surveyed the area, and let the dogs out the back. Then Raul came around to her side of the vehicle and opened the door, but he held up his hand as she moved to exit. "Best to stay inside the car. We'll be talking right here but you should stay in the protection of the vehicle for as long as possible."

He left the door partially open and stood beside her with Taz between them. They were parked on a service road at an elevation high enough to give them a distant overlook on several properties.

"Where are we headed?" Mali kept her voice low. She didn't know if it was out of fear of being overheard by their enemies or to avoid disrupting the conversation Zu was having with Todd Miller.

The team's kennel master had met them at the corporate office and followed them in a small Jeep. He'd swapped out his usual prosthetic for one that looked high tech, maybe one for being outdoors. Ann and Dan were with him, and the two hounds trembled with eagerness to be put to work. Come to think of it, Taz was extra alert, too. She didn't know Buck well, and the dog was as unreadable as his master, Zu, to her. But overall, she had the feeling all of the dogs were as prepared as their handlers to dive into action. She only wished she was as ready.

"The big plantation down the hill and to the left from here." Raul didn't point, but he shifted his stance so she could see over his shoulder. "This is close enough for us to proceed from here on foot."

"Okay." It looked far to her, but then again, she figured her perception of everything from here on out would border on the surreal. Her challenge would be to keep it together enough to react when they needed her to and not slow them down. She was on her feet and walking for the better part of every day when she was gathering testimonials for her research. She could do this.

The sound of an approaching engine freaked her out, but

Raul looked calm. Taz took a few steps forward, the big dog putting himself between them and whatever was coming—probably for Raul, but it felt like for her, too.

A woman arrived on a motorcycle, the femininity of her form unmistakable in her brown and khaki denim with a fitted cargo jacket. When she removed her helmet, Arin flashed a fleeting smile of encouragement before her features returned to her neutral façade.

"I brought supplemental firepower." Across her back, Arin had a ridiculously large duffel bag, the kind hockey players or baseball players carried.

King rushed to greet her, and Arin dropped a hand on the huge dog's shoulders. He was bigger than Taz, taller at the shoulder, and Arin could rest her hand on her dog's shoulders without crouching or bending at all. He'd ridden with them in the SUV but it was obvious he preferred to be with Arin at all times.

Arin strode over to Raul and Mali, transferring her duffel from her back to her side. She lifted her chin at Raul. "I'll stand here. Assess the lay of the land with Zu and Todd."

"Thanks." Raul turned to Mali. "Be right back."

Mali bit down on the urge to try to go with him. There wasn't any point in her inserting herself in that conversation. Raul joined Zu and Todd where they had established themselves, laying flat at the edge of a sharp drop on the hillside. The three of them lay shoulder to shoulder, using binoculars and glancing down at their smartphones at the satellite images Pua had provided. It was hard enough to consult with each other when it was two people. Three in that position would require strained whispers. Her as a fourth made no sense at all.

"He'll tell us the outcome of whatever discussion goes on," Arin said.

Mali tore her gaze from Raul. Taz lay a few feet away under the cover of thick undergrowth. "Okay."

"Good." Arin tossed her duffel bag into the footwell next to Mali and unzipped the bag. Reaching in, she pulled out a series of components and began fitting them together. "You know the overall plan anyway. All they're doing is making refinements based on what we can see in real life, right now."

Mali stared at the thing Arin was putting together. "That's...a big gun."

"Rifle." Arin started to apply tape to certain parts of it. "Every team has people assigned to roles to make responsibilities clear. Zu is in the lead with Buck. Raul and Taz will be providing escort to you and taking on the primary search for your teammates. On this team, I'm the sniper. If I do my job right, I'll be able to keep the bigger picture in my sights for all of you and take out a threat before it gets to you."

Arin's gaze hit Mali full force. Yes, her sister had been talking about the team but that last statement had been specifically focused on Mali. Her sister would be looking out for her, even from a distance. In fact, Arin was better at protecting Mali from far away.

The implications knocked the breath out of Mali. She nodded, unsure of what she could say. Well, there was something. "Thank you."

Arin paused and glanced at her. "It's what I do."

There was a lot in that statement. It could've been about Arin's job. It felt like more.

"If there's going to be a good time, this is it." Raul returned and stood at arm's reach, facing both Mali and Arin. "It's the hottest part of the day. We've got line of sight on people inside the main house taking siestas. There are guards on patrol and at the main entrance, but they're all hating the heat. They'll be sluggish."

"We're making the best of a shit situation." Todd Miller strode over to join them.

It was getting crowded on this side of the vehicle. Mali scooted farther into the SUV but leaned forward enough to still hear the discussion.

"It'd be better if there was more time to study this place," Todd continued.

Arin shook her head. "We don't often have the luxury. Assessing and going in at risk is always going to be standard operating procedure for us."

Todd grunted. "It's still too far away to get good detail on the level of resistance you're going to encounter inside the courtyard area. You're going to need to find a closer vantage point, maybe get up on that roof."

Arin nodded. "I'd be better at a distance but I can go in closer if necessary. I'll do what's needed when the time comes."

Yes. That. Mali worked to solidify her internal resolve. She would do her best to do the same.

*   *   *

The plan was ballsy and relied primarily on Taz's ability to locate the research team. Once Taz had the trail, it would be up to Mali to provide positive identification and coax the hostages into coming with them. There were times when a hostage could be so frightened or traumatized that they'd refuse rescue. They didn't have enough resources to remove Mali's research team if any of them balked. So having her with them made sense. Raul had gone through it in his head over and over on the ride here.

Miller stepped around Raul and Arin, grabbing the driver's-side door of his Jeep. "There's already one distraction in place but I can add to it. Shouldn't disrupt what you have planned already but could thin out their security at the front gate some in case you have to make your exit out the front door. It won't take long to drive by them and get them worked up, maybe lead them on a little chase. The bigger the distraction I can provide, the better the chances for all of you."

Zu joined them with Buck at his side. "Better than waiting here for us. I like it. Circle back to meet with the group on time, though. We need you mobile and ready to pick up anyone who gets separated from the group."

This change to the plan had always been an option but Raul wondered why Zu had waited until Miller made the choice on his own. Zu liked to keep his thoughts to himself more than anyone realized. This wasn't a formal military unit, and it was still new. In a lot of ways, Zu might be establishing himself as their new lead gradually, similar to the way Raul was integrating himself with the team. Things like that took time.

Arin finished her preparations and zipped up her duffel. Instead of leaving it in the trunk of the SUV, she pulled it back out and strode over to the undergrowth to hide it at the base of a nearby tree.

"I'll head around to the far side of the water reservoir and choose a position." Arin slung her rifle across her back and grabbed her helmet. "I should be able to get in closer from that angle if it becomes necessary."

Zu nodded. Raul did the same. Neither of them wished her luck. She was their luck.

"Be careful."

At the sound of Mali's quiet words, Arin paused. "You stick with Raul and come out of this whole and unharmed."

Raul bit back a grin. Mali frowned but hopefully there'd

be time to explain it to her after all this. Arin wasn't going to be careful because being too careful could get a person killed. She excelled at walking the tightrope. She didn't hesitate. She assessed a situation, plotted a course, and executed before the variables had a chance to change too much. It was all split-second decision making.

He didn't plan on being careful either. He also wouldn't say as much to Mali. None of them made promises they wouldn't keep.

"I'll ride down in the SUV to the edge of the property by the main road." Zu moved to the back of the SUV and opened it, signaling for Buck to hop up. "I'll get in position to start my distraction tactic once Arin is in place. It'll give Raul and Mali the best chance to get in and get out with minimal opposition."

"You got it." Miller settled himself in the driver's seat and closed the door. Moments later, he'd pulled back onto the service road and headed toward the plantation at a lazy Sunday driver speed.

Raul gave his best encouraging smile to Mali. "Here we go."

Her gaze settled on him and held for a long moment. His heart stopped in his chest. Damn, he needed to keep her safe through this. Then she returned his smile with one of her own, and the world started moving again.

CHAPTER TWENTY-ONE

Mali did her best to breathe as Zu put the SUV in drive. This was it. They were going in to a place to find her coworkers and get them out before the worst possible thing could happen.

Or the worst possible thing could happen to all of them.

She closed her eyes as they pulled back onto the main road. No. It was one thing to intellectually acknowledge possible scenarios. It was a bad idea to defeat them all before they got started by giving too much power to the scarier possibilities.

"Once you two get out of the car, we'll switch to comms." Zu's eyes were reflected in the rearview mirror as he addressed her. "If any of us speaks, it should be audible, but won't be loud enough to give away your position even if someone is near you. If you can't answer one of us right away, we will assume danger is imminently near you. Try to answer us as soon as you can. If we can't see you, we need to rely on communications to make sure we can help you."

She nodded. They had all done this kind of thing before. Arin had gone over it with Mali back at headquarters when they'd fitted Mali for a comm. But she had to admit that it was a relief for Zu to go over it with her again. The reinforcement would help her remember what to do in case things got crazy. The reminder that someone was listening for her was a comfort, too.

Todd's car was barely visible ahead of them, far up the road and approaching where the main gate was supposed to be. The Jeep dipped out of sight as the road curved and Zu pulled to a stop.

"Delta team at the front gate." Todd's voice whispered in her ear. The comm was a good fit, nestled in her ear, and he wasn't loud enough to distract her from her immediate surroundings.

Zu responded, "Copy. Team Bravo, go."

That was them.

Mali opened the passenger-side door as Raul did the same from the front seat. They both hopped out of the SUV, and Mali hurried to follow Raul to the limited shade provided by the tall hedge bordering the property. Taz jumped out to the roadside on his own and even turned, rearing up and closing the vehicle door with his front paws. In moments, the big dog had joined them, and Mali stared as Taz sat grinning up at Raul.

In her ear, Todd's voice took on a coarser tone. "You boys look like you're overqualified for gate duty. Stand around here all day and you're going to lose your edge."

There was a pause. Maybe whoever Todd was talking to had answered. Probably. The mic he was wearing didn't pick it up. It only brought them his words. Zu pulled the SUV away and drove off the road in the direction of the plantation fields.

"Hard to find potential talent unless we catch soldiers coming off active duty. I came out here recruiting." Todd fell silent again and then laughed, a hard, mocking sound. "Hey now, none of you can think for yourselves? Or maybe you want to stand around all day mouthing off to an old man."

This time they could hear a faint voice. Someone might've approached Todd.

Raul touched her shoulder. "Be ready."

Mali nodded.

Zu's deep voice came across the comm. "Alpha team in position."

Alpha was Zu. Mali hadn't heard her sister yet, but she didn't know if they were supposed to. Arin's role was the one she'd listened to and had understood the least about. Based on the plans, her sister was the most autonomous. She might not need to check in.

"Lazy." Todd barked the word. "You don't know anything about me but I have plenty of intel on you and your employer. Sloppy work. I sure as hell am not getting out of this vehicle. Want to know what I know? Fucking making me get out of my vehicle."

There was the sound of rubber squealing against black top. "Delta team, on the move. Looks like four guards are coming after me in two different vehicles."

"Copy," Zu responded. "Bravo team proceed."

Raul kneeled beside Taz, the two of them staring through the gaps in the hedge. After a moment, Taz seemed to lean forward. Raul murmured a word. "*Revier.*"

Taz shot forward through the hedge, a streak of black with tan blurring his form.

"What the fu—" a man's voice cut off with a surprised cry and the sound of growling.

Quickly, Raul forced his way through the hedge, holding

some of the thicker branches of the hibiscus to make it easier for Mali to pass through. She slipped through as best she could, ignoring the light scratches of the branches. As soon as she was clear, Raul pushed her into a crouch next to the hedge. Then he rushed ahead.

There was Taz, struggling with a man dressed in some sort of deep green camouflage. Taz had the man's arm in his jaws, and there was blood. As Raul reached them, he kicked something away—a gun.

"*Aus*." Raul issued the command in a quiet, assertive tone, full of authority and confidence.

Taz immediately released his target.

"Down on the ground. Now." This was clearly aimed at the injured man. "He didn't break your arm but he could. Get down now. No talking."

The man clutched his arm to his chest and dropped to his knees. Awkwardly, he lay forward on the ground, holding his injured arm away from the reddish brown dirt.

"*Pass auf*," Raul murmured again. Taz took a few steps forward and sat, staring at the other man intently. "Stay still and my partner will leave you alone. Move in any way and he will be on you faster than anything you can think to do. Understand?"

No answer but the man remained still. Apparently, Raul was satisfied because he placed his gun back in his shoulder holster and approached the other man. Pulling zip ties out of his pocket, he bound the man at the wrists and ankles and dragged him over into the minimal shelter of the hedge.

When Raul and Taz returned to Mali, she wasn't sure what to say but she felt she had to say something, anything, to reestablish a connection to these two. Otherwise, they were becoming very scary strangers in her mind. "That was kind."

Raul paused and looked at her, his expression a brief flash of sadness, and then he was urging her forward along a line of cultivated banana trees toward the main house. "That wasn't kindness. He needed to be out of immediate view so another guard wouldn't catch sight of him and raise an alarm from a distance."

"Oh." Mali fell silent. It made sense. Of course it did.

*   *   *

Raul set his jaw and urged them forward. There were a lot of possible outcomes for today, and while he was prepared for the worst, he hoped for the best for Mali's sake. Even if he'd had to agree with the rationale for her being here, he didn't have to like it. The best he could do was to get her through this mission as safely and quickly as possible.

"This way." He urged her along the line of banana trees, keeping her between him and the trees to provide her with as much cover as possible on the move. She was wearing a bulletproof vest but it wouldn't save her from a head shot. He and Taz needed to minimize her chances of becoming a target as much as possible.

Mali followed his directions silently, her eyes wide open. Her breathing was normal for now but he was monitoring her closely. She'd taken in the sight of Taz mauling the guard's arm in a detached, almost clinical fashion. For now, that was good. Later, a negative reaction could kick in, and he wanted to be ready to help her through it. So far, though, she seemed to have her mind on the plan.

"Bravo Team, this is Alpha." Zu's voice came in quiet but clear on the comm. "I am in position and have eyes on you."

"Copy," Raul responded.

It was good to have the reassurance of coverage but

Raul didn't relax. Zu was at a distance. Arin was somewhere out there, even farther away. They knew from
the attempt on Mali's life at the beach that there was
at least one other sniper to deal with as part of the opposition. Arin's main objective would be to neutralize
the sniper threat and identify additional issues from a
distance.

This was a simple plan. The faster they were able to ex-
ecute it, the better their chances of success. As time passed,
things would get more complicated.

"Bravo Team, this is Charlie." Arin's voice came across
the comm, smooth and cool. "I am in position and have eyes
on."

Mali let out a small noise. It sounded like relief but Raul
glanced back at her to be sure. She gave him a tremulous
smile and a thumbs-up. Okay then.

They reached the end of the banana trees and had to
dart into the shelter of a stand of solar panels. In his ear,
Raul heard Zu. "Place has enough power to go off grid if
necessary."

It was good to note. If they'd tried an incursion at night,
cutting the power lines from off-site wouldn't have disabled
their target as much as desired. Hopefully, they wouldn't
need to come back, but if they did, they had additional intel
on the premises.

There was a garden at the edge of the solar panel units.
They made it into the lush greenery bordering the garden
without incident.

"Incoming. Not armed. Possibly a gardener or other do-
mestic." Arin's warning was crisp.

Mali crouched down in the greenery, looking to Raul for
a hint about what to do next. Good. He signaled for her to
stay with an open palm facing toward her. Then he peered

through the broad leaves of the plants around them to get a line of sight on their visitor.

Mali tugged at his pants leg, and then she whispered into her comm. "I know her. She's part of my research team. Terri."

Raul nodded. "I'll get her."

Mali glanced at Taz and back at him.

He frowned. "Not the same way as the guard. I'll leave Taz with you and get her."

Mali made a slight motion with her hand, waving away his comment. "I know it wouldn't be the same. But just you would scare her, too. She doesn't know you, and she's already been kidnapped. We don't know what else happened to her."

He wasn't sure either but this Terri was walking unaccompanied in a garden. There were some ugly possibilities as to why.

"No time." Arin's voice cut in with a more strident note. "There's a guard coming around the other end of the garden. If he walks in, you'll lose your chance to intercept the girl."

Raul clamped a hand down on Mali's shoulder as she gathered her feet under her. "Taz, *Geh vorhaus.*"

Taz left cover and walked ahead a few steps.

Raul called out, keeping his voice too low for any people to hear from a distance but the dog would hear him. "Taz, *blieb.*"

Taz came to a halt and stayed just as he was.

The woman, Terri, came around the corner and several steps closer before she noticed Taz and stuttered to a stop. She was medium height and build with pale white skin dusted in freckles and brown hair cut short around her chin. For someone in captivity for the last forty-eight hours plus, her makeup was on point. How? She wasn't immediately afraid of Taz, thankfully, but she definitely didn't know what to make of him.

Raul gave Mali's shoulder a squeeze at the same time Zu's voice came across the comm. "Bravo Team, Mali is to stay put. Sá to retrieve the target."

Mali settled into her crouch. Raul thanked her silently for listening in the heat of the moment.

Raul slipped through the vegetation to a position just behind the woman as she leaned forward to look farther down the path, probably for someone from the house who might be accompanying the dog. Taz chose that moment to cock his head to one side in doggy curiosity. The woman let out a huff of laughter and tilted her head to the side to match.

Gotcha.

Raul left cover and wrapped his arms around the woman, one hand over her mouth and the other arm around her waist. He didn't waste time dragging her, instead lifting her off her feet and pulling her back into the landscaping. As soon as they were hidden from casual view, he dumped the woman on the ground and pinned her.

"Taz, *hier.*" He called and Taz answered immediately, returning to his side.

He kept his hand clamped over the woman's mouth as she tried to scream. It would take her a few seconds before she'd take a breath and give them a chance to get through her fear.

Mali rushed over, pushing Taz aside so she could kneel near Raul and Terri. Mali glared at him hard enough to punch a hole through him. He kept a neutral expression and looked pointedly down at Terri and back at Mali.

Mali narrowed her eyes at him, but her shoulders dropped as she turned to get into Terri's field of vision. "Terri, it's me. Shh."

Terri didn't respond at first, still struggling against Raul's weight on top of her. Mali had to try three times to get Terri's attention. As Terri settled and finally nodded understanding, Raul slowly removed his hand from her mouth.

He grimaced at the smeared lipstick on the inside of his palm and wiped it off on his hip. Hopefully, the stuff wouldn't mess up his grip.

Mali started talking, low and urgent. "We're here to get you and the others out."

Thankfully, Mali didn't mention how many were included in "we."

Terri swallowed hard and tried to push up into a sitting position. Raul didn't let her up. Something about her wasn't right.

The woman darted a glance up at him, then at Taz over his shoulder, and then directed her attention to Mali. "Are you crazy? The university is handling this. The insurance will cover our ransoms. You could get us all killed."

Mali sat back on her heels, startled by the anger in Terri's tone. "The men who grabbed everyone were obvious. None of them wore masks. You think they're going to let all of you go when you can identify them?"

Terri blinked and then pursed her lips. "You don't understand. If I'm missing, they could hurt the others."

"We're going to get them now," Mali assured her. "You can show us where they are."

Terri laughed, almost too loud. "This isn't a game. You can't just run in there and save everyone. It's not that easy."

Mali held a finger to her lips. "You're making this harder. Why?"

Raul breathed, inwardly relieved. Mali might not be experienced but she was smart and observant. This Terri woman had gone from angry to patronizing, but in no way was she relieved to see Mali.

"Let me go and get out of here." Terri tried again to push up against Raul. "I won't tell anyone I saw you. Just let things go as planned, and everything will be fine. Don't ruin it."

Like hell. He didn't let her up, but it was Mali who reached out with both hands and grabbed the sides of Terri's head. "Where are they?"

He'd never heard that kind of intensity from Mali before, and apparently, Terri hadn't either.

Terri's face twisted into an ugly scowl. "They're fine. They're here right next to the main house."

"Why are you allowed out here and they aren't with you?" Mali wasn't letting Terri turn her head, keeping the woman captive and focused on her.

The bravado left Terri in a rush of words and hot air. "I...I'm special."

"Why?" Mali sounded hurt and angry and dangerously quiet all at the same time.

"Because she helped," Raul answered when tears started to spill out of Terri's eyes in rivulets of black mascara. "She's cooperating now, too, probably keeping her host happy. She probably thinks she's going to get a cut of the ransom, maybe a new job in his organization."

Every guess appeared to hit home. Terri started sobbing. "If you already knew, why are you asking me?"

Raul clamped down on his disgust. "You confirmed a few guesses. Who the hell has access to makeup and everything else it took for you to keep looking like this? Kidnapping victims don't come out without some wear and tear. You weren't planning to go home with the rest of the team."

The question was whether she knew what was really going to happen to the team. Even if they asked, they couldn't be sure she wasn't lying. They had no leverage to be sure she'd tell the truth. Her whole plan was toast.

A mean glint shone through Terri's tears. Her chest expanded, and he clamped his hand down over her mouth again before she could scream. That did it; she'd been about to do her best to expose them.

"Mali, back away."

Mali did as asked but she whispered, "What are you going to do?"

"I'm not going to kill her."

CHAPTER TWENTY-TWO

Mali stumbled back, unable to look away from Terri's hateful gaze. She didn't want to believe the accusations, but Terri's face was twisted and flushed in an angry mask beneath Raul's hand. The woman's nostrils were flaring, and she seemed to be seething.

Raul shifted off Terri and pressed something against her at the same time. Terri jerked, her scream choked off in her throat as her whole body spasmed. Then she was still. He quickly turned her on her belly and zip-tied her hands behind her back. It took another moment for him to secure her ankles, too.

"She'll be okay." Raul gave the reassurance as he pressed two fingertips against Terri's neck. "I used a taser to subdue her for a short time. We need to get moving."

Mali swallowed hard and nodded. "Too many questions. There's no time to ask them."

Raul smiled with sympathy in his eyes. "Not right now, no."

To be honest, she was sure she didn't want to hear the answers at the current moment either. Reality wasn't an easy thing to face, and while she wasn't going to hide from it, she could recognize when she was going to need more time to deal than they had here. She was already a risk for the team, and she needed to do her best to keep up. Think it all through later.

"Bravo Team is moving out." Raul made the statement more deliberately. "One hostage identified as a traitor. She is neutralized, and we are proceeding to the main house."

That was right. The team was listening via the comms. They might not have heard Terri, but they'd heard Mali and Raul talking to her.

"Copy." Zu's deep voice was a balm as Mali struggled to put one step in front of the other. "We have eyes on the garden, and your path is clear."

Raul murmured a command to Taz, and the big dog moved forward. Raul turned to her, and his face had taken on that neutral, almost cold mask again. "Stay as close to me as you can."

They moved out of the landscaping and onto the path, following Taz toward the main house.

"Initiating phase two." Zu's warning still startled her, even though she'd known the plan.

Gunfire erupted nearby but out of sight, and then something exploded out in the fields. Even knowing it came from a distance, Mali flinched and ducked her head. If Zu was causing a distraction now, who was watching their progress?

"Multiple guards headed your way, Alpha." Arin sounded oddly genial. "Bravo Team, I have eyes on, and your path is clear."

Of course.

Shouts rose up from inside the main house. Not all of

them had the sharp, efficient cadence of orders. Some of them were panicked.

"This is Delta Team, headed back for a second pass at the front gate. Those initial guards couldn't drive for shit." Todd was still gruff but his words were lighter, more energized.

"Copy." Arin chuckled. "Bonus."

How were they all joking around right now?

And yet, their levity kept Mali hopeful. If they were joking, things were going well, and there was a chance they'd get through all of this with the best possible outcome. They had prepared her for the worst. They'd been pragmatic and realistic. In the midst of all this, they were optimistic. It was a strange, very effective balance.

Raul urged Mali forward. "Couldn't have asked for better timing. Let's keep going before our luck runs out."

They approached the entryway Pua had spotted from the satellite images. It was a doorway set into a low wall that bordered a covered walkway connecting the main house to one of the secondary buildings. Hopefully, they would encounter few guards based on the distractions being provided by Zu and Todd on the other side of the complex.

Raul pulled Mali beside the door, making sure her back was pressed against the wall as he partially covered her. From the side, he opened the door a few inches and peered through the space to see as much of the walkway as possible. Then he looked down at Taz and gave a command. *"Revier."*

Taz slipped through the door and looked both ways before proceeding forward and to the left. Raul rushed her in after Taz and shut the door behind them. At this point, she felt more exposed than she had when they'd been out in the garden, with all of the greenery providing places to hide. Here, in the courtyard area, anyone inside the complex could catch sight of them. The courtyard had some ornamental trees and a fountain in the center, but otherwise, it was very open.

Raul kept her between him and the wall as they moved down the walkway toward the nearest secondary building. They'd gone a few steps when Taz paused ahead of them, leaning forward and almost trembling with eager attentiveness. He'd had that posture earlier, first when he'd taken down the guard at the hedge and again when he'd scented Terri approaching.

Mali shrank back as Raul moved forward with his gun up and ready.

There were two men in casual clothes standing on the opposite side of the fountain, having a smoke. Only luck had prevented them from seeing Raul, Taz, and Mali enter through the garden door because the fountain had been between them. They were facing the somewhat distant sound of chaos going on in the fields but they must have heard something because they turned at the same time and caught sight of Raul. Both of them were armed.

Mali's knees buckled. Raul couldn't shoot both of them at the same time, and Taz was fast, but not fast enough to get to the men before they fired a shot on Raul or Mali.

They raised their guns. Raul fired first. Both men jerked with the impact of a bullet and went down in different directions.

"Bravo Team, you are clear in the courtyard. Proceed." Arin's voice came across the comm, cool and steady.

Mali hadn't realized how directly Arin could protect them from a distance. The second man on the ground was proof.

Both men lay where they'd fallen, not moving. They hadn't been tased. They'd been shot. Raul and Arin had shot them.

Mali swallowed hard. "Are they dead?"

Something cool touched her hand, and then Taz's warm muzzle slipped under her palm. The big dog wedged himself between the wall and her hip, pushing her, urging her, back to standing.

"Let's go." Raul's tone was quiet. His words were short and grim. He proceeded ahead of them, gun up, turning to look into every window around the courtyard and up toward the rooftop and then back down and around them again.

*   *   *

Shit way for Mali to come face to face with who and what he really was. Oh, she'd known intellectually. Maybe. She'd known he'd been a soldier and what being a soldier deployed overseas could mean. He'd done his best to make it clear he hadn't served from behind a desk.

But nothing could prepare a person for seeing death first-hand.

This was a major reason he hadn't wanted her to be here, with the team, with him. He'd wanted her out of danger, first and foremost, and he hadn't wanted her to see what he and the team might have to do.

"This way." He motioned for her to stay close to the wall as they moved toward the nearest building. It was a long structure and had looked like stables from the satellite pictures but was enclosed with ornamental bars over the windows. It was a good bet this was the "guest" house. Once they got inside and had a small, relatively safe space clear, he'd give Taz the scents of Mali's research team again to see if his partner could find a trail at all.

When they reached the door to the building, he pulled her behind him so that they were both stacked up at the edge of the doorframe, pressed as close as possible. "Okay, Mali.

This door opens out. You're going to scoot over to the other side. When I nod, you open it. Keep the door between you and anyone inside who might see you. Got it?"

There was a long pause. Then Mali answered him with a barely audible "okay."

He nodded and tried to give her a smile of encouragement as he listened hard for any warning sounds from inside the building. A moment later, she did as he instructed. He gave her a nod, and she opened the door in a smooth motion, keeping it between her and anyone inside just as he'd asked.

He lunged partially through the doorway and pulled back, getting a quick look at the interior as he did. A shadow moved against the far wall, whoever it was giving away his position as he flinched at Raul's feint.

Raul barked out a command. "*Fass.*"

Taz darted in the door, a dark streak against the shadows, launching over a table in the center of the room and contacting with the man Raul had seen.

"C'mon." Raul reached around the door and grabbed Mali's shoulder, moving them both inside the building and out of the open doorway. Doorways were kill funnels. They needed to move quickly while Taz had their unknown occupied. Raul kept her behind him but made sure they stayed out of a corner, giving her space to move if they needed to.

The room was a high-ceilinged open area with a massive table. It was built sturdily and had seen some rough use but could've seated a large number of people down its length on either side. At the end of the room was a hallway with a set of stairs on either side arching up and coming together over the first floor hallway. Two choices.

First, Taz. Raul moved along the wall, holstering his primary weapon and drawing his sidearm with a silencer. Indoors, he wanted to maintain as much of an element of surprise as possible. Mali had caught on and was following close on her own, staying between him and the cover of the wall as much as possible. Taz's target was cursing and struggling to reach something he'd dropped on the floor: a radio.

Taking careful aim, Raul shot the radio. The man choked on a shout, disrupted by Taz shaking his arm.

"*Aus.*"

At Raul's command, Taz let go of the man. The sleeve of his work shirt was shredded, and blood was beginning to soak the fabric. He sat there, clutching his arm to his chest and glared at Raul.

"Don't m—"

Even as Raul was telling him not to, the man lunged at the radio. Broken or not, Raul wasn't going to take a chance of the guy getting a call out. Raul took two quick steps forward and kicked the man in the head. The man slumped the rest of the way to the floor.

For Mali's benefit, Raul growled. "One man inside, unconscious. Room is clear."

"Copy," Arin responded.

Mali surprised him, taking the zip ties from his hand and moving to secure the unconscious man. He kept watch as she finished, looking out the windows for anyone approaching the building.

"We're moving toward the rooms now," Raul said to Mali. "It'd help if you could keep eyes on my six. We may not have time to tie up every person we take down from here on out."

Mali's glazed look faded as he gave her a call to action. He needed to keep giving her things to do so she didn't have time to think too hard about what she was seeing. "Six?"

He nodded. "As we go, you keep a lookout on what's behind us. Just keep physical contact with me so you move

when I do. Keep your hand here, on my hip, so you don't accidentally impede any motion I need to make with my arms."

More alert, less numb, she nodded her understanding.
"Okay."

"Stay with me." He meant it both physically and mentally. She'd been withdrawing as they'd progressed further
and further into this mission. As the moments of action es-
calated, she'd appeared to be going into shock. He needed
to keep her engaged and responsive or this was going to become way more complicated very quickly. He'd been watching for it, though. Even trained soldiers experienced dif-
ficulties, sometimes froze, their first time in combat. For
someone with no training, Mali was doing better than anyone could've asked of her.

The three of them crossed the room quickly and started
clearing the lower hallway. Two of the rooms were empty
of people and looked to be storage for firearms and random
piles of clothing. The third held a worn, stained mattress.

As they reached for the first door on the other side of the
hallway, Taz whined and sat in a deliberate, passive signal.
There were people on the other side of the door.

Raul motioned for Mali to wait on the other side of the
doorway from him as he tried the door. Locked. He pointed
his sidearm at the ceiling. Maybe in television shows it
worked to shoot the lock, but in reality, a bullet wasn't going
to solve this. He studied the door. It was older. The whole
building looked updated and kept up from the outside, but
the interior was run-down. He took a step back and kicked
the door just below the doorknob, hard.

The door gave on the first kick, and he pushed it the rest
of the way open.

Inside the room, at least six to eight people huddled in
the far corner. It wasn't a big space but they were doing their

damnedest to stay clear of the door and as far away from him as possible. All of them were Asian, dark-haired and terrified. Their clothes were torn. None of them looked like they'd had a decent meal in a long time. The scent of un-washed bodies and human excrement hit him in the face.

"There's not enough room in here for them all to lay down at the same time," Mali whispered from behind him. "They've been using that bucket in the corner."

"No time to talk to them." He backed out of the room with his sidearm pointed at the ceiling so they'd know he wasn't about to shoot them. "If they can get up the courage to leave on their own, they have a good chance right now. It's the best we can give them."

It wasn't enough. Damn. But they had an objective.

"We're putting together the intel to tip off the police." Arin's words were meant to reassure Mali, but they soothed him, too. "My line of sight is obscured, Bravo Team. Charlie is moving to a new position."

They needed to move fast then, while Arin wasn't able to watch the building to warn them of any approaching hos-tiles.

The other two rooms left in the hallway were similarly filled with frightened people, mostly from Southeast or East Asia. Raul took the risk and left their doors wide open to give them a chance to escape if they could bring themselves to take the opportunity.

The horror of slavery was that, sometimes, people who'd become slaves couldn't bring themselves to run for freedom. The fear of not having a place to go would keep them where they were. He and the Search and Protect team couldn't take them out of this place yet.

"We're not going to forget them."

He took Mali and Taz up the stairs. Two rooms had open

doorways with no occupants, just relatively clean mattresses on simple bed frames. Another door revealed a full bathroom. Taz paused at the fourth door and sat, turning back to look at Raul.

Mali moved to the opposite of the door without needing to be asked. She watched him expectantly. He studied the door, looking for any signs to set this one apart from any others, any potential danger. Nothing.

He kicked in the door and heard exclamations this time. He kept his sidearm up and took a good look at the people inside the room. The people were Caucasian, better dressed, but still looking the worse for wear. Their faces were gaunt from lack of sleep, and their lips were cracked from dehydration. Several of them, man or woman, sported bruises on their faces. They'd been roughed up at some point, either when they'd been taken or during the time they'd been held or both. All of them were frozen and staring at his gun, some with eyes wide in fear. One or two had the glazed expression of hopelessness or shock.

Backing up a step or two, he glanced at Mali and back down the hall, and then he studied the captives again. "Don't go into the room. Just come around behind me and look over my shoulder. Is this everyone?"

Mali stepped away from the side of the door and took up the position he'd asked. Her sigh of relief washed over him, and her hand briefly rested on his shoulder. "Yes."

"Mali." The oldest man in the room stepped forward, his expression a mixture of happiness and worry as he drew heavy brows together. His jaw was covered in salt and pepper scruff, and a huge bruise blackened the area around his cheek and eye. "What are you doing here? Have you seen Terri?"

The man paused. "Are you cooperating with her?"

"No!" Mali spat out the word, the horror and disdain in her voice coming across loud and clear.

"Bravo Team, you have a hostile approaching from the south door." Arin's voice. "Wrap it up and get out through the courtyard. Stat."

"Copy." Raul lifted his chin toward Mali's principal investigator, or at least he was assuming so. The older man was at least the person who was acting as lead for the group of captives. "There's no time. Leave with us or take your chances here. If you've seen any faces since you were taken, I strongly recommend you leave with us."

He was not dragging anyone out of here, except Mali if he had to.

CHAPTER TWENTY-THREE

Move now. Talk later."

Mali gave her PI a pleading look. He was a reasonable man most of the time, and sure he could be stubborn on occasion, but this would be an awful, awful time for him to dig in his heels.

Her PI seemed to flinch and deflate. He waved his hands, almost shooing the rest of their research team around the room and out the door toward Mali.

"Mali, lead them back the way we came in." Raul stood to one side. "Taz will go with you, and I'll bring up the rear. Listen for me in case I have to give you instructions."

She hurried forward, and her colleagues followed her like ducklings. She tried to give an encouraging smile but, other than their PI, no one spoke. No one even looked up to meet her gaze. They all looked bruised and worn, with ragged edges from days of fear.

If she and the Search and Protect team could pull this off, they'd all be safe. There'd be time to recover from this.

Then, maybe, she could address the nagging guilt starting to poke at a part of her mind. No time for it now.

She hurried down the stairs, glancing down the lower hallway at the open doors. None of the other captives had emerged. Another pang of guilt hit her in the gut, harder.

"Straight to the door." Raul's voice called to her. "Save the group we've got with us now."

Or fail to save any of them. The possibility hung in the air over Mali's shoulders. They'd been here too long. The whole thing was already insanely risky. Zu and Todd, her big sister, all of their dogs, were here to help her. Any stupid decisions at this moment could waste all of their efforts, maybe result in irreparable harm to them.

Raul was here with her, and he was right. She headed straight for the door. The research team scuffled behind her, strung out in a bedraggled line of escapees.

As she approached the door, she paused, uncertain. There was no telling what was beyond the door right now, and Raul was bringing up the rear. She hovered in a precious moment of indecision. Then Taz moved ahead of her and stood in the doorway, crouched low to the ground. He sniffed the walkway first and then lifted his nose to the air.

"Bravo Team, this is Charlie. I see Taz." Arin's voice came over the comm, a soothing presence. "Courtyard is clear. Safe to proceed."

"Copy." Raul answered in Mali's ear but she didn't wait for him to tell her what to do next.

She darted out into the courtyard and ran along the wall, toward the garden entrance, trusting her sister to watch over her. As she neared the entryway she paused, and her colleagues piled up behind her, instinctively pressed against the wall. Adrenaline had been pumping through her in repeated rushes throughout this entire experience until Mali's head buzzed with the hyperawareness.

Arin's voice, steady and cool, came over the comm again. "Mali, give it a count of three then you can proceed into the garden. Try to get into the cover of the landscaping as quickly as possible."

"Okay," Mali whispered. Arin had broken her protocol to talk directly to her, and the difference was huge in Mali's mind. She could do this.

One one-thousand.

"Bravo Team, this is Alpha. You have hostile headed back from the fields and coming your way." Zu's message was delivered in a terse tone.

Two one-thousand.

"Copy," Raul responded. "We have the package. Proceeding with extraction."

Three one-thousand.

Raul passed her and opened the entryway, holding the door open and falling into a crouch beside it. He held his firearm close to his body and turned his torso in an arc as he studied the outer area. "Go, Mali."

She darted forward and headed directly into the large gathering of landscaped trees and bushes, returning to the place where they'd left Terri. Mali stopped short, and her PI let out a curse as he skidded into her. Terri was gone.

The rest of the group joined her and gathered around her, shuffling their weight from one foot to the next, every one of them ready to bolt. It was a good thing, too, as long as they all came with her and Raul and didn't scatter to just anywhere.

"Bravo Team, this is Alpha, distraction is complete. Returning for retrieval."

"Alpha, this is Bravo Team. We are one minute from extraction point." Raul's response comforted Mali.

He joined her a second later, and she pointed at the ground where Terri had been, unwilling to mention the woman's name in front of her PI and colleagues. There'd be questions and no way to explain fast enough.

Raul frowned but shook his head. "Probably went to raise some kind of alarm. We're out of here anyway. Let's hope we get out before whoever was alerted makes it here. Let's keep moving."

They headed out again, back the way they'd come, with Mali and Taz in the lead and Raul guarding their rear. It was different once they left the concealment of the landscaping. Different from the courtyard. They were out in the open, and Mali shrank inside as she pushed herself to continue despite the exposure. Far off to one side, smoke rose up over the fields, evidence of the earlier explosion.

"Bravo Team, this is Charlie. Your path is clea—" Arin's voice cut off.

"Charlie, say again," Raul barked into the comm.

Nothing.

The SUV pulled up right next to the hedge, the driver's-side window rolled down to reveal Zu. Mali dove right through the hedge and yanked the side door open as the back door also opened. The entire group piled in. Raul helped a few of them as they clambered into the vehicle, shoving in limbs and closing the door.

Raul tucked Mali in right behind the driver's seat. He met her panicked gaze with a serious one of his own. "Charlie, this is Bravo Team. We are with Alpha. Copy."

Nothing. His mouth pressed into a grim line. He closed the vehicle door firmly, keeping Mali inside the vehicle.

From the driver's seat, Zu made the call. "Stick to the plan. We go to escape and evade."

Raul ran around the back of the vehicle and jumped into the front passenger side. "Go."

*   *   *

Raul wondered if he should text Brandon Forte over at Hope's Crossing Kennels for some tips on building relationships with the local hospital personnel. Forte and his people had gotten involved in enough unusual activity to need emergency medical care multiple times in the last year or so.

When Raul arrived at the hospital, every one of his charges—including Mali—had been hustled in through the ER and past the check-in desk. The nurse at check-in was small yet formidable. Both he and Zu had opted to step back and not crowd the woman, instead answering her questions as best they could, remaining calm and helpful as she informed them that the police were on their way.

Pua arrived before the police did, happily. She was in the process of providing pertinent information on all of the research team and connecting the hospital with their university affiliates on the mainland for access to any medical information necessary to treat the team now that they'd been recovered.

The nurse still wouldn't let him by to check on Mali.

"Family only." The woman hadn't quite snapped at him, but he was starting to envision a dragon sitting behind the counter.

He respectfully backed off. It might be for the best, in any case, because he had no word from Arin yet. Mali would ask, and he didn't have any answers.

Pua approached him and Zu, a pleasant smile plastered on her face but worry in her eyes. "Transferred all the information we had, Boss."

Zu nodded. "Monitoring the situation back at the plantation?"

"Yup." She slipped between them so she could show them her tablet. "I put in the call to the police about the explosion in the plantation fields and shots fired. They arrived on the scene about ten minutes after our team left the premises. Video evidence from the cameras shows their men fired shots that ignited the fuel barrels out by the fields."

Raul grunted. Zu had skills. Not only could the man create a diversion, but he had also manipulated their opponents to trigger it. Arin's targets had been taken out at a distance, and she'd have been careful not to be caught by surveillance. It was possible she'd been delayed removing any additional evidence linking her to the dead men.

There was nothing captured on video to pin on the Search and Protect team except trespassing on private property. But since they were ostensibly following search and rescue dogs on the trail of missing persons, well, that might not stick either.

"Has Charlie checked in yet?" Zu asked the question Raul had been thinking about constantly.

Pua shook her head. "Not y—"

"Here." Arin strode into the emergency room, covered in dust. "I caught a ride with one of the local police teams headed here."

She jerked her chin back at two uniforms entering behind her. One of them made eye contact and nodded. "Zu."

"Officer Kokua."

Raul recognized the man as one of the local police officers Todd Miller had initially introduced to Mali the other night. The other man apparently recognized Raul, too. "Good to see you again in one piece, young man. We should have a talk about you immobilizing a suspect, dropping my name, and leaving the scene before officers arrive."

Raul kept his peace and just nodded. There'd be a mess to untangle from that incident, for sure. It'd be best if they all just got along.

"I'd like to take you and your team aside for statements to add to our investigation," Kokua addressed Zu, his tone courteous. "We can do it here in the waiting room while your team member checks on her little sister."

Zu nodded. "Appreciated."

Arin spoke up. "I gave most of my statement in the car on the way here. TLDR version: my comm broke when I had to engage in a direct confrontation with one of the hired private resources. He encountered me while I was check-ing out an elevated area as my canine partner remained on the ground. We exchanged...introductions... and it came to his attention that the property he was providing security for was being used for human trafficking. He claimed he was unaware and immediately withdrew both himself and his team."

Raul raised his eyebrows, and even Zu cleared his throat in surprise. That was definitely the redacted version, and they probably both wanted to hear the detailed version. Still, if she'd been on a roof or up at a high vantage point with King down on the ground level, it explained why someone had gotten close enough to take out her comm.

If there had been another private contract group on site, he and Mali had been lucky not to encounter them. Things would've gone much harder. Fortunately, the men they'd en-countered guarding the human...stock...hadn't been much more than thugs on the payroll. Those must've been working directly for the main man. The professional private security must've been responsible only for securing the perimeter of the property. The less the hired help knew, the better.

Kokua cleared his throat. "I have a much more detailed report from the ride here. I'd like to get your reports as well."

Raul's eyebrows might take up permanent residence around his hairline for the rest of the day. The professional courtesy Kokua was offering was incredible. Some of it might have to do with his longstanding friendship with Miller. The rest, who knew? But Zu seemed all for cooperating so Raul followed his lead.

Arin didn't wait for anything more. She strode right past the dragon nurse and headed back into the ER in search of Mali.

As they settled into seats at the far end of the waiting room, Raul stared at the doors leading into the rest of the Emergency Room. Family was here. Mali and her team were safe. The mission was complete.

"After we're done here, I'll head back to HQ with Pua." Raul looked at Zu. "They don't need all of us taking up space in the waiting room."

Zu regarded him with a neutral gaze and then nodded. "Might be for the best."

It was the right thing to do. So why did he hate the idea the minute he'd committed to it?

CHAPTER TWENTY-FOUR

What comes next?" Mali sighed.

Across the living room, King lifted his head from his paws to look at her.

"Sorry," she mumbled. "I wasn't talking to you."

King studied her with some sort of inscrutable canine stare for a long minute and then wagged his tail in a single swish across the floor. He turned his attention to the front door, let out a long whoosh of air, and lowered his head to his paws again.

He was a good dog. All of the Search and Protect dogs were. But King was her sister's dog. He had eyes only for Arin, and sometimes she was the only person he obeyed. Most specifically in this moment, King wasn't Taz.

Mali missed Taz. She missed talking out loud to him because he really listened to her. There was something incredibly helpful in the way she could sift through her thoughts with a doggie sounding board. There were about a million thoughts running through her head in what seemed like a mental infinity loop. She could benefit from a long talk with Taz right about now.

Petting him was soothing, too. She'd never had a pet, not really. She hadn't had the budget or the time to have one as she'd focused on her academic studies, and growing up, the family pets had really been taken care of by her older sister. It only made sense that the pets had always seemed closer to Arin.

But when she'd met Taz, he hadn't been attached to her older sister, hadn't preferred her. He'd been attentive and friendly. Okay, she should admit she was transferring some of her feelings. She also missed Taz's owner.

Raul hadn't returned to the house with her, Arin, Todd, and their dogs. Instead, Raul had hung back to go to the team headquarters in town with Zu.

The thing that'd been burning between them was left suspended. For once, she was too tired to differentiate between her intellectual thought process and her emotional reactions.

Her heart ached.

Through this whirlwind of activity over the last couple of days, she and Raul had reacted naturally to the chemistry between them. With the stress and adrenaline, the rational part of her brain figured it was perfectly understandable. Logically, once there was enough time to slow down the pace, the intensity of her feelings would ease back to something manageable, too.

But she didn't want it to.

She didn't know exactly what she was feeling, and there was no road map ahead of her to tell her where this was leading, but she wanted to explore this more than any line of research she'd ever encountered in her life. A few days ago, she'd have considered the idea of a whirlwind romance improbable or crazy. Now?

Nothing made sense, and that was incredibly enticing.

Every minute, every hour she'd spent with Raul had been like discovering herself for the first time. Her responses to him, her thought process—everything had been a new perspective. It'd given life a vibrancy she'd never known, but now, in the lull after the insanity, she missed it. Even after he'd told her about the horrible things he'd done in the past, she'd been drawn to him. She'd been shocked, frightened by what he'd said, and later at the plantation, by what he'd done. But she'd also seen the way he'd done those things out of necessity, for the mission, for her.

She missed him. His voice, his face, definitely the smoldering intensity of his gaze, his touch, his mouth...

She shook her head. If she went on, she was going to come up against an inventory of every body part, and there was a particular part of him she was missing in some very graphic ways.

Her desire to see him again clashed with the hard fact that she'd be leaving soon, and she was right back to her original thought process. Whatever they'd shared had been transient, impulsive, and not sustainable considering their very different career paths. Maybe this was better, being apart now that the situation was resolved and her colleagues were safe. Up until now, their tryst had been balanced on a fine line of enjoying each other without making the mistake of any false commitments. They could go their own separate ways thinking well of each other, no harm done.

Maybe. Her chest tightened and ached. The idea of never seeing him again hurt more than she had anticipated.

Finding a reason to see him again didn't make sense. To her sister's point, it also wouldn't be fair. It was crazy to think they could find a way to make a relationship happen,

long distance, with ocean and the majority of a continent between them.

King rose to his feet, startling her. The big dog was staring at the front door, ears forward, but he didn't make the
eager whine he usually did when Arin came back to the
room. Nails click-clacked on the floors in the hallway as
Ann and Dan joined King.

The three dogs positioned themselves in the foyer area,
a few feet from the front door, between the door and Mali.
Now that was a little unsettling.

Mali shrank back into the couch. A few days ago, she
wouldn't have paid any attention to what the dogs were
doing. But she'd seen how much they could sense and anticipate. No doubt, they were ready to protect her from
something. There was a relief in that. But a tiny part of her
brain shouted for Taz and Raul.

The knock at the front door made Mali jump out of her
skin.

"Coming." Todd came down the hallway. He gave her
his version of a reassuring smile and waved for her to stay
where she was. "Catching up to the welcoming committee.
You should be fine where you are."

Still, he angled his body to block her line of sight as he
opened the door.

Cautious. They all lived their lives with such hyperawareness of what could happen.

A female voice carried from the doorway. "I'm Makani
Hills, working for the Hawaiian state department. I'd like to
speak with Mali Siri, please."

"Todd Miller, Search and Protect Corporation." Todd's
tone was gravelly and grouchy. "We've had an exciting couple of days, so you'll understand that I have to ask for your
credentials, please."

"Of course."

There was a pause.

Todd grunted. "Wait a minute."

He closed the door in the woman's face. Mali sat forward. He couldn't, could he?

Todd turned to her. "Credentials look legitimate. Do you want to meet with this woman?"

Mali realized her mouth was open. She snapped it shut, took a deep breath, and then blurted out, "What will you do if I don't?"

Todd shrugged. "You go into your sister's room, and I tell her to leave. Then me and the dogs will make sure she really does."

Easy as that.

In Mali's world of academia, no one would've risked insulting anyone else that way. It simply wasn't done. And all of the circling around each other with all the words and considerations and circumspection was exhausting. Here, it was as direct as whatever decision each of them made. So how should she react?

"I'd like to know what this woman wants." Mali said the words before she had the thought clearly formed in her head. But hey, nothing about her thought process was normal recently.

Todd nodded. Then he turned to the door and opened it, gesturing for the woman to step inside.

Mali stood to greet her.

"Miss Siri, I'm Makani Hills. It's a pleasure to meet you." The woman held out her hand.

Mali studied the smooth skin of her palm and the impeccable manicure and then took the woman's hand in her own for a quick but firm shake. "Call me Mali."

"Thank you. Please call me Makani."

They stood for an awkward moment.

Todd shook his head. "Why don't we sit here and my wife might bring some tea?"

Mali smiled then. Todd wouldn't leave her alone but he'd made his statement loud enough to carry into the kitchen. Still, he hadn't said his wife would do something, only that she might. He didn't dare say what Kalea would and wouldn't do.

So all of them sat, three humans and three dogs. Ms. Hills—or Makani—seemed unintimidated faced by Todd and the dogs deliberately placing themselves between her and where Mali tucked herself on the far end of the couch. Points for her.

Kalea appeared, carrying a tray bearing a pot of tea, teacups, and a plate of golden bars. They smelled of toasted coconut and butter. Butter mochi. While Kalea poured tea, Mali snagged one and nibbled at a corner.

"Mmm." Mali smiled her thanks as Kalea handed her a cup of fragrant black tea. The steam rose up and tickled Mali's nose with the delicate perfume of jasmine.

Kalea gave her a warm return smile. "Seems to be a household favorite."

"Thank you." Makani accepted her tea politely.

Todd simply leaned forward and snagged a bar, consuming it in a single huge bite. He sat back, chewing thoughtfully.

Once Kalea returned to the kitchen, Makani cleared her throat. "A new commission has been formed to gather data on enforced labor and human trafficking on the Hawaiian islands and to conduct a thorough analysis. In light of recent events, I've come to invite you to join a team here in Hawaii."

Mali blinked, startled. Her bite of butter mochi stuck in

her throat, and she hastily sipped tea. It took her a minute or two to recover. "I'm a postdoctoral researcher still working on my first academic publication."

Makani nodded. "So your principal investigator informed us. He shared the purpose of your research team here on the island, including the observations and data gathered by both his postdocs. I was impressed by your work. The position I am offering you is part of a multidisciplinary team appointed to prepare a series of studies. It's an opportunity you might not otherwise find in your current academic path."

Mali didn't know what to say so she sipped her tea.

"The offer is for a salaried position. You'd conduct your research mostly here on Oahu, with some travel to the other Hawaiian islands."

Mali set down her teacup. "I don't feel comfortable leaving my current research unfinished. I'm scheduled to submit my work for publication. It could be published in the next few months."

It would be important to her career to publish her first paper. As a postdoctoral scholar, she was expected to produce multiple publications as a result of her ongoing research.

"Recent events, in which you have been very much involved, have brought a higher level of urgency to various members of the Hawaiian government." Makani also placed her teacup on a nearby table. "The formation of this commission is only one of several actions taken to address a serious issue here in Hawaii. I read your work. Your observations reflected an empathy that was absent from those of the rest of the research team. Some might mistake it for bias but I view it as an expanded understanding of the circumstances victims of human trafficking find themselves in, where they are hesitant to come forward because there aren't enough protections in place to prevent them from being prosecuted for actions they were forced into taking to survive. Your perspective could make a significant difference here as we bring these issues to light."

"My research could make a difference at my current academic institution." Mali bit her lip. She'd felt compelled to defend her university, or at least stand up for the influence the academic institution could have. But Makani was offering her the kind of position to influence actual government action, different from the audience garnered by academic journals.

"You're absolutely right." Makani hadn't lost the earnest expression, though. "But you have multiple opportunities. I'm offering one of them. I can send you further information on the commission and the studies to be conducted. Would you take some time to look them over and consider?"

Well, opportunities were truthfully harder to come by than most might realize. Makani Hills seemed like the sort of person who would know how competitive the world of academia could be for postdocs in her field. What she was offering was a really tempting position, and she was willing to give Mali time to absorb the situation.

The question was, what did Mali want and why was it so hard to look at the choices sitting in front of her and make a decision?

The memory of Raul and Taz rose to the fore in her mind, arriving to find her hiding in plain sight out on the beach. They'd come to Hawaii for a reason. She had, too. She wasn't going to resolve how she felt about Raul if she left things unfinished everywhere else in her life.

"My first priority is to complete my current research and paper." Mali met Makani's gaze steadily. "Once I've submitted for publication, I'll be able to direct my full attention to your offer. Would that time frame be acceptable?"

It would've been comforting if Taz had been there at the moment for Mali to pet. It'd be a way to hide her intense desire to fidget. And if Taz had been nearby, then Raul would've been close, too. Just the thought of Raul took the edge off Mali's spike of nervousness.

Makani's pleasant countenance shifted to a much more relatable expression as her lips spread into a wry grin. "I want to tell you sooner is better than later, but I also would think less of you if you didn't finish your current objectives. So I have to say your proposed time frame is absolutely reasonable."

"Well, then." Mali sat up straighter. "If you send me your contact information in addition to the materials you mentioned, we'll keep in touch."

* * *

"New life, next step, find a home." Raul sat at his desk, in his office, at Search and Protect headquarters in town.

Taz grunted in response to Raul's statement and rolled from his belly onto his side with a groan.

"Yeah. House hunting isn't fun." Damn. He'd known Hawaii had a high cost of living but it was a completely new experience to be considering places to live with his own budget in mind. No wonder so many people had two and even three jobs here. Search and Protect paid well and would pay even better with bonuses from future contracts but he preferred to live within the means of his base salary.

Pua had quizzed him on a few key things he was looking for in a new home and done a preliminary search for apartments and condos fitting his criteria. She'd even made notes on considerations for each neighborhood based on her local expertise. They were things like ease of access to good food within walking distance at odd hours of the day and night or traffic getting into town or out to the team house. Happily, he could afford to choose from a couple of safe, reasonably well-kept, modest places that were dog friendly.

He just couldn't choose between them, and the prospect of going out to each of them to walk the premises in person was not sounding fun, no matter how smart it would be.

He should be excited about this. It was the next step to getting settled in here. It was time to get back to taking care of all the logistics he should've been handling in these first few days after his arrival.

Shit. What he should—or should not—be doing had been ruling his mind since the day he'd arrived, and he wanted to be angry and resentful about it. But he couldn't. Every minute since he'd received Mali's call for help had consumed him, and he had no regrets about any of the time he'd given her.

Mali hovered at the edge of his awareness sleeping and awake. Either he knew exactly where she was when he was in her presence or her absence left him cold and aching.

Fine. No regrets falling for her. It'd take time for the memory of her to lose its edge and fade to good memories. In the meantime, his thoughts of her were sharply detailed, amazingly vibrant, and left him in serious need of a cold shower or a private moment. His time with Mali, even under fire, had been bright moments of joy.

But he had a future here. He could even be happy with this life.

He had a place with an elite team, serving under a commander he could respect. His team had welcomed him with warmth and sincerity. He'd had the opportunity to prove his potential to his colleagues. His partner was everything he could ask for, and there was a lot to value in Taz's unconditional companionship.

Taz lifted his head and got to his feet, standing at Raul's left. Raul buried his hand in the thicker fur around Taz's shoulders in silent thanks for the early warning. The dog's ears were forward, and his mouth was open with his tongue lolling out in a relaxed doggie grin. He was alert, not alarmed.

A minute later, Zu appeared in his office doorway with Buck. It was interesting being around so many handlers and their dogs in an office setting. Sure, Raul had been in training and even out in the field with multiple pairs, but the polished atmosphere of their headquarters was a new experience. Another thing to be happy about in this new way of life.

He was counting up the happy. It wasn't the same as what he'd experienced with Mali but maybe he should make do. It was better to give her a simple send-off back to her life.

Zu hadn't bothered to knock, but he lifted his chin in acknowledgment. Standing in the doorway, his broad shoulders almost filled the space frame to frame. Raul returned the gesture and waited. He was learning that around Zu, words came at a minimum use, maximum impact.

"We had a visit from a representative from the Department of the Attorney General here in Hawaii." Zu crossed his arms. "It was interesting."

"Yeah?" Raul stood and came around his desk rather than leaving it between them. He figured it was a good idea to engage in a conversation rather than maintain a distance.

"They've got a task force to combat human trafficking in the islands. There's a new commission, too, but that's separate from this task force."

Raul raised his eyebrows. "Were they happy or mad about our latest excursion?"

Zu snorted. "The task force considered it a positive demonstration. They want a Search and Protect resource on retainer for their activities here on Oahu and the neighboring islands, especially Maui and Big Island."

Interesting. Raul waited. Obviously this had something to do with him.

"We demonstrated speed in mobilization, which is a goal for them," Zu continued. "We also have more experience in coordinating efforts for tactical advantage. It's a challenge for them from island to island."

"Makes sense." The possibilities immediately started running through Raul's head. There was a lot of meat to an assignment like this, requiring more strategic planning and interpersonal relationship building than one-off contracts.

"It's outside the original scope of this corporation." Zu rubbed the side of his neck with one palm, leaning his head to one side to ease an ache. "But I think the coordination with this government department would be a strong value for us in the long run."

"It's also a task force worth supporting." Raul hadn't even realized the level of conviction he had until the words were out. What he'd seen in those rooms as they'd searched for Mali's colleagues had haunted him. Those people had been rescued, finally, by local law enforcement today during a dawn raid triggered by the rescue and statements of the research team.

Zu smiled suddenly, a startling contrast to his usual serious expression. "Glad you feel that way."

Ah. "I'm assigned?"

"Not forever." Zu let his hand fall to the back of Buck's head, giving the ridgeback a scratch behind the ears. "I'm thinking each new resource should do a stint with this task force, letting the local authorities get to know us. Say, trial for six months and check in to see if that's enough time to build confidence or maybe extend to a year, or even two. Then you have the choice to join missions elsewhere. Could be the mainland. Could be international. You and Taz would be detailed on retainer to this task force to assist in search and rescue efforts, also providing an element of protection to the task force personnel in joint operations. You and Taz demonstrated a wide range of skills. Excellent search capabilities, effective defensive and offensive tactics used with a keen eye for the appropriateness of the situation, and good split-second decision making."

Pride expanded Raul's chest with Zu's assessment. That was maybe the most words he'd ever heard anyone on the team string together on one topic yet. Except for Pua, maybe. She spoke so fast that she could fit a lot of words into a miniscule amount of time. Raul took a moment to savor it but didn't let it expand his ego too far. Instead, he nodded. "Thank you. I'm game."

Contributing to this task force would help assuage his guilt from the tough decision to leave those people behind on that plantation when he'd had to extract the research team. He might never be able to make up for the additional suffering those people experienced in the hours until the police raid liberated them, but it could've been a lot worse. He personally knew how little time it took to do irreparable harm.

"Good." Zu stepped away. The advantages to Search and Protect Corporation were also obvious, but Zu had an idea of both Raul and Arin's service history, both the official and the shadowy details. "I'll set up the introduction meeting and have Pua put together a briefing package."

"Thank you." Raul could concentrate on this for six

months. He could make progress in proving to himself he had a right to more than just what he should be doing. He could gather the resources to be able to offer more than he ever had in his life.

Maybe by then, he could do something crazy, like what he wanted to be doing.

CHAPTER TWENTY-FIVE

Y our party is already seated. Just follow me, please."

"Thank you." Mali slipped out of her heavy overcoat as she followed the waitress through the main dining area toward a more private nook at the back of the restaurant.

It hadn't snowed yet but winter was definitely settling in, and Cambridge, Massachusetts, could be brutal at this time of year. She hadn't seen sunlight in at least a couple of days because of the dreary cloud cover, and the wind had bite to it coming off the Charles.

She'd thought wistfully back to the warm ocean breezes of Hawaii every single day of the last six months. It'd been easier when the weather had been warm and the sun had been out more in Cambridge. And the autumn foliage had been spectacular. But warm or cold, Mali had walked the streets of the city feeling displaced and out of step with the pace of the people around her.

This wasn't home anymore.

She caught sight of her PI first. He stood as she approached, smiling with his arms open to give her a light hug. "Congratulations on your first public talk and publication."

She smiled broadly in answer. It'd been nerve-wracking preparing her presentation. She'd presented the unique aspect of her studies as part of his research team and her analysis of the findings. The talk she'd given had been before an assembly of not only her peers but also colleagues from across the globe.

Before she could get any closer to the table, the rest of her research team surrounded her, giving her hugs and exclamations of pride. This dinner was for her, to celebrate. The full detail of today's presentation had been discussed in her first academic paper, published in a very well-respected journal. It was a major milestone.

So why was she already wondering how long she'd need to stay before she could excuse herself and leave without hurting anyone's feelings?

Finally the first round of congratulations was over, and people started to head back to their seats. The restaurant had no large tables so several small ones had been moved together with chairs pulled up and around for everyone. She had a chance to draw a deep breath, and she caught sight of not two, but four figures hanging back from the rest of the crowd.

Raul stood, not smiling, staring at her as if he would devour every part of her if he could just look at her long enough. She didn't mind one bit because she was taking him in the same way. He was tanned now, maybe even more fit than the last time she'd seen him, with the full Search and Protect team seeing her off at the airport. He looked better than she remembered, more steady, more real.

Taz sat at his side, panting slightly. The big dog's ears

were up and forward, and he gave her his big doggie grin, his tail switching across the floor.

Next to both of them were Arin and King.

Mali's eyes burned, and she blinked hard, repeatedly, to keep tears from falling.

"We wanted to come congratulate you in person," Arin said, holding out her arms.

Mali rushed to her sister and slammed into her hard enough to knock the air out of them both. They hugged each other tight.

"It's a damned good paper," Arin whispered.

Mali had sent copies to their parents, too. Her parents had expressed pride, said all the right things. But Arin had read it. Understood it. Mali was sure Arin had absorbed the content in ways that went beyond academic analysis.

"Your presentation was really good, too." Raul's words were quiet, but even if he'd spoken in a whisper, she thought his voice would've resonated in her sternum.

Her sister released her, and Mali turned to him. "You listened?"

He nodded, still not smiling, but his eyes sparkled. "It was a big lecture hall. We had the dogs lying in between the rows so they wouldn't catch your eye."

That explained why she hadn't spotted them in the sea of faces. She'd been so nervous that she hadn't been looking for anyone familiar. She'd been looking out and above the assembly.

"Wow."

Arin chuckled. "Used up all your words in your presentation?"

Mali smiled. "I might have, yes."

She had no idea what to say to Raul. She had spent nights thinking about what she wanted to say to him. It'd been months. Right before she'd left, he'd taken her hand and told her he'd keep in touch.

After what she'd said about them going their own ways, he'd proved to her that distance and time zones weren't obstacles to him. He'd texted every day. He hadn't needed responses from her, hadn't asked for anything. He'd simply sent her fun pictures of Taz and Arin and King and the entire Search and Protect team. He'd sent her images of sea turtles and endless variations of shaved ice desserts. Every text had brought a smile to her face. When she'd asked him questions, he'd texted responses. It hadn't mattered what she'd asked or how inconsequential her inquiries might've seemed to her. He'd always been out there, answering her.

He hadn't called, though. She'd gotten the impression he'd wanted to give her the space and the choice. She hadn't called him. So they'd just texted and it'd given her the space to recognize that she'd been afraid of what they could be.

He'd been a surprise, an unpredictable variable, and a threat to her carefully planned academic career. She'd been in a living nightmare when her research team had been kidnapped, and he'd stepped into the middle of it. Once the nightmare was over, she hadn't been able to separate him from the experience, even if she had wanted to.

So he'd let her go. And he'd proven he'd still be there if she wanted him. It'd been huge. She still hadn't worked through all of her apprehension yet. But hell, she figured he deserved her if he wanted her, and she deserved to be happy. More than happy.

She stared up at him. "I am so glad you're here."

He smiled then, slow and incredibly sexy. None of his texts had indicated anything but light flirtation with no expectations. She'd wanted him to cross the line, even hint to her that he wanted more. Here he was, and just his smile was doing bad, bad things to her ability to remain standing.

"After dinner, can I see you home?"

Yes. Oh yes. Maybe by then, she could manage to pull together all the things she'd been wanting to say to him.

*   *   *

She wasn't just beautiful. She was everything. He'd soaked in Mali's talk as she'd presented her research findings and analysis. The sound of her voice had soothed a six-month-long ache. It'd been a good idea to watch her from the back of the hall at first and then to stand back as she'd entered the restaurant. He'd enjoyed the play of expressions across her face, ranging from nervous to professionally serious, passionate with the conviction of her research, and gracefully relieved once she'd arrived at the restaurant for drinks with close colleagues.

He'd refrained from trying to give her a hello hug because he'd have held her too tight, been too much, too soon. Instead, he'd savored every little touch she'd given him through the drinks and chatter. Every brush of her fingertips over his wrist or the light bump of her knee against his. She'd continued to rest her hand against his shoulder as she'd given him driving directions to her apartment, leaning close through the drive.

Now, standing behind her as she fit her key into the deadbolt lock of her front door, he was close enough to catch the scent of her hair and the hint of perfume she wore. She didn't smell of beach sand and sea salt anymore, but there was the faintest hint of plumeria. She leaned back into him briefly before opening the door and letting Taz precede them into her home.

He'd given her a fair chance to fade in his memory. She hadn't. The chemistry between them hadn't changed gradually to friendship the way it could have. It was time to explore the "what ifs"—if she was willing.

"Careful of the step here. This is just sort of an entryway between the outer door and the inner door to my place. The lightbulb in this hallway went out, and I never got up there to replace it." A faint light flared from her hand as she used her smartphone as a kind of flashlight.

"I could change the bulb for you," he offered automatically.

"Oh, don't bother. It's really not worth it." She stepped out of tiny heels, placing them on a shoe rack next to the first step from the landing, and he wondered what shoe size she must be. They had to be more than three inches high. He strongly approved of the way they'd changed her walk from a smooth gait to a sexy stride, where her hips rolled as she moved. He wanted to commit her size to memory because it'd be fun to buy her all sorts of sexy heels in the future if she liked them.

He bent and took off his own shoes, chuckling as he slid them under the shoe rack. The size difference was crazy. It'd look ridiculous to put his big shoes on the top rack next to the neat collection of small footwear.

As he straightened, she was standing there waiting for him within arm's reach. Her eyes shone with anticipation.

He reached out, careful, and caught a loose strand of hair near her jawline. "Hey."

She rose up on her tiptoes and pressed a kiss against the corner of his mouth. He set his hands on her hips to steady her, bending his head to follow as she settled back down on her heels. He returned her kiss with a longer one of his own, reveling in the warm softness of her mouth and the sweet taste of her. "I had a question for you."

"Mmm hmm." She slipped her hands under the front of his shirt and coasted them over his abs until her palms lay flat against his chest.

Words. What were words?

This time, they kissed as if they were drowning. They breathed each other in, tongues exploring and tangling with each other. He pulled her close against him, and she ground her hips against him in response.

Damn. He was going to bust out of his own dress pants.

He bent his knees, sliding his hands over her tight ass, and lifted her. She spread her legs and wrapped them around his waist. He was careful to keep hold of her as she leaned back, unable to hold on with her hands still trapped against his chest. He took a step forward and braced them both against the wall. She was wearing the barest bit of silk or satiny something under her cocktail dress. He wondered how mad she'd be if he tore it off her.

Mali trailed kisses along his jaw and then gently bit the side of his neck. He groaned into her hair, squeezing her ass while he rolled his hips against her.

"T-Taz will be fine inside the kitchen." She didn't make it a question. She only freed an arm and flailed somewhere in the dark, her phone clattering to the floor as she somehow found the inner door on the opposite side of the entryway and swung it shut in his dog's face.

He probably grunted something in agreement. He'd made a noise. He was sure of it. If he didn't taste more of her in the next few seconds, he was going to rip their clothes to shreds.

Her hands were on his shoulders now, pulling at his polo. She was breathless as she gave him her next request that wasn't a question. "Off."

Yes ma'am.

He let her down carefully and pulled his shirt over his head, surrendering it to her. "Now I get something of yours."

"Wh—"

He kissed away her question. She'd find out in just a minute. He ran his hands over her shoulders, her soft breasts, over her ribs and her waist. As he explored with his hands through the fabric of her perfect little dress, he kneeled down before her and prepared to do the only kind of worshipping he ever did. And he planned to put everything he was into it.

He buried his face into her belly, glad when her hands caressed his hair. He pressed kisses into the inner hollow of her hip as he slipped his hands under her skirt, finding the sides of her panties. She gasped as he pulled her panties down and she stepped out of them for him. Looking up, he watched her gaze go dark with lust as he tucked her underwear into his pants pocket.

Her lips were parted, and she was watching. Good.

Lifting her skirt to expose her, he nuzzled her first. She whimpered. He grinned up at her then and wedged his shoulder between her legs, forcing her to widen her stance and present herself even more to him. Her hands landed on his shoulders as she braced herself. He blew a puff of air against her most private flesh.

"Please," she whispered.

He raised an eyebrow, nuzzled her again, and then darted the tip of his tongue between her delicate folds.

She balled up her right hand in a fist and brought it down on his shoulder in a credible *thwack*.

He chuckled. She was riled up, frustrated, for him. There was nothing in this world so tempting. He parted her folds with his thumb and ran his tongue up her slit.

She gasped.

He lunged forward then, and he feasted on her. She cried out, grabbing his shoulders and leaning back against the wall as he explored, tasted, nibbled, and sucked. He relearned the sounds she made, reminding himself of exactly where to press the tip of his tongue to get her to whimper and just how to tease her entrance to make her moan. He grasped her ass in both his hands and squeezed as he darted his tongue wickedly inside her. She called out, exciting him further.

He let her go as he licked her folds and she gasped for air. Then he circled her clitoris with his tongue, tickling her with his fingertips.

"You are so mean." Breathless with need.

But he wanted to hear more from her.

He clamped his lips over her clit and suckled as he thrust a finger into her, groaning at her tightness. And whatever sexy sound came out of her as he pumped his finger inside her—he had no idea how to describe it—but it was exactly what he wanted to hear.

Her hands were in his hair, and her hips were moving whether she was aware of it or not, helping him, encouraging him, as he stroked her with his finger and mouth. He steadied her with his other hand when she tensed, right on the edge, and he kept up the rhythm of his finger inside her until she crested and her orgasm took her in a shuddering release.

He sat back, taking her into his arms as she collapsed down on top of him. But then she rolled and pulled him over her on the hallway floor. "I want you inside me."

"Anything you want." He barely got his agreement out before he undid his belt and pants, keeping just enough presence of mind to free his wallet and retrieve a condom.

His brain stuttered as she lifted one leg over his shoulder. She was showing him exactly how she wanted this, and he only hoped he could give it to her before she sent him into a stroke. In a split second, he had the condom out of its wrapper and rolled over his length. With his hand at the base of his cock, he guided himself into her; a groan of his own ripped from his throat with her tightness around him.

Her hand landed on his hip and grabbed hold, urging him, and he was not about to argue. He drew back and drove into her, balls deep, and she cried out with the pleasure of it. Again. And again.

"More," she gasped. "I missed you so much. I want you. Harder."

"Everything." His voice had dropped to a growl. "You can have everything." Because he loved her, this woman who could embrace everything about him. She'd seen every aspect of him and hadn't pretended she understood. She'd acknowledged him and hadn't hidden. And here she was, with him now, wanting him.

He thrust into her, fast and hard, picking up the pace at her encouragement until fireworks started firing off behind his eyes. She arched to meet him, taking him in as far as she could. When he thought he wasn't going to make it, thought he was going to lose it before her, she tensed under him again.

"Come with me," he urged her.

Her eyes went wide, and they went over the edge together.

It took them a few long moments, raggedly gasping, to come back to themselves. He eased her leg down from over his shoulder and gathered her into his arms. It was a good thing this was a private foyer.

Hooking his arms under her knees and behind her back, he lifted her as he got to his feet. Kicking his clothes aside, he got them both to the inner door. She had draped an arm around his shoulders as he cradled her but she reached out with a free hand and opened the door for him.

He carried her inside and froze.

Taz lay on top of a large box across the room. Actually, there was nothing but boxes. No furniture. No appliances. Nothing, not even food, on the shelves in the kitchen. Well, there was a candy bar on the kitchen counter.

"What?"

Her arms tightened around his shoulders. "I've been packed. I was leaving tomorrow morning."

His heart stuttered. But no. It didn't matter. He'd adjust course. Whatever it took.

Before he could pull his wits together to ask any of the fifty questions whirling through his brain, she pressed a kiss against his cheek. "I have a one-way ticket to Honolulu, over there. See?"

There was a sheet of paper, an e-ticket printed out.

She tapped his lips until he looked down into her dark gaze, sparkling with joy. "I was going to come to you. I figured it's an island; how hard could it be to track you down? If Arin didn't know where you were exactly, I was going to make her and King help me find you right away. I didn't plan to wait."

She'd been ready to come to him.

"And then you both were here, tonight. I couldn't have dreamed of better timing." She was laughing now, quietly, and pressing kisses against his jaw between words. He tightened his hold on her. "I love you."

"I love you."

They'd said it at the same time.

"I was going to come to you, you know." He whispered to her. "I was ready to do whatever it took to help us work. I was ready to wait as long as you needed to decide if you wanted to be with me. But I was going to wait nearby."

She snuggled into him. "We both made the big gesture. I like that. Puts us on even footing."

"Yeah."

There was a pause and then she asked, "What are you looking at?"

He grinned. "I'm counting how many rooms you've got here."

She drew back to stare at him quizzically. "Why?"

He chuckled. "Well, if we're leaving in the morning, I figure we've got enough time to do right by every room in here. You know. As a send-off."

She gasped. Then she bit her lower lip with mischief and hunger in her eyes. "I like the way you think."

Acknowledgments

Thank you to Alex Logan and Courtney Miller-Callihan for working with me to bring Raul and Mali's story to life and for your amazing patience.

Thank you to Christopher Baity, Executive Director of Semper K9 Assistance Dogs, for your insight into working dogs. Any exaggerations or errors are my own—because sometimes we writers need to stretch a few truths to make things work—but hopefully the story is plausible thanks to you.

Thank you to Katee Robert and Allison Pang for helping me in those crazy moments where I lost the beats of my story. Your help in finding them again was invaluable.

Thank you to Matthew for being the heart in which mine finds home even when we're far apart.

And finally, thanks to my readers. The True Heroes series is continuing because of you, and I hope you'll enjoy.

After multiple tours of duty, Brandon Forte returns to his hometown on a personal mission: to open a facility for military service dogs like Haydn, a German shepherd who's seen his share of combat and loss. It also brings him back to Sophie Kim, a beacon of light in his life...And the one woman he can't have.

Please see the next page for an excerpt from *Absolute Trust*.

CHAPTER ONE

It was a quiet Tuesday afternoon in New Hope. Few people were out and about on the main street when it was this cold out, which was perfect for Brandon Forte. The jet-black German Shepherd Dog walking just ahead of him needed space for this excursion, a couple of things to look at but not too much to excite him. A few people to see was good for them both, too, so long as they weren't going to be overwhelmed with requests to pet or take pictures.

Besides, the bake shop all the way down on this end of town tended to have day-old baked goods at a discount, and the shop owner occasionally gave Forte a cupcake or cookie on the house along with special home-baked dog treats for whichever dog was with Forte. It gave the dogs and him something to look forward to on the walk.

Today, it was Haydn. Haydn was a seasoned veteran and one of the dogs Forte had trained on active duty for the Air Force. Now, Haydn had come to Hope's Crossing Kennels for a new kind of training. The black GSD had a lot of physical therapy ahead of him. He'd been fitted with a prosthetic to replace his front left leg prior to arriving, but it was up to Forte to help Haydn figure out how to use it. The big dog had walked the kennel grounds fine but was obviously getting bored. It happened with intelligent animals, the same way it could with people. Both of them were more than ready for a change of scenery and terrain.

Thus, the outing and the very slow walking.

Besides, it took skill to stuff a chocolate cupcake with cookie dough frosting dusted with sugar in one bite. A man needed to practice once in a while to make sure he could still manage it.

And it was a necessary skill, as far as Forte was concerned. Sophie tended to bring her own cooking and baked treats to Hope's Crossing Kennels every weekend. She was a close friend to everyone at the kennels, an integral part of what made the place home to each of them, and she was…more to him. If she caught him partaking of other sweets, she'd never let him hear the end of it.

Now if it was about dating, she never had a word to say about any of the women he saw or the one-night stands he indulged in now and then. He'd bumped into her once in a while in Philly on the weekends. They both dated, and it couldn't matter less to her who he chose to spend his time with, as far as he could tell. But take a taste of someone else's baking, and he was in for a world of hurt. Thus, the one-bite-and-inhale technique. Because she had a knack for popping up out of nowhere.

Which made it more fun when he took the risk and did it anyway.

Of course, he had a long history of crossing paths with Murphy's Law, and apparently, this was his day for it because who would be walking down the street but the very person he was thinking about?

Sophie Kim was five feet, two inches of nonstop energy, usually. Today, though, her shoulders were slumped and her steps lacked the brisk cadence he'd always associated with her. She was heading out of a small art gallery with a large paper shopping bag, and despite the difference in her body language, she was still alert. The woman had expansive peripheral vision and excellent spacial awareness.

Which meant she spotted him and changed course to head in his direction immediately.

Forte swallowed hard.

She must've come directly from work because under her very sleek black trench coat, she wore a matching pencil skirt. Three-inch red heels popped in contrast to the severe black of the rest of her outfit. Which did all sorts of things to him. Naughty things.

The kind of things that were so good, they were really bad. Especially when a woman was off-limits.

"Hey! Is that the new guy?" Sophie slowed her approach, keeping her gaze locked on Forte's face.

She'd been around tiny dogs all her life, but she'd spent enough time at Hope's Crossing Kennels over the past couple of years to have learned how to meet the much bigger dogs in Forte's care. Training working dogs was his thing. Or in Haydn's case, *re*training.

Always a work in progress.

Sophie had been there when he'd come back from active duty, too battle weary to continue deploying. She'd helped him with the accounting when he'd established Hope's Crossing Kennels and had generally integrated herself into the private world he'd created for himself, Rojas, and Cruz while they all rebuilt lives for themselves.

Some people might've assumed he'd spent a lot of years running from New Hope between high school and now. He'd been away a long time, explored a lot of different places around the world. But there'd been no question about where he'd end up between deployments. He always came right back. And her friendship, her smile, had always been waiting for him.

Sophie's bright smile faded as she waited for him to answer. She always sensed when he got too caught up inside his own head.

"Yeah." Forte came to a halt and murmured the command for Haydn to sit.

Instant obedience. Despite his injury, surgery, and current need for recovery, the dog was as sharp as he'd been on active duty. The mind was eager, ready to work. The body, not so much.

Sophie's smile renewed, the brilliant expression stopping his heart, the way it had every time he'd seen her since they'd first met way back in high school. She came to a stop in front of them, barely within arm's reach. "He must be doing well if you've got him out here for some fieldwork."

Haydn remained at ease, unconcerned with her proximity, as Forte and Sophie stood there. Curious, even, if Forte was any judge of body language. And he was. For dogs, at least.

He shrugged. "Easy going with Haydn. He needs a lot of light walking, over different kinds of surfaces, to get a feel for his prosthetic. We're not out for too long. I don't want to tire him out or put too much strain on his legs."

Sophie nodded in understanding. "Glad to meet him, though. I thought I was going to have to wait until I stopped by this weekend."

While they spoke, Haydn watched them both. Then he

stretched his neck and sniffed the back of Sophie's hand, which she'd been holding conveniently within reach.

Introductions were simple with dogs. Stay relaxed, let the dog know the approaching person wasn't a threat via body language, and give the dog time to investigate on his own. Sophie's body language was naturally open and non-threatening. She had learned from Forte not to look his dogs in the eyes. The dogs he trained tended to be dominant and aggressive, and they required a more careful approach than the average pet on the street.

Usually, he preferred if a person asked to be introduced, but this was Sophie. If she'd approached anyone else, she'd have requested permission to say hi to the dog. But this was him and her. Between the two of them, everything was an exception. She spoke to him and took it on faith that he'd tell her if she needed to keep her distance. But then again, he also wouldn't bring a dog out in public that wasn't ready to be socialized.

It showed how well she'd come to know the way he worked in the past few years. He'd changed with every deployment. It happened. And she'd adjusted and accepted those changes in him without a word when he came back. She was the steadfast forever friend.

He'd never told her why he'd left in the first place or why he'd come back. She was so good at just accepting him that she might never know. And he was a coward for not telling her.

"What's your plan for him?" Sophie glanced down at the dog, now that he'd sniffed her hand. "Haydn, right?"

Forte gave her a slight nod, and she ruffled the fur around Haydn's ears. The big dog's eyes rolled up, and he leaned his head into her hand for more enthusiastic scratches.

Definitely no problems socializing. Then again, in Sophie's hands, most males turned to Silly Putty.

Or... he needed to stop thinking about what could happen to him in Sophie's hands.

"Yeah." Forte cleared his throat. "He's got a couple of weeks of physical therapy first. Then we need to coordinate with the Air Force on his adoption."

"Ah." Understanding in one syllable. She had the kind of caring heart to fill in the gaps when something went unsaid. "His handler didn't make it?"

Part of why Sophie was one of the only people Forte felt easy around was because she got it. Only needed to explain once. And she *listened* the first time. Sometimes no explanation was required at all.

Forte shook his head. "Same IED that injured Haydn took out his handler. The deceased's family has been contacted, and they'll have first choice to adopt. We haven't heard back yet on their decision, but those kinds of things can take some time coming through the communication channels."

Sophie nodded and looked down at Haydn. "We'll give you time to figure things out while all the paperwork goes through, huh? It's nice to meet you, Haydn."

The black GSD leaned into her, his tongue lolling out in response to the attention and the use of his name. Haydn knew when someone was talking to him and, apparently, he liked Sophie's voice.

Every bond between working dog and handler was unique. Haydn was dealing with the loss of his handler in his own way, mostly by being generally friendly with the trainers and those to whom he was introduced. But there was friendly and there was truly affectionate. A deeper level of affection was something Haydn seemed to be holding in reserve. This physical training period would give the dog the time he needed to be ready to bond with someone again, too.

If he decided to. It was always the dog's choice.

"Where's your car?" Forte was not going to stand around long enough to be jealous of a dog. Not at all. "We'll walk you."

"Right across the street." Sophie jerked her head in the direction of a small parking lot.

They headed over, Sophie falling into step next to Forte. She didn't try to take his hand or tuck her own around his arm. They weren't like that. Besides, she knew he didn't like to be all wound up with a person when walking out in the open. It was another way her understanding of him manifested. It was a regular reassurance. A comfort.

Better than free cupcakes.

"Has Haydn met Atlas?" Sophie asked casually.

The first rehabilitation case at Hope's Crossing Kennels had been Atlas, a dog suffering from PTSD after his handler had died. One of Forte's trainers and close friends, David Cruz, had worked with Atlas and still did now that the dog had become a permanent part of the kennels. But Atlas's challenges had been psychological. With the help of Lyn Jones's approach to working with dogs, Cruz had successfully brought Atlas back up to speed.

"Briefly." He glanced at Sophie and caught her making a face. "The dogs don't need group therapy sessions."

The psychology aspect of the rehabilitation was something Forte was willing to entertain only so far. Lyn got results with her work, yes, but he was not going to go all the way into the deep end with the dog whisperer approach.

He made a stupid face right back at Sophie. "You do not

need to come over and sit Atlas and Haydn down to compare notes on what they've been through. Souze doesn't need counseling, either."

Souze was Rojas's partner, a former guard dog turned service dog helping Rojas face the challenges of reintegrating into civilian life.

Sophie was silent a moment, a sure sign his guess at her thought process was on target. "Well, they do need to play with each other sometimes, right?"

"Dogs are social creatures, and, yeah, some playtime is good if they can socialize with other dogs that way." He'd give her that. Forte made sure the dogs trained at Hope's Crossing Kennels could socialize well with both human handlers and other working dogs. "Haydn's the second military working dog to come to us for help after active duty, but his challenges are mostly physical. We have to watch him carefully with the prosthetic on until we all know what he can do with it, including him. But, yeah, he's gone out with Atlas and Souze on a couple of group walks without the prosthetic."

Honestly, Haydn was pretty spry even without the prosthetic. The dog just had better mobility with it.

"Okay." Sophie let it go. "I just think you and your working dogs could use a little more playtime in your lives. Like a doggie field day or something."

He snorted.

Sophie's car was a sensible sedan, the sort to blend into a lot of other normal, everyday cars. What made it easy to spot was the pile of cute stuffed animals across the back. Not just any stuffed animals—a gathering of cute Japanese and Korean plush characters from her favorite Asian cartoons.

As they approached, Sophie juggled her shopping bag to pull her keys out of her purse and triggered the trunk.

"Need help?" Forte came up alongside the car, scanning the area around the parking lot out of habit.

"No worries." Sophie lifted the trunk door and carefully placed her shopping bag inside the deep space, leaning in to move things around to where she wanted. "I need to make sure this is arranged so stuff doesn't shift. It's delicate!"

He was not going to admit to anyone, ever, how much he was willing to stretch his neck to catch sight of her backside while she was leaning over.

Haydn sniffed the side of the car. The big dog was very engaged, his relaxed attitude changing over to a sharper set of movements. Forte tore his attention from Sophie. Actually, the black dog was very interested in the car.

Forte tuned into the dog's body language, changing his own to match. He leaned forward a fraction, his balance over the balls of his feet. He kept his limbs loose, ready to respond to the unexpected. It didn't matter that they were in a sleepy town on the edge of a river in the middle of a peaceful country. It didn't matter that there shouldn't be any real danger there.

Haydn had detected something out of place. Something wrong. Forte's stomach tightened into a hard knot. Nothing wrong should be anywhere near his Sophie.

His attention centered on the sniffing dog. Whatever Haydn did next, Forte would act accordingly.

Haydn deliberately sat and looked up at Forte. It was a clear signal. One Haydn had been specifically trained to give as a military explosives-detection dog.

Shit.

"Sophie. Step away from your car." He'd explain later. Be afraid later. Rage. Worry.

Later.

She popped up from the trunk. "Huh?"

"Do it."

They had to move now.

Sophie always listened to him, Rojas, or Cruz when they were urgent. She complied, thank god. He gave Haydn a terse command and circled around to grab Sophie and get more distance. He steered her across the parking lot toward a big Dumpster. It'd serve as good cover. Then he reached for his smartphone.

They got a couple of yards away, and Sophie craned her neck to look back at her car, even as she kept moving with him. She always did as he asked immediately, but she had a brain, and she insisted on explanations after she complied. "What—?"

Behind them, the trunk hatch came down with a solid *thunk.*

Forte let out a curse and grabbed her, pulling them down to the ground and rolling for the cover of other cars as an explosion lifted the entire driver's side of her car.

* * *

Sophie screamed. Maybe. She was pretty sure she did, but wrapped in Brandon's arms and smooshed up against his chest, she wasn't sure if she'd gotten it out or if it'd only been in her head.

The explosion was crazy loud. The concussive force of it slammed into her and Brandon despite the shelter of the cars and the Dumpster he'd pulled them behind.

He covered most of her, one of his hands tucking her head protectively into his chest. His other arm was around her waist. They were horizontal.

Not the way she'd daydreamed this would happen.

After a long moment, all she could hear was the ringing

in her ears. Her heart thundered in her chest. And she thought, maybe, Brandon's lips were pressed against her temple.

Or was it her imagination?

His weight lifted off her, and his hands started to roam over her, gentle but with purpose. Looking for injuries.

His voice started to penetrate the roaring sound filling her head. The words slowly started to make sense. "Are you hurt?"

"Haydn?" She sounded funny in her own mind, but Brandon met her gaze for a moment and jerked his chin to one side.

"Don't turn to look until I check to see if you hurt your neck or head." His admonishment came through sharp. It was the way he talked when he was worried. People thought it was meanness, but it wasn't. He was frightened. For her. "Haydn's right here. He's fine; a little shaken up by the blast, but his training will help him keep his shit together. He's fine."

As Brandon continued, a cold nose touched her cheek. Big ears came into view, and warm, not-so-sweet breath huffed across her face.

"I'm glad you're okay," she whispered. It was for both Brandon and the dog.

A brief whine answered her. Then a large, furry body lay down next to her, just barely touching her shoulder and side. A fine tremor passed through the big dog and then he pressed closer to her.

"He's going to stay here with you." Brandon rose. "Can you lay here until the ambulance comes, Sophie? Please? He'll be calmer if he has you to watch over."

Then she realized things hurt. Her right shoulder, her hip. Pain shot from her right ankle. Maybe the only thing that didn't hurt was her head. Brandon wasn't just worried about Haydn.

"Is it bad?" She stared up at Brandon as he lifted his smartphone to his ear. Sirens were already approaching.

Brandon held out his hand. "Give us space, please. Stay off the blacktop!"

People must have been gathering. He was stepping out to take command of the situation. He was walking away from her. Again.

"Don't leave me," she whispered. She always said it quietly. Because she didn't want him to actually hear her.

A soft *woof* answered her instead. Careful not to turn her head, because Brandon had asked her not to, she looked as far to her side as she could. There was Haydn lying next to her. His eyes were dark, almost as black as his fur. And his gaze was steady on hers. Calming. He wasn't going to leave her.

"Okay, Haydn," she whispered to her new friend. "We'll wait right here for him."

It was what she'd always done. And this time, she had company.

ABOUT THE AUTHOR

Piper J. Drake is an author of bestselling romantic suspense and edgy contemporary romance, a frequent flyer, and day job road warrior. She is often distracted by dogs, cupcakes, and random shenanigans.

Play Find the Piper online:
PiperJDrake.com
Facebook.com/AuthorPiperJDrake
Twitter @PiperJDrake
Instagram.com/PiperJDrake

Fall in Love with Forever Romance

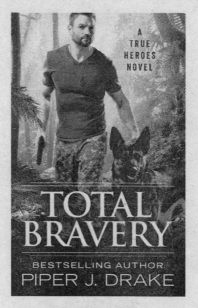

TOTAL BRAVERY
By Piper J. Drake

Raul's lucky to have the best partner a man could ask for: a highly trained, fiercely loyal German Shepherd Dog named Taz. But their first mission in Hawaii puts them to the test when a kidnapping ring sets its sights on the bravest woman Raul's ever met...Mali knows she's in trouble. Yet sharing close quarters with smoldering, muscle-for-hire Raul makes her feel safe. But when the kidnappers make their move, Raul's got to find a way to save the life of the woman he loves.

Fall in Love with Forever Romance

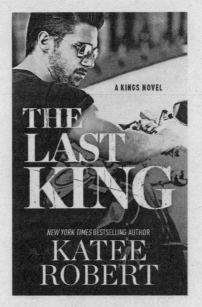

THE LAST KING
By Katee Robert

The King family has always been like royalty in Texas. And sitting right at the top is Beckett, who just inherited his father's fortune, his company—and all his enemies. But Beckett's always played by his own rules, so when he needs help, he goes to the last person anyone would ever expect: his biggest rival. Samara Mallick is reluctant to risk her career—despite her red-hot attraction—but it soon becomes clear there are King family secrets darker than she ever imagined and dangerous enough to get them killed.

Fall in Love with Forever Romance

THE AMISH TEACHER'S GIFT
By Rachel J. Good

Widower Josiah Yoder wants to be a good father. But it's not easy with a deaf young son who doesn't understand why his mamm isn't coming home. At a loss, Josiah enrolls Nathan in a special-needs school and is relieved to see his son comforted by Ada Rupp, the teacher whose sweet charm and gentle smile just might be the balm they *both* need.